need you now

need you now

Emma Douglas

St. Martin's Paperbacks

This is a work of fiction. All of the characters, organizations, and events portrayed in this novel are either products of the author's imagination or are used fictitiously.

NEED YOU NOW

Copyright © 2017 by Emma Douglas.

For information address St. Martin's Press, 175 Fifth Avenue, New York, NY 10010.

ISBN: 978-1-250-11098-5

Our books may be purchased in bulk for promotional, educational, or business use. Please contact your local bookseller or the Macmillan Corporate and Premium Sales Department at 1-800-221-7945, ext. 5442, or by e-mail at MacmillanSpecialMarkets@macmillan.com.

Printed in the United States of America

St. Martin's Paperbacks edition / September 2017

St. Martin's Paperbacks are published by St. Martin's Press, 175 Fifth Avenue, New York, NY 10010.

10 9 8 7 6 5 4 3 2 1

*For those who make the music
and those who love it*

acknowledgments

I've always loved music and musicians so thanks to Eileen Rothschild and everyone at St. Martin's Press for giving me a chance to write about them. Thank you also to Miriam Kriss, always an awesome agent. To all the writer buddies who got me through the hard parts and celebrate the good parts and the friends who put up with me becoming a writing hermit at regular interval, smooches. To the big torti for continued excellent writer kitty services and the little torti for joining the team and providing much amusement. And last, but certainly never least, to all my fellow bookworms who support writers like me, by reading, sharing, and loving books, the biggest thank you of all.

And the cloudlines
Rise in your eyes
And I am lost again
And drowning

from "Cloudlines,"
released by Blacklight April 6, 1990

chapter one

Faith Harper stared down at the bright green and red Lansing Island ferry edging up alongside Cloud Bay's long dock and tried not to fidget. The atmosphere in the streets below was starting to buzz with pre-festival crazy, like it did every year, and, like every year, that buzz made her . . . itchy.

Itchy like her skin was too small and her clothes were too tight. Itchy like she needed something she'd never quite been able to describe to anyone.

Just a few more days.

A few more days. Then CloudFest would start and she could, as always, hand over the zillion and one details of running one of the country's most popular—and hardest to get tickets to—music festivals to her crew and just show up to do her intros and meet and greets and enjoy herself. And after that, she could leave Lansing for a few days.

Go to L.A. or New York, maybe. Relax.

But a few more days were still a few more days, and she had at least a million of those zillion details to nail down before Thursday.

"Spotted any talent yet?" Ivy Morito asked from behind her.

Faith shot a grin over her shoulder. Ivy sat behind her desk, typing at warp speed while watching Faith over the top of the bank of four slim black monitors that formed a wall of IT along the edge of her desk. Knowing Ivy, she was probably simultaneously working on a client's security problem, messaging at least three of her friends, *and* designing a website in her head. This week her hair sported blue and purple streaks flaring through a jet black bob. The colors clashed with her acid green glasses, and the overall combination gave a sort of angry mermaid impression but one that didn't distract from the curiosity in Ivy's brown eyes.

"I'm waiting for Lou." That and trying to remember whatever it was that was giving her the nagging feeling she'd forgotten to do something. But no, all the major pieces were in place. All their permits had signatures and dotted i's and crossed t's, even if Lansing's new mayor had made that process more complicated than usual. "Good daughters pick up their mothers when they come home from vacation." Seeing Lou safely home would be one more detail ticked off the list.

"You're a good daughter. Lou's a good mom. Neither of those things precludes you checking out the tourists to see if anyone cute is coming to town." Ivy mimed something that Faith assumed was meant to be a hunter stalking its prey. Which was pretty funny when you considered she was doing so while wearing an

Elmer Fudd T-shirt that proclaimed that she was "hunting wabbits."

"I don't have time for cute," Faith reminded Ivy.

Ivy looked appalled. "That's just plain sad." She chewed her lip, made a gesture on the touchpad by her left hand. "How's Ricky?"

"Still getting married," Faith said drily.

"Le sigh," Ivy said. "He sounded nice."

"He is nice." Ricky was the guy Faith had been hooking up with occasionally for a few years when she went to L.A. He was nice. And good in bed. And worked for a record label, which meant they could talk shop. But neither of them had been looking for love, so other than being cut off from the good sex part, Faith had been more than happy for him when he'd told her he'd met someone—wait, had that been before Christmas? More than six months ago?

God. She needed to get off the island.

" 'Nice' isn't helping you if he's marrying someone else. Thousands of people are about to invade the island. There must be a few nice ones. Who are also hot."

"The majority of them are about nineteen."

"Not all of them," Ivy objected.

True. CloudFest attracted a mixed audience. It skewed young like any music festival, but Blacklight had been huge for decades. Their fans spanned those decades as well. And those fans came to CloudFest whether any of the surviving members of the band were playing or not.

"I don't do island, you know that," Faith said. "I'll take some time off after the festival." Every year she rewarded herself for all the hard work that went into keeping the family legacy running and CloudFest happening by taking a vacation. In the past—pre-Ricky—occasionally there had been a vacation fling. A guilty pleasure.

Or really, totally nonguilty pleasure. She liked sex. She wasn't married. She didn't intend to ever be married. So she had a few flings. Flings she'd kept off-island because she learned young that privacy was hard to come by when you were (a) the daughter of a rock star and (b) lived in a community of only a few thousand people. But somehow, she'd settled into a habit with Ricky. Ricky was simple. And since Ricky, well apparently she'd forgotten about sex altogether.

Of course, she'd been neck-deep in the festival for most of that time. So what if she hadn't had time to have sex lately? That wasn't a crime.

"Tourists aren't island. They leave. Thereby fulfilling the criteria for the perfect Faith Harper man," Ivy said.

"Yeah but they leave and then they decide to sell their story to the newspapers." Faith said. "No thanks." She knew she sounded paranoid but she had no desire to become a tabloid sensation. She'd had enough of paparazzi and scandal growing up with Grey Harper as a father.

"Maybe you should try an island guy for once," Ivy said.

"I'm pretty sure if any of the guys who live here lit my fire, I would have realized it by now," she retorted. Ivy didn't share her views on island guys. She was newly moved in with her boyfriend. She had a bad dose of love cooties.

"When's Matt back?" Faith asked.

"Don't change the subject," Ivy said, shaking her head.

Busted. "I'm not," Faith protested. "You get cranky when Matt's off-island." Matt Hanlon was one of Lansing's two deputy sheriffs. He was attending some sort of police conference in L.A., taking advantage of the calm before the storm—as the locals tended to view the weeks before CloudFest.

"I'm not cranky, I just know you," Ivy said but she was smiling again now, no doubt thinking of Matt. "And Matt's catching the last ferry tonight, if everything goes to plan. How did Lou's trip go?"

"I've hardly heard from her, so I'm assuming pretty well," Faith said. Her mom also took the opportunity to flee the island for a few weeks before the festival and go soak up some peace and quiet and culture in San Francisco or Los Angeles or farther. Lou claimed it was her right as a teacher on vacation to escape for a proper holiday for at least some of the summer. Faith couldn't argue with that though she had a sneaking suspicion that Lou was mostly avoiding helping out with tying up the endless last-minute issues that went with the festival.

Her right to avoid being sucked into the insanity was also hard to argue with. Lou and Grey had been divorced for a long time before he'd died. True, she'd never truly broken away from Grey. She'd decided to stay on the island so that Faith didn't have to choose between her parents. But she had kept herself out of the circus that surrounded Grey and Blacklight as much as possible.

The only times Lou had voluntarily waded into

Grey's business once she'd divorced him, was when she thought something that affected any of the three Harper kids needed to be straightened out. Even though two of them weren't technically hers.

But that was Lou. Easygoing until she turned into a ferocious mama bear. Five foot three of implacable will, not to be messed with when she wanted something for Faith or her siblings. She was one of the few people willing to tell Grey when he was being an asshole. Pity. Life might have been easier if there'd been a few more of those in her dad's life.

Faith turned back to the window, humming under her breath. The second-floor office that Ivy ran her IT empire from was the perfect vantage point. The view to the long dock where the ferry came in was unimpeded. It meant Ivy had to put up with being blasted by the ferry horns signaling arrivals and departures eight times a day, but that never seemed to bother her. The ferries were ingrained into the noise of Cloud Bay, being the only means on or off the island unless you had a boat or could afford to charter a small plane or helicopter. Not many of the locals bothered with any of those options though the skies would be busier than usual over the next few days, bringing CloudFest attendees who had money to burn to Lansing. The marina's spare moorings were already full.

The ferry was just starting to lower the car ramp, which meant the passengers would begin to disembark any moment. So she should really head down and find Lou.

Normally she wouldn't have been shy about waiting down at the dock but for some reason this year she wasn't quite ready to put on her public Faith Harper-famous-daughter-of-dead-rock-star face just yet.

Lansing Island and Cloud Bay—the island's one real town—attracted a steady stream of Grey Harper and Blacklight fans making a pilgrimage to one of the pivotal places in the band's history all through the year.

And Faith was the face of the Harper clan on Lansing, given her older brother Zach hadn't been home for more than a day or two in years and her little sister Mina had made a career out of avoiding being recognizable as one of Grey's kids. So Faith was used to dealing with fans, but the CloudFest crowd could sometimes take Blacklight hysteria to a whole other level. She needed to be ready for that level of hyperenthusiasm to deal with them. With her famous girl clothes and attitude firmly in place.

And today she just wasn't feeling it.

She glanced back at Ivy, who was still typing away madly. "I should go."

Ivy nodded, fingers pausing. "Estimated chance of us getting to hang out for more than ten minutes before the madness starts?"

Faith made an apologetic face. "Low maybes? Let me see how today goes."

Ivy shrugged. "Figured. You know, one of these days you can let someone else take up a bit more of the work of this whole circus." She looked back at her screen, frowned, and starting typing again with finger-blurring speed.

"I will if you will," Faith said. Ivy looked up and grinned. Faith grinned back. People didn't get why she and Ivy clicked sometimes. And they rarely understood

when they heard the story of how the two had met. Ivy—
who'd run away to CloudFest—had tried to pick Faith's
pocket in the festival crowd when they'd both been fifteen. Or why Faith had dragged Ivy off to her house to
stay for the week instead of taking her down to see Sheriff Lee. Sometimes like just called to like.

The sound of a honking horn—there was always one
idiot in the line of cars who couldn't wait—blared
through the open window, and Faith twisted around to
see what was happening. Sure enough, the first car was
easing down the ramp from the ferry. "That's my cue,"
she said. "I'll drop your passes off tomorrow."

She blew Ivy a kiss and left the office. Taking the old
wooden stairs two at a time, she popped out the door
beside the boutique below Ivy's office before the second
car had even reached the road. As she stepped onto the
pavement she pulled her straw cowboy hat—snitched
from one of the festival crew as camouflage—more
firmly over her hair. Despite the hat, the heat made her
head start to sweat almost immediately and she shoved
her sunglasses into place and craned her neck looking
for Lou. Who, being sensible, would probably wait for
the hordes to disembark while she sat and chatted to
Magda, who operated the tiny coffee concession on the
ferry, before making her own way down onto dry land.

Sure enough, there was no sign of Lou's close-cropped
silver hair in the steady stream of people making their
way, so Faith faded back against the building, out of
the way of the new arrivals, and entertained herself by
watching the cars easing their way off the ferry and
trying to navigate through the crowd of pedestrians. So
far none of the drivers of the mostly shiny and expen-

sive vehicles had lost their cool. Though all it would take would be some tourist whacking an overpriced side mirror with a backpack for someone to crack.

Most of the cars had their tinted windows up, which, given how hot it was even in the shade where she stood, she kind of envied. Air-conditioning would be nice right about now. The old truck she was driving today, tucked neatly into the lone parking space behind Ivy's building, was no doubt getting hotter by the second under the midday sun. Maybe she should text Lou. Tell her she was waiting for her. But that would spoil the surprise of coming to meet her.

The car now opposite her—a screaming red Porsche—blasted its horn, snapping her attention back to the traffic. The driver accelerated, and she shook her head at his impatience. Lansing Island was only a couple of miles long. Nowhere took very long to get to, so a few seconds of waiting for a pedestrian to cross his path was hardly going to ruin his day.

She was tempted to give his taillights the finger, but that wasn't going to magically transform him into a non-moron. Life was too short and she had too many things to do to worry about jerks whose actions weren't affecting any of those things. She started to turn her head back toward the ferry and as she did, she caught the gaze of the passenger in the black SUV behind the idiot's Porsche. He was apparently the exception to the rule of not winding your window down.

Blue. That was all she could think for a moment. His eyes were stupidly blue.

Her heart gave a little bump at the sensation that he was looking right at her despite the sunglasses and the fact that she was half in shadow under an awning and there were people walking between them.

Hello.

She blinked, feeling an involuntary smile spring into life.

He started to smile, which made her realize that the rest of the face was pretty good too. He had a cap on, which meant she couldn't tell what color his hair was— the stubbled beard outlining his square jaw was lightish brown—but his skin was tanned and the teeth flashing in that smile were very white. An odd sense of déjà vu tugged at her, like she'd seen him somewhere before, but then the car was moving on and she turned to watch it go.

Apparently Ivy had been right. There were cute tourists. Beyond cute. The Jeep had a CloudFest permit sticker on its back windshield, so presumably he was going to the festival.

She shook her head. He might be going to the festival, but she didn't have time for cute or beyond cute, even if she'd felt inclined to break her keep-it-off-island rule.

"Faith? What are you doing here?" Lou's voice came from behind her and Faith whirled around to hug her mom, forgetting all about blue eyes and hot smiles. For now.

In retrospect, a small island crowded with thousands of people for a music festival probably wasn't the best place to hide out.

Caleb White tugged his baseball cap further down his head as he looked at the throngs of people already

crowding the streets. Cloud Bay was apparently the island's only proper town or village or whatever the term
was for somewhere where the population was only a few
thousand people for most of the year, but right now it
looked more like downtown San Francisco or Los Angeles. Too many people.

Despite the crowd, he had to fight to resist the urge
to lean out the window to try and catch a better glimpse
of the girl in the battered straw cowboy hat.

The one whose smile had just sucker-punched him.

Damn. She gave good mouth. Her eyes had been hid-
den behind huge mirrored sunglasses, and the hat
pulled low on her head made it hard to see much of her
face through the crowd. But that mouth had been killer.
Full lips curving into a delighted smile that was somehow sexy as hell. He'd thought she'd been looking at him
but it was hard to tell with the glasses.

No way of knowing now that they were slowly making
their way down the street, leaving her behind. Beside
him, Liam was focused on the road ahead, his fingers
drumming the steering wheel as he paused every so often to let a pedestrian cut across their path. Feeling
vaguely disappointed, Caleb leaned back in his seat
and hit the button to roll up the window. The tinted glass
was a barrier between him and the rest of the world that
he was happy to exploit for now.

He was under no illusions that he could make it
through the whole festival incognito, but surely he could
just hole up and relax at the place Liam had borrowed
until CloudFest actually started.

Normally Caleb was fine with the fact that people
knew who he was and having to deal with fans but

apparently announcing your retirement from tennis just after reaching the semifinals at Wimbledon created a media shitstorm. And he didn't feel like dealing with paparazzi or well-meaning members of the public trying to convince him he was still at the top of his game.

He wasn't. He had the scars from last year's shoulder surgery and the opinions of his world-class doctor to prove it.

He'd still fought back to the number-two ranking after his surgery but it had been freaking hard work, and lately he could feel the downhill slide starting. Didn't matter how hard he worked, his shoulder was never going to be as good as new. Worse, he could feel it starting to go again. It had been agony after his last few matches. And screw being the guy desperately trying to hold onto former glory.

He'd seen too many guys do that in his time on the tour. It never worked.

So he'd decided to bow out.

He was fine with his choice.

The rest of the world didn't seem to be.

Golden Boy of Tennis Loses His Shine

White Goes Dark

What's Wrong with Caleb White?

The headlines had been endless and the media crush outside his house in Santa Monica relentless. Not even a minor scandal involving the actor who lived three

doors down and the just-legal daughter of a U.S. sena-
tor had shaken them from his doorstep for more than a
few hours.

Mostly because the actor in question had left town.

Caleb had dug in. Until Liam had rung with the news
that he had tickets to CloudFest and a house on Lansing
Island until early August.

His precise words had been, "Get your ass down here,
White, we're going to have fun. You remember fun,
right?"

Caleb had remembered fun. He was no longer in
training; no tournament start dates loomed in his cal-
endar. For the first time since he had started taking his
tennis seriously as a scrawny twelve-year-old, his time
was his own. So he'd decided why the hell not?

Now, staring through the darkened car windows at all
the tourists who would be joining them at the festival,
he was starting to rethink that choice. He shifted on the
seat, suddenly edgy. Maybe he'd go for a run once they'd
settled into wherever they were staying. Or a swim.
Blow off some steam.

"Lots of people," he said to Liam, whose finger tapping had sped up as they waited for the car ahead to turn
onto a cross street.

Cloud Bay was larger than he'd been picturing in his
head. And more upmarket. Both sides of the street were
lined with stores that looked expensive even while
housed in the old-fashioned wood two-story buildings
that seemed to be the town's style. No sign of any chains,
but there were sleek clothes and art in most of the store
windows. Any place that wasn't a store seemed to be a
hipster café. And there were people *everywhere*.

"Yup," Liam agreed. His head swiveled to Caleb. "Don't worry, the house has good security. It belongs to one of the Blacklight guys. No one's going to hassle us."

"O-kay," Caleb said. He hadn't asked where they were staying, knowing that Liam would have found somewhere decent. But he hadn't expected it to be a house belonging to one of the guys from the band that had made Lansing Island famous. Blacklight had started the whole CloudFest thing back in the nineties. "Doesn't he need it for the festival?"

He wasn't surprised that Liam knew someone from Blacklight. An entertainment lawyer whose dad had been a studio bigwig, Liam had grown up peak Hollywood. Rubbing shoulders with the who's who of California. And Blacklight had been a very California band. Caleb had spent his teens focused on tennis but the Blacklight juggernaut had been too big for even him to miss. He owned most of their albums. "Cloudlines," which had made them their fortunes and cemented them as superstars, was still one of his favorites.

"Dude, Blacklight haven't played at CloudFest since Grey Harper died. I don't even know if any of them have played together at all since then." Liam eased the car forward.

At this rate they would be arriving at their destination in about five hours. His jaw tightened and he made himself relax it. Vacation. He didn't have anywhere to be. He needed to chill.

Liam aimed a satisfied smile at Caleb. "So one prime island hideaway is all ours."

Just them and—no doubt—a bunch of other people Liam had either invited or decided to party with. "So who runs the festival, if none of the band are here?" He'd never been to CloudFest though it, like the band who'd started it, was something everyone knew about. He'd just never given much thought to how music festivals happened.

"Harper's oldest daughter. Faith. I don't need to explain Faith Harper to you, do I?"

Caleb shook his head. He knew who Faith Harper was all right. She hadn't followed in her father's footsteps musically, but she'd been in a couple of the band's videos when she'd been about eighteen. She was beautiful—or no, maybe "arresting" was a better word. All long legs and a mane of wavy sun-streaked hair and her father's famous gray-green eyes, huge in an angled face, drifting through the moody landscape of the clips. He wondered what she looked like now. "The name sounds familiar."

Liam snorted. "It really is a good thing you've retired," he said. "You have about twenty years of pop culture to catch up on. Danny told me he has a sweet home theater. Maybe I'll give you a crash course."

Danny being Danny Ryan, Blacklight's lead guitarist, presumably. "I was playing tennis, not living on the moon. I know about pop culture. How do you think I passed all that travel time?"

"If I know you, watching video of your competition playing so you could figure out how best to totally annihilate them."

Liam apparently knew him a little too well. Because he couldn't deny that he liked to win. And would do whatever he needed to do to make sure he did. But that didn't mean he was a robot. "You can't do that one hundred percent of the time. Sometimes you have to watch stuff blow up instead." Or sleep. He'd gotten pretty good at sleeping on planes. It didn't hurt that these days he generally got to travel first class. But he'd learned the trick in cattle class in his early years on the circuit.

"There's more to pop culture than action movies."

Caleb grinned. "Yeah. There's Sci Fi as well."

Liam rolled his eyes. "Well, at least we can bring you up to date on music this weekend."

Caleb nodded, hoping his sudden lack of enthusiasm for the idea of being surrounded by so many people didn't show. "Looking forward to a couple of quiet nights before then. Not sure I've caught up on what time zone I'm in since I got back from London." Jet lag was a reasonable explanation for the fact he hadn't been sleeping well. It just wasn't the actual explanation.

"Don't tell me you're getting boring in your old age."

"Boring is better than eventful right now."

"You can't hide forever. Besides, between that cap, your sunglasses, and that lame beard, no one's going to easily recognize you."

"My beard is not lame." He'd been growing the beard for only two weeks—since his announcement in fact. Part of his fool-the-press attempts. So far it hadn't actually fooled anyone. It just looked scruffy. And it itched. He was nearly ready to give up and shave.

Liam rolled his eyes. "Hipster is not your look. Stick to all-American."

"You're more hipster than me." Liam had grown his dark hair out to nearly shoulder length. That had to be annoying as hell to deal with all day but apparently it worked for Liam. He never lacked female company.

Girls apparently liked long hair. Of course, Liam was a pretty son of a bitch, so that helped.

"Maybe, but on me it looks good. Ginger whiskers aren't cool."

"My beard isn't ginger."

"It's ginger in bits." Liam rubbed a hand over his own smooth chin. "Gingers don't get the girls."

"I'm blond."

"Your beard isn't."

"I'm also not here to get the girls." He thought again about the girl near the ferry and that smile. Well, maybe if she crossed his path again he might be interested. Perhaps an island fling would be just what the doctor ordered to distract him from life without tennis.

"Why the hell not? You're retired. Time to live a little. Don't tell me you're getting cold feet. You can't be missing getting up at dawn to train and eating rabbit food."

"No." He definitely didn't want to go back to his old life. Though he still kept waking up before six a.m. Apparently the habits of a lifetime were hard to break.

"Good. So it's time to get with the program. And the program while we're here is good music, good booze, and pretty girls. You can figure out the meaning of life and Caleb 2.0 later."

Liam had a point. And, more important, Caleb didn't have a better plan right now. So maybe it was just time to let the fuck go and see what the hell happened.

chapter two

Faith had almost reached Lou's house when her cell rang. She flicked her eyes to where the phone lay between them on the bucket seat. She'd taken Grey's old pickup out of the garage this morning rather than using the Prius she usually drove. She never knew quite what she might have to end up ferrying around the island in the last few days before the festival opened, and the pickup was far more practical than the Prius for that. But it lacked some modern amenities. Like Bluetooth. And air-conditioning.

"Do you mind?" she said to Lou, nodding at the phone. "It's probably festival business. Things are getting hectic." She had a hard-and-fast rule about not using her phone in the car when she didn't have it on speaker. She rolled up the window to cut down the noise of the truck's engine, cutting off the flow of air as well. The temperature inside immediately felt twenty degrees hotter.

Lou shook her head but reached to hit the answer button, flicking it onto speaker.

"Faith?" Theo King's voice came through the speaker. "Did you take the pickup this morning?"

"Yep," she confirmed. She fanned herself with one hand, feeling sweaty all over again. "I've been at the site. Going back there shortly. What's up?" She'd been too busy for her normal five-minute morning check-in with Theo, who ran things in the Harper Inc. offices. Technically he was the COO, but given there were only six of them in the office, everyone tended to pitch in when things got busy.

"The keys to Danny's place are in the glove compartment," Theo said. "I tossed them in there last night. He called to say he'd loaned his house out for the next two weeks. I was going to take the keys around to Leon this morning so he could let whoever it is in, but things got busy and I forgot. I didn't even realize you'd taken the truck until just now."

Faith didn't look at Lou. "Well, I'm almost at Lou's house. So I guess I can keep going and take the keys out to Danny's."

The Harper offices were near the Harper house. Which was further around the island than Danny's. She'd have to drive past Danny's place to take Theo the keys so he could run the errand. Which made no sense.

Damn. She'd been looking forward to stealing thirty minutes with Lou to catch up on her mom's trip before Faith was due back at the festival site for the first sound checks and now she wouldn't be able to. She made an apologetic face at Lou, who waved her off.

"Cool. And, sorry. I should have told you last night." Theo said.

Faith ignored that. They were all run off their feet. She tried not to let the little churn of disappointment that Danny would be a no-show ruin her day. She'd known it was unlikely that any of the remaining members of Blacklight would be coming home. Most of them had avoided the festival since Grey had died. Danny still turned up on Lansing a few times a year but never really let anyone know when he might next appear.

So she shouldn't really be sad that he wasn't coming, but she was. She shoved the feeling down, determined not to let her day be ruined. Because this year, one good thing was happening. Zach was coming home for Cloud-Fest. He was doing a secret solo set on the final night. But more importantly, he was going to be on the island for more than a couple of days for the first time in longer than Faith cared to think about. He was arriving Thursday, not leaving until the Tuesday after. Which would give her a chance to not only catch up with her brother but to have the all-three-Harper-siblings-required discussion she needed to have about what she wanted to do next with the family business.

"Did Danny tell you the name of whoever it is he's loaning the house to?" Faith asked.

"Liam Sullivan," Theo said.

He didn't offer any more, which probably meant he had no more information to give her. Faith filed the name away. It didn't ring any bells, which didn't mean anything, really. Danny had what could only be termed "a gigantic circle of friends and acquaintances" and he was the kind of guy who'd lend his place to one—or twenty—of them on a whim. "Right. One key delivery coming up," she said.

Theo sounded relieved as he said goodbye before hanging up.

She looked ruefully at Lou. "I wanted us to have some time to talk before I had to go back to the site. Do you want to come with me or do you want me to take you home?"

Lou shook her head. "I don't mind the drive. I'm only going to unpack and do laundry and putter around the house this afternoon anyway. And I told Danny I'd check that the place was okay when I got back."

"You saw Danny while you were away?" Faith asked as she took the turn to Danny's place rather than continuing on to Lou's little house on the outskirts of Cloud Bay.

"Just for a quick lunch. He was in L.A. the same day as me."

"How is he?" Faith asked. She missed the rest of the band. They'd been around for most of her life. Like a bunch of wild and unruly uncles, always in motion around Grey. Never a dull moment. And many, many wonderful ones. Until Grey had died and suddenly it felt like everyone who'd ever been part of her family—other than Lou and her sister, Mina—had vanished along with him. Like she'd lost not just her dad, but the rest of her family as well.

She'd seen Danny and Billy and Shane more off the island than on since then. None of them had ever said anything, but they kind of acted like the place was radioactive. It was too much of a reminder of the hole in their lives Grey and Blacklight had once filled. So they'd run back to the one thing that had always got them all through. The music. They'd agreed that Blacklight was done. Shane had a whole new band to support his solo career, stepping into the lead singer spotlight Grey had never really been that keen to share. Billy had taken over as drummer of Erroneous when their drummer had passed away six months after Grey. And Danny toured solo and stepped in for other acts who needed an emergency lead guitarist. All three of them seemed to be on the road as much as ever.

Faith understood them wanting to leave the reminders of what they'd had with Blacklight behind.

Didn't mean she entirely forgave them for leaving her behind too, though.

But Lou, ever the peacemaker, kept in touch with everyone. She was the only one of Grey's wives who'd always gotten along with the other guys. Zoe, Zach's mom, hadn't stayed around long enough to really bond with any of them, and Mina's mom, Emmy was . . . well, Emmy was mostly interested in what she could see through her camera's lens. She'd lasted longer than Zoe but not by much. And she'd left Mina with Grey, which by default meant that Lou had raised all three of them.

Lou was good friends with Billy's wife Nina, and with Shane's longtime girlfriend, Claire. Danny had been married once early on around the same time that Grey had married Zoe. Unlike Grey, he'd decided once was enough after he'd gotten divorced.

Faith realized she wasn't listening to Lou, who was giving her an update on Danny. Something about a tour to England kicking off soon. "Uh-huh," she said, hoping Lou hadn't noticed her distraction. They were headed along the coast road toward the north end of Lansing. The ocean to their left ebbed and flowed in deep blue-green waves under the sun, putting on a show for the tourists as it curled onto the beach.

Faith put her foot down a little. She knew this stretch of road intimately. Had traveled it thousands of times. And every time she reached this particular spot, she always wanted to go a little faster. To fly around the curves and dips and crests of the road.

The road that led home.

Home. The Blacklight guys had returned to Lansing after "Cloudlines" had made them all rich and bought up a substantial chunk of the island, including, in Grey's case, the land where the house they'd recorded the album in had stood. That house had burned down, but over the years Grey had turned it into something more like an estate than just a home. The land was dotted with the main house and several guesthouses for ex-wives and guests and whoever else might turn up. He'd built his tiny personal studio where that first house had stood. Not to mention an office and a real recording studio on another parcel of land nearby. There was even an old lighthouse on the headland, where Mina now lived.

Danny's place was to the left of Grey's, and Shane's was to the right. Billy's property flanked Danny's. It was a little world all of their own, where they could come and not be hassled.

Home.

Still Faith's home, even if most of the other residents had deserted her.

She shook off the mood. No time for memories. It was a beautiful day, her mom was home, and she had way too much to do to waste time reminiscing. She tightened her grip on the steering wheel and started asking Lou about her trip.

Lou had just finished telling her a long and complicated tale about how she came to meet a pet alpaca somewhere in the canyons of Hollywood when they reached the gates barring the long drive up to Danny's house. She lowered the window and leaned out to enter the code into the security system. The gates swung obediently open, and she drove more slowly down the winding drive. But when they pulled up outside the house, there were no cars in the semicircular sweep of paving stones that fronted the building. Apparently Danny's guests hadn't arrived.

She reached for her phone as she and Lou climbed out of the car. "Theo, no one's here. Any idea where Danny told these people to find the keys? Or if he gave them the code for the house?" Hopefully he'd at least told them how to get through the gates.

"Crap. No. He didn't tell me much. Just said they were meant to be on the midday ferry. They're not there?"

"No," Faith said. "Maybe they stopped to stock up on groceries." Or booze, more likely, knowing Danny's friends. "Is Leon supposed to be here?" There was no sign of Danny's caretaker/gardener, who would have normally appeared by now to investigate a car pulling up.

"I was going to give the keys to him. Maybe he thought that they weren't coming after all when I didn't turn up."

That wouldn't be unusual. Danny was the king of the last-minute change of plans. Worse than Grey had been, even. She chewed her lip, pondering options. Of course, on Lansing it was probably safe to leave the keys in the front door itself, but you never knew when some fan might just decide to try and sneak onto the property, particularly now that the festival crowd was arriving. The festival site—another piece of land Grey had purchased—started only a mile or so from the edge of Billy's land, and there were always Blacklight faithful curious enough to try getting a closer look at where their heroes had lived.

She could wait a little longer for whoever Danny's mystery guest was, but after that, she might have to coax Lou into waiting here for the visitors. Faith could send one of the temps they had helping out in the office to pick Lou up and drive her home once she'd handed over the keys.

"I'll figure something out," she said to Theo. "I have to meet Ziggy back at the main stage by one thirty. I'll be back in the office about four." She hung up as she reached the front door and let herself in, pulling off her sunglasses and tucking them into the neckline of her T-shirt. But when she entered the security code in the alarm system, the lights stayed stubbornly red. Dammit. She hauled out her phone again.

"Ivy? It's me. I'm at Danny's. Did you change the house code again?"

"Yes," Ivy said. "Danny called and said he was having guests, asked me to change it for them. Didn't he tell you?"

"Not so much," Faith said. "But I'm here to drop off

the keys and all your super gadget alarms are going to go off any second if I don't put the code in."

"It's eight-seven-six-five-three-five." Ivy reeled off the sequence without a pause. Her memory for numbers was a little scary at times.

"Thanks," Faith said, keying in the code. The lights turned a welcome green. "And if the system sent out any sort of call for help, cancel it." The Cloud Bay sheriff's department, such as it was, had enough to do over the next week without following up false alarms. For one thing, Faith tying up the police for no good reason would only piss off the mayor. Angie Rigger seemed determined to make life difficult for CloudFest. She couldn't stop the festival altogether because it was the island's biggest source of income, but since she'd stepped into the job last year, things had become a lot more complicated.

Angie had never really liked Faith and that hadn't changed since she'd taken office. But Angie wasn't her problem right now. All CloudFest's permits were signed off on. So she wouldn't have to tangle with Angie again until next year.

"Sure thing," Ivy said. "No cavalry will be dispatched. So be careful out there."

Faith laughed and ended the call. Lou had followed her into the house and was busy opening windows in the huge living area that ran half the length of the house.

"Mom, it's hot." She pulled off her hat to fan herself. "Shouldn't we just turn the air-conditioning on?" Something Leon would have done already if he'd been here today. So, definitely no Leon to leave the keys with if she needed to.

Lou shoved another window open. "Fresh air first. It's stale in here."

Faith couldn't smell anything but she knew better than to argue with Lou about housekeeping. So she left her to it and wandered down to the kitchen to check that Danny had remembered to tell Leon to do the basics like turn on the fridge and leave out the little binder of instructions on how everything worked. The fridge was on, at least, and cool. The binder was on the counter. So maybe Leon had left to run an errand or something. She could call him, of course, but she and Lou were here now so there wasn't much point bothering him.

She wandered out of the kitchen, looking for Lou. She was just about to follow the noise of doors being opened upstairs when she heard the sound of an engine outside. Yay. Something was working out today. She could dump the keys and get her and Lou back on the road.

But when she stepped back outside, she quickly forgot about what she was supposed to be doing that day. Because she recognized the big black SUV rolling to a stop in front of the house and the silhouette of the man sitting in the passenger seat. Mr. Very Nice Smile from the ferry.

Right here on what was practically her doorstep. Maybe it was a sign.

Nope. On second thoughts, if the universe was sending her a sign to suggest that perhaps she could break her rules for once and hook up with a guy on the island, it would have waited to deliver him directly to her. Or, at a minimum, arranged for her to meet said guy at a time when she was wearing something a little more flattering than cut-offs and a well-worn Rolling Stones concert T-shirt and didn't have sweaty hat hair.

She ran a hand through her hair quickly as she watched two men get out of the car. The driver was cute too, with olive skin and straight dark brown hair that fell almost to his shoulders. Very L.A. cool guy chic in expensive-looking black cargos, leather slides, and a charcoal T-shirt. But it wasn't Mr. Cool making her pulse bump a little and focusing her attention.

No, that honor belonged to his big blond—well, dirty blond—friend, the one walking around the SUV with an easy loose-hipped grace that caught her attention as surely as if he'd been standing in a spotlight. The sun seemed to bounce off him, producing a halo effect around his long, suntanned limbs.

She was briefly tempted to ask him to put the cap he held in one hand back on, if only to stop them all being blinded by too much male perfection in one place.

But only briefly. After all, a woman would have to be crazy to deprive herself of the sight of him. Especially once he pulled off the sunglasses and hit her with a straight-on stare from eyes that she could tell from twelve feet away were an even more ridiculous shade of blue than she'd noticed back at the dock.

"See, told you there'd be cute." She could almost hear Ivy's voice snarking in her head. But no. Despite what Ivy might think, handsome faces weren't enough. In fact, sometimes they were too much. She knew about beautiful men. She was the daughter of one and had met too many other too-handsome-for-their-own-good rock gods not to know how they operated. They were the center of their universes and everyone else had to revolve

around them. She had no interest in being the satellite to someone else's sun.

Still. That face.

God.

It was both glorious and gloriously familiar but she couldn't immediately figure out who he was.

Behind her, Lou cleared her throat and Faith realized she was quite possibly staring at the man. Sure, he was definitely worth staring at, but she usually preferred a more subtle approach. Particularly when she didn't want to give the man any ideas.

She conjured up what she hoped was a normal welcoming sort of smile. Not one that was dazzled. "Hi. I'm Faith. Welcome to Lansing."

"Faith? As in Faith Harper?" The dark-haired guy hit her with a smile she was sure was supposed to be charming. Unfortunately for him, her attention was still caught by his blond friend.

"Guilty," she said. "Which one of you is Liam?" She looked from dark hair to light and felt her gaze linger just a little too long on blondie.

The other guy held up a hand, his smile dimming a little. Faith made herself focus on him, hoping he was the only one who'd noticed her staring.

"I am," he said.

"Nice to meet you," she said as she tossed him the keys. "That's my mom, Lou." She nodded back toward Lou who was standing a few steps behind her still. She figured if he knew who she was, he probably knew the history of the Harper clan. He might even recognize Lou even though she'd avoided the spotlight as much as possible.

"Nice to meet you," Liam said. "This is—"

"Caleb White," Lou blurted out. Faith turned to look at her. Lou was not a blurter. Or a gusher. And Lou's tone had been distinctly gushy.

Then the name sank its way through her subconscious. Caleb White. She had pretty much zero interest in sports but even she knew who Caleb White was. Mostly because Lou loved tennis and told Faith far more about it than she ever wanted to know. Including, in the week just before she'd gone away, all the news about the shock retirement of one of the sport's top male players.

The man her mom was now staring at with a distinctly fangirly expression. When you lived around rock stars, you got the fangirl thing knocked out of you fairly quickly. Lou had met musicians and movie stars and politicians and hell, even royalty in her time. But apparently Caleb White trumped all that if the multiple shades of pink her mom's face was turning were any indicator.

Faith turned back to face Caleb. Okay, she couldn't really blame Lou for her reaction. The man was hot.

Faith had seen him before, of course. In the pages of glossy magazines, looking casually elegant sporting some ridiculously expensive watch or lounging next to a ridiculously expensive car in advertisements. No doubt companies fell over themselves to secure that face to promote their products.

She'd even seen him play occasionally when Lou had forced her to watch a match or game or whatever they called it in tennis on TV. It had vaguely registered with her that the man was quite attractive but apparently the camera had never really captured just how damned hot he actually was.

Especially when those blue eyes were firmly fastened on her. She fought the smile that threatened to spread across her face again.

"Guilty as charged," he said as he held out his hand. "I'm Caleb."

Before Faith could take the proffered hand, Lou stepped past her and grabbed hand it. "It's lovely to meet you. Danny didn't tell us who he was expecting."

"That's because I borrowed the house," Liam said. He looked at Faith then back at Lou with an expression somewhere between amusement and resignation. Apparently he was used to his famous friend getting all the attention.

Lou didn't respond, still looking up at Caleb with a can't-quite-believe-it expression.

"Well," Faith said brightly. "How about we give you a quick tour of where everything is, and then we'll get out of your hair and you can settle in and enjoy your vacation. It is a vacation, isn't it?" She studied Liam. She couldn't remember meeting him before but that didn't mean he wasn't connected to the music scene somehow. After all, he knew Danny.

"Definitely," Liam said. "We're here to hang out and enjoy the music."

"Then you're in the right place," Faith said. She hooked her arm through Lou's. Lou blinked and apparently had managed to return from Planet Starstruck because she started asking Liam polite questions about their journey to Lansing as they all walked to the house.

Faith gave the guys the five-dollar tour. Lou came

with them, occasionally glancing at Caleb. As Liam and Caleb walked ahead of them out onto the deck surrounding the pool, Lou dug her elbow into Faith's side. "He's very attractive, isn't he?"

Caleb, at that moment, bent down to test the temperature, dragging his hand back and forth through the water. The movement made his shirt ride up a few inches. His torso was as tanned as the rest of him. The bare skin on display gave an extremely good demonstration of the muscles of the male back. Damn.

She shouldn't be looking. She made herself turn away. Focus on Lou. "Mom, quit it."

Lou shrugged. "He's only a few years older than you. Well, he's thirty-four."

"Six years is not 'a few.' Not that I care how old he is."

"Honey, if I was your age, I'd care."

When Lou had been Faith's age, she'd been knocked up by a rock star. But Faith wasn't going to point that out. Though it was a strong argument for why it might be a good idea to avoid really gorgeous charming rich guys. Too much like her father. Who was all those things but also destructive and selfish.

"Mom. Do not get any ideas. They're only here for a week. Not that I am interested," she added in case Lou misinterpreted.

"A week with that man would be . . . fun." Lou sighed.

"Mom, did you get sunstroke while you were away?" Lou was normally the one dropping hints Faith should find someone serious and settle down, not have a fling.

"Honey, sometimes you need a little crazy." Lou

grinned at her. "After all, without a little crazy, you wouldn't be here."

"I am not in the market for crazy. And I'm definitely not in the market for babies. Drool over the man all you want but leave me out of it."

"You're no fun," Lou said. She turned back to look at Caleb again.

"Mom, I mean it. Do not start. Or I'll start inviting Seth to dinner every week."

Lou's head snapped back around, blue eyes turned steely. "Don't you dare."

"Well then, how about you let me manage my love life and I'll leave you to manage yours?" Faith returned, hiding a grin. Seth Rigger was Cloud Bay's only lawyer. He was the one who'd helped Grey and the guys buy their houses back in the day and Harper Inc. still used him for local issues.

He was also Lou's tennis partner in the local competition—at least when she played mixed doubles—and he was clearly willing to play any other games Lou might want to play. Everyone on the island knew it. Including Mayor Angie. Who was definitely less than pleased with her father's choice of infatuation. Which, Faith suspected, was a big part of the reason why the mayor had been such a pain in the butt about CloudFest this year.

But until Lou made up her mind about whether she was ever going to let Seth out of the friend zone, Faith was willing to put up with the annoyance of dealing with Angie, who seemed outraged at the idea of her dad moving on after her mom's death. Given Clementine Rigger had died about five years before Grey, Faith figured

Angie needed to grow up. Seth was sweet. Lou deserved sweet.

But Lou seemed stuck on ignoring the fact that sweet was an option, so Faith and Mina tried to pretend they didn't know how Seth felt around her. Except when the knowledge came in useful for cutting off Lou's maternal instincts when they started to run wild.

Lou sighed. "Fine. But I think you're missing an opportunity."

"I think I'm about to be late if we don't get this over and done with." Faith went to join the guys by the pool before Lou could start matchmaking again.

Both men smiled as she joined them. Lou was right, she decided, the two of them definitely presented a pretty picture. She waved her arm at the pool and the stretch of rolling lawn that led down to the beach. "Everything you need."

"It's a sweet view," Liam agreed.

"The scenery makes up for some of the less exciting parts of island life," Faith said. "It can be pretty boring around here."

"Not at this time of year though," Lou interrupted with a wide smile. "Never a dull moment around the festival."

"Looking forward to it," Caleb agreed. He bounced on his toes a few times then seemed to catch himself and stilled.

"You know, if you get tired of crowds and music, Faith has a tennis court at her place. I'm sure she wouldn't mind if you wanted to use it. She's just next door." Lou smiled sunnily at Faith.

Who suddenly had to fight a severe urge to push her mom into the pool.

" 'Next door' is a relative term, Mom. It's a bit of a hike from here, you know that." Danny's house didn't sit on quite as much land as the Harper's did, but it was a couple of miles between the two houses. A bit longer if you took the path along the beach instead of cutting across the land. But she wasn't going to encourage that. "Besides, Caleb's here for a vacation. I'm sure he doesn't want to play tennis."

Crap. Did that sound rude? Like she didn't want him to use the court? She wasn't sure if she liked the idea of him on her home turf or not. Not that she'd be likely to run into him. She only came home to sleep and change clothes during festival week.

It shouldn't bother her if Caleb White wanted to play a few games on her court. Well, Grey's court. It was still too weird to think of the house as hers, not her dad's. Even six years later. And technically, it wasn't hers. Grey had left all three siblings equal shares in his estate. But Mina had wanted to live with Adam once they'd gotten married and after the accident, she'd refused Faith's offer for her to move back home. Instead, she'd claimed the cottage at the base of the lighthouse and moved in there.

"I mean, he probably gets sick of tennis and wants a break," she said hastily. Lou winced and Faith remembered that Caleb had recently quit the game for good.

Yikes.

Talk about opening mouth and sticking foot in. After all, "retired" could be code for a lot of things these days.

Much like "taking time off to find new inspiration" or "suffering exhaustion" could be in the music trade. She wondered exactly what had driven Caleb from the sport he'd ruled over for years. Injury? He seemed pretty healthy to her. So was there a less-appealing reason? Drugs? Drink? Depression?

Pretty outside didn't always equal pretty inside.

"I'm taking a break from tennis for a while," Caleb said, his voice politely friendly.

"Okay, then," she said brightly, hoping she didn't sound as awkward as she felt. What was it about this guy? First he'd sent the normally unflappable Lou into a flap and now she was turning into a moron around him too. Normally she could do small talk with strangers in her sleep but today she was seriously off her game.

"Liam plays sometimes," Caleb added when she didn't say anything else. At least one person in the conversation had his act together. Or had been raised with excellent manners. Not that she herself hadn't been raised that way. No child brought up by Lou Henry got away with being anything less than polite and respectful. And, gah, now she was rambling again. In her own head. While there were three people waiting for her to say something intelligent.

"Oh," she managed. Brilliant. *Pull it together.* "Well, of course, you're welcome to use the court if you want to." There didn't seem to be any way to avoid issuing the invitation now without turning the conversation into a complete train wreck. "I'll let my guys know, so no one hassles you. The court is easy to spot. Look for the lights." Because of course, Grey, who had briefly flirted with tennis in the early stages of his relationship with

Lou, had to have the best. She added "tell security about Liam and Caleb" to her mental list of things to do. Normally she tried to get away with the minimum she could security wise but there had been enough incidents when Grey was alive with overly enthusiastic—or sometimes straight out crazy—fans trying to get into the house for her to be able to argue that some reinforcements weren't required. After all, you couldn't exactly completely fence off a property that had the ocean on one of its sides.

"Speaking of security, I guess I should give you these." She pulled the keys out of her pocket and tossed them toward Liam. Who caught them neatly. "And the security code is—"

"I'll never remember it if I don't write it down," said Caleb. "Why don't you text it to me?"

He grinned at her, eyes suddenly very blue, and she went still, a little coil of heat flaring to life in her stomach. Smooth. The guy was smooth as well as pretty. "I don't have your number," she said, pretending not to recognize the invitation implicit in his offer. "I'm sure Danny has Liam's. I'll text it to him."

Caleb opened his mouth to say something else. She wasn't sure she wanted to hear it. Or that she could resist giving him her number if he flat out asked for it.

"And now, we have to be going," she said a little frantically before he could speak. "I have an appointment at one thirty. C'mon, Mom." She moved toward the far end of the pool, where there was a path that led back around to the front of the house where her truck was parked. "It was nice meeting you," she threw over her shoulder, not quite able to resist one last look.

chapter three

"And lo, the queen looked out upon her kingdom and saw that it was good."

"Damn, right it is." Faith Harper bumped her shoulder against Ziggy Ives's bicep and craned her head back to grin up at his lanky form. "I work damn hard to keep it that way." She took a couple of steps nearer to the edge of the main stage. "And the rest of you have worked damn hard too."

Ziggy grunted, as if to say, "Well, what do you expect?" as Faith stared out over the long, mostly deserted space in front of the stage.

It wasn't totally empty. The massive sound deck sat about three quarters of the way to the security barrier that ringed the main stage area, separating it from the other parts of the sprawl of land that CloudFest occupied each July. And despite the lack of any actual audience, there were still plenty of people moving over that space. Sound techs, lighting techs, the always-there road crews, security people, and her own team overseeing the whole production. But all those didn't add up to anything like the ten thousand music fans who'd flood the space and make it seem tiny in just three more days. But enough of that—just like it did every year, the sudden feeling of "how the hell will we pull this together in time?" swept over her.

Six years she'd been running the festival, and she'd been attending it since she could barely walk, and yet bringing the whole circus of bands and audience and crew together each year took ridiculous levels of organization and more than a sprinkle of sheer luck and magic. But they were nearly there, she reminded herself.

Every year everything fell into place. This year it all would too. Besides, contemplating her mile-long to-do list would stop her from thinking about the very blue eyes and very nice face of Caleb White.

The fact that he kept popping back into her head was annoying. Because she didn't intend to do anything involving getting to know that very nice face any better, so she needed to focus.

So. Massive to-do list contemplation was just what the doctor ordered.

"Any issues I need to know about?" she asked.

Ziggy shook his head. "We're on schedule." He hesitated a moment. "Saw Ryan earlier. Wandering around."

Faith frowned. "What did he want? We've got everything signed off, right?" Ryan Beck worked for the mayor's office.

"In triplicate," Ziggy agreed.

"So what did he want?"

"I didn't talk to him. He spoke to Dell, asked him a

question about the sound deck apparently, but he'd gone before I got down there."

"Everything's within noise limits."

"I know," Ziggy said, spreading his hands out. "Maybe he's just being extra thorough."

Ryan was a newcomer to the island, someone Angie had hired. "Thorough" was one word for him. Faith could think of less polite ones. "Maybe." Faith said. "Or maybe Angie's just trying to bust our balls some more."

"She's not dumb enough to interfere with the festival once it's underway," Ziggy said. "Too many locals make too much money from us. She'd be voted out fast enough if she messed with that."

"She still has three years in her term after this one."

"She can be recalled."

Faith lifted an eyebrow. "You been studying local politics?"

"I pay attention," Ziggy said. "Spent enough time here over the years."

Ziggy technically lived in L.A. but he also owned a tiny house on the island, not far from Lou's. In reality, he spent a lot of time on the road when he wasn't working on CloudFest. After years of being Blacklight's tour manager, his skills were still in high demand. But he devoted a couple of months each year to CloudFest. Faith wasn't entirely sure she'd be able to pull the whole thing off without him.

"Well, let's hope it doesn't come to that. Angie is just going to have to get used to the fact that CloudFest isn't going anywhere." Angie had made life difficult last year after there'd been an accident caused by a couple of festival goers driving back to the ferry after the festival ended. No one had been killed but there'd been a couple of injuries. Not anything CloudFest could have prevented, but Angie had used it as an excuse to make Faith jump through many extra hoops to get all her permits signed this year. Not to mention increased the fees for getting those permits.

But when push came to shove, CloudFest formed a major part of Lansing's economy. Angie couldn't afford to lose the festival. So she was stuck with Faith and Faith was stuck with her.

Faith turned back to look out at the site. At all the people working. Her family had started this. Over the years hundreds of thousands of people had traveled to Lansing and shared their love of music. That wasn't going to change any time soon. Not while she had anything to do with it. She walked closer to the edge of the stage, pictured the audience singing, hands waving, faces lit up.

She knew that buzz. The indescribable exhilarating flow of energy between the audience and the music, and the musicians.

She'd loved it from both sides of the stage. Just about the best feeling she knew. So Angie Rigger could bite her.

"You going to sing this year?" Ziggy asked, his bass voice resigned.

So it should be. He knew the answer to that question. She hadn't sung at CloudFest since her dad had died. With no Grey around to charm or cajole her to perform, her singing was pretty much limited to the shower, the car, and the odd drunken karaoke session these days.

She shot Ziggy a "don't start" look over her shoulder.

He held up his hands, skinny fingers spread. The sunlight glinted off the thick silver rings gracing each long digit to the knuckle. "Just askin'. Miracles happen." He rubbed a hand through his spiky graying hair and then grabbed his smart phone out of a pocket, pulling up one of his endless lists. Which was his way of telling her he was dropping the subject.

"You can console yourself with the fact that Zach decided to grace us with his presence this year." She tried to keep the happiness at the thought of seeing her brother out of her voice but she couldn't help doing a quick fist pump.

That made Ziggy look up from his screen, eyebrows drawing down over pale blue eyes. "He's definitely coming?"

Faith shrugged. "Haven't heard otherwise." She turned back toward the front of the stage. Where Zach would be standing Sunday night. Doing his thing.

Which once had been *their* thing. But that was ancient history.

She dug her fingers into the back of her neck, trying to dismiss the sudden envy that bubbled up in her chest. She could take the damn stage any time she damn wanted. Trouble was, for her, music was a team sport. And her partner had ditched her many years ago. To be fair, she hadn't exactly fought him on it.

Nope, she'd come home to lick her wounds and stayed here ever since. She couldn't blame Zach for that.

And having Zach home and watching him play was still pretty good. She turned back. Hopefully the sunglasses shielding her eyes from the heat of the midday California sun also hid her disappointment from Ziggy. Probably not. He'd known her all her life, after all.

Determined not to think of Zach and what might have been, she focused back on the people moving around the space, checking that everyone was doing what they were supposed to. An unexpected face near the security barrier past the sound deck caught her eye.

"Speaking of miracles." She bent and boosted herself down from the stage, heading toward the dark head before it disappeared.

"Mina!" she yelled, flicking the mic pack she wore—the first sound check was starting in an hour—on. "Mina!" she yelled again. This time her voice boomed through the sound system like a thunderclap.

Faith ignored the puzzled faces pointed in her direction as she jogged across the space. Dust puffed up around her worn red Converse, sticking to her sweaty legs. Lansing Island hadn't been quite as badly hit by drought as the rest of California—but it was dry enough, and the fields that housed CloudFest were mostly dead grass and dry dirt in the height of summer. The catering contractors were going to do well selling water this year. She made a mental note to double-check that the stock of water—and other beverages—backstage and for the crew was larger than normal.

She rounded the corner of the sound deck and almost crashed into Mina standing in the shade cast by the structure. She turned the forward motion into an enthusiastic hug, wrapping herself around Mina's shoulders. Mina returned the embrace for a few seconds before slipping free.

Faith let her go. She missed Mina's hugs, but Mina was the widow, not Faith, so Faith was sucking it up and giving her sister whatever space she needed. Mostly.

"You bellowed?" Mina said, pushing short black hair back off her face.

"I did not bellow. I spoke normally and the sound system did the rest." Faith lifted her own mane of hair off her neck and scrabbled in her pocket for a hair tie to secure it into a pile at the back of her head, envying her sister's pixie cut for once. The heat was turning her into a sweaty mess. She wanted nothing more than to head down to the beach and let the salt water wash the dust off her sticky limbs but there was way too much to do to even think about playing hooky.

"You bellowed. I heard you the first time."

"Well, I wanted to make sure I caught you." She waved an arm at all the hoopla around them. "What do you think?"

Mina looked around and shrugged. "Looks good."

"Are you going to come see some of the sets? We've got some great bands this year." Faith stopped herself from giving a list of their starring acts. Mina paid about as much attention to the music scene as Faith did to tide charts and rescue techniques. Still, Mina usually showed up to at least one or two events at the festival. Faith half-suspected Lou talked her into it. Gave her a speech about supporting the family biz or something.

Those maternal instincts again. Lou wasn't Mina's mom, but given Emmy had only stuck on the island until Mina was four and the siren song of her jet-setting photography career had been too much to resist, Lou had earned the right to maternal interference.

Thank god for Lou.

Without her, the three of them would have been

screwed. "I'll get Theo to send you all the times and stages, if you'd like."

Mina hesitated, then another shrug. She shoved her hands into her pockets, the motion tugging down the waistband of her old green cargo pants, revealing a frame that still looked way too thin for Faith's liking.

"I have to wait and see. I'm on call this weekend."

No doubt that she'd volunteered for that particular duty. CloudFest was the biggest event of the year for Cloud Bay and most of the residents—even the ones who ran the businesses that benefited most from the influx of festival goers—tried to come along and see some of the show.

Because Grey had started the festival that had revolutionized sleepy Lansing Island's economy all those years ago, Mina's boss would have let her have time off if she wanted. "No one's going to need search and rescue, everyone's going to be here at the festival."

"You say that every year but every year, some idiot and his friends go swimming or hire a boat or a jet ski and get their drunk asses into trouble."

"Maybe this year will be your lucky year," Faith said, hiding her sigh. Mina would far rather risk life and limb hauling some stranger's ass to safety on the ocean than brave the crowds at the festival. Which was just wrong. And Faith was determined to start coaxing Mina out more often. She'd had three years of being a virtual hermit by Faith's standards. Surely that was long enough?

Mina gave yet another shrug.

"At least take your passes—" Faith paused, as she remembered the VIP passes were in her purse, which was currently somewhere back on the stage. "Come up to the stage with me and say hi to Ziggy and I'll give them to you. Then I promise to stop nagging."

"That would be a first," Mina said, but she smiled as she spoke, so that was okay.

Faith slipped her arm through her sister's and started back toward the stage before Mina could change her mind.

"Look who I found," she called to Ziggy, who had his nose in his phone again. She clambered up the metal stairs at the side of the stage and Mina followed.

"Hey, darlin'," Ziggy said, grin cracking his tanned face as he spotted Mina. He came toward them, looking cool despite his black jeans, black boots, and black T-shirt. Just looking at him made her feel hotter, but Ziggy looked like he was standing in an air-conditioned room. She had no idea how he did it. Maybe after forty odd years of life under huge stage lights you developed immunity to high temperatures.

Mina stood on tiptoe to kiss Ziggy's cheek. She was a couple of inches taller than Faith, but Ziggy had giraffe in his blood somewhere.

"Hey, yourself," Mina said. "Hope you're not letting Faith work you too hard."

"Never."

Liar. Ziggy was more of a workaholic than Faith was. He was sixty-three and showed no signs of slowing down. The only time he stopped was when he lost himself in a book or stole a few minutes to sketch something in the battered leather notebook he carried around everywhere.

Now he was turning his artist's eye on Mina. "You look tired."

She waved him off. She'd pretty much waved all of them off whenever they expressed concern for her at any time during the last three years since Adam had died. "I'm fine. You're the ones working the crazy hours."

"All for a good cause." Ziggy was grinning again.

"You two talk, I need to find Mina's passes." Faith left them to it and went in search of her purse. It was tucked in between a guitar case and several coils of electrical leads farther back on the stage. As she rummaged for the passes, she watched Mina and Ziggy. Mina laughed at something Ziggy said, her face lighting up. Thank god for Ziggy. He got Mina, who liked books and art as much as he did. He'd always understood her way better than Grey had. And looked after her.

But Ziggy, like everyone else in the immediate vicinity apart from Mina, had rock 'n' roll running through his veins. And he followed its call. Mina was always going to be the odd one out when it came to music. Faith's fingers closed around the passes, pulling them free. There were people who'd kill for all-access passes to Cloud-Fest. But Mina would probably avoid using them. Which only went to show that genetics was a very weird thing.

Faith would never be able to explain the electric charge she got from live music to her sister any more than Mina would be able to convince Faith that going out in boats in storms or spending hours alone with a paintbrush—the two things Mina spent most of her time doing these days—were fun.

But Mina's musical indifference didn't matter to Faith. It had mattered to Grey, but Grey was gone. And Zach was gone ninety-nine percent of the time too. Which meant that Faith was going to be thankful for the family still around her, different as they might be. The ones who were smiling at her when she walked back over to join them.

"Here you go." She slipped the lanyard—which had a tiny version of the iconic CloudFest logo stamped along its length—over Mina's head. "Try and come to something, okay? You don't have to fight the crowds or anything if you don't want to. You know that. The gate guys can get me any time you get here and I'll come grab you and we can hang out backstage."

"Of course," Mina said. She just barely avoided sounding like she thought mingling backstage was a fate worse than death, but Faith knew she was thinking it. But she shut up. Enough sisterly hassling for one day.

"What brings you to the madhouse, darlin'?" Ziggy asked. "We haven't seen you around lately."

Faith gave herself a mental slap. In her happiness at seeing Mina, she hadn't stopped to wonder what had brought her sister down to the festival site. It was out of her way and not the sort of place where Mina hung out by preference. She made an apologetic face at Mina. "Sorry, I kind of railroaded you there. Was there something you wanted to talk to me about? Or were you looking for someone else?"

Mina kind of winced. Her hand went to her neck where Adam's wedding ring hung on a thin silver chain.

Crap. Faith's stomach sank. Mina didn't exactly have a poker face and she only played with the ring when she was nervous. Or uncomfortable. Or had bad news.

"What?" Faith asked.

Mina lifted a hand. "Don't shoot the messenger, okay?"

"What?" Faith asked again, hearing her voice go grim.

"Zach called me."

Well, crap, that couldn't be good. "And?"

"He said that the band got offered a last-minute slot opening for some big act this weekend. At Madison Square Garden. So he can't make it."

Goddammit. Faith bit back the string of extremely bad words that floated through her head. It wasn't Mina's fault that Zach had used her as a go-between. She felt her hands curl into fists.

"Faith?" Mina said cautiously.

"Did he say who they were opening for?" Faith managed. Beside Mina, Ziggy's face was carefully blank.

"No. I didn't think to ask," Mina said, looking guilty.

Faith tried to think if she knew who was playing the Garden this weekend. She usually had a good idea of clashes with CloudFest for major artists because it meant they got crossed off the list of potential invitees to perform for the year. But apparently being filled with rage was bad for her memory. "Did he say why he couldn't call me himself?"

"He said he'd tried. That you weren't answering. He had to jump on a plane, then they were going to be in rehearsals. Said he wanted to make sure you had plenty of notice."

That was a complete crock. There was no trace of Zach in her call log. She'd have noticed. Nope. He'd just not wanted to have to deal with the fact he was leaving Faith in the lurch. Again. Fuck.

Intellectually she understood. Zach's band, Fringe Dweller, was starting to get some serious traction after working their butts off for years. Any chance for a high-profile gig was good for them. It had been a bit of a fluke that they'd had a break in their touring schedule so that Zach could play at CloudFest this year anyway. But her brain wasn't in charge right this moment. No, right this moment what she really wanted was to punch Zach. Hard. Mina and Ziggy were both watching her like she was a bomb that might explode at any second.

"He said it shouldn't be a big deal, because he was the secret gig, right? You can get someone else?" Mina said hopefully.

Faith breathed in through her nose. *Not Mina's fault,* she reminded herself. All Zach's.

Mina really had no idea what went into pulling the festival together. Zach, on the other hand, knew exactly the kinds of logistics involved. And what it meant to have to find a fill-in performer who'd be a big crowd-pleaser at the last minute and get them, their gear, and everything else to Lansing. Or else not have a secret gig this year, which would disappoint all the fans. Sneaking in an unannounced act or two was part of CloudFest tradition, all the way back to the very first CloudFest in 1992 when Grey had somehow convinced Kurt Cobain to do a short solo set right at the peak of Nirvana hysteria. Traditionally the secret act played on Sunday, just before the closing act. And it was already Monday afternoon. Which didn't exactly give her a lot of time to find another act and get the logistics sorted. The ferries were all booked solid at this time of year, even with the extra services they ran, so she'd have to charter something to get whoever she could find here, let along their gear. Fucking Zach.

Not Mina's fault, she thought again as she pulled herself together. Made herself meet Mina's worried gaze.

"Sure," she said, ignoring Ziggy's raised eyebrows.

Mina's expression turned relieved, and Faith made herself smile.

"I should get out of your hair," Mina said, glancing back toward the exit.

Faith didn't try to stop her. If Mina stayed, she was just going to see just how upset Faith was. Which neither one of them needed. Normally Faith would've tried to coax Mina into hanging around a bit longer, but now it was better just to let her go. "Okay," she said. "But make sure you come and see some of the festival. I want to hang out with my baby sister."

"I'll try," Mina said.

Which wasn't the same as "I'll be there." But Faith knew when to back off. Sometimes.

"You try not to work too hard," Mina said as she stood on tiptoe to kiss Ziggy's cheek.

"That's a promise," Faith replied. As much as she worked like a dog leading up to the festival, when it actually started, she tended to hand over the micromanaging to the various stage managers and crews and—barring dire emergencies—immersed herself in the week-long party, soaking up the music and catching up with the performers and VIP guests she knew. But Mina didn't need to know that part—well, she did know but she didn't need to talk about it. Mina was the married-to-the-childhood-sweetheart-at-eighteen type. Faith was . . . not.

She watched Mina making her way to the exit, trying to relax. Or at least stop plotting ways to kill her brother slowly and painfully.

Behind her, Ziggy cleared his throat. "You okay?"

"Do you want the real answer to that question?" She pasted on a smile and turned back to him. The sympathy on his face was clear. She didn't want sympathy. She wanted a voodoo doll of Zach and some very large and pointy pins. Just for a couple of minutes.

"Darlin', Zach's just doing what he has to do."

"You mean he's doing what's good for Zach."

That earned her a hitch of his shoulder. "You know what the business is like. Fringe Dweller needs to keep the hustle going while they've got some momentum."

She did know. She learned those lessons from the time she'd been old enough to understand what it was that made her daddy vanish from her life for weeks at a time, only heard occasionally on the end of a phone line or as the name on a card on the parcels that used to arrive whenever Grey had a rare fit of paternal guilt and decided to send his kids the latest toy or gadget while he was on the road. And as much as she really didn't want to admit it was true, it seemed as though Zach was growing more like Grey every day.

So. Fuck him. She'd been stupid and had gotten her hopes up. Believed Zach was coming home. She wasn't going to do that again.

She drew her shoulders back and shoved her sunglasses into place, determined that Ziggy wouldn't see any stupid lingering shreds of hurt in her eyes. It was doubtful he didn't know exactly what she was doing, but the illusion of maintaining some dignity made her feel a little better.

"So," she said. "Who are we going to call to fill this damned slot?"

chapter four

"Right, that's it," Faith said many hours later. "Everybody out. We all deserve a night off." The clock on the wall told her it was already past ten. "What's left of the night off," she amended.

Across the table, four pairs of eyes regarded her as if she'd just lost her mind.

She slammed the laptop shut. "I'm serious."

Theo tapped the open notebook in front of him with his pen. "We have half a hundred things—"

"All of which can wait until morning." In fact, if the mood she was in had anything to do with it, it could wait forever.

She wanted to snarl. Had been wanting to snarl for hours even as she had sweet-talked and cajoled her way through her little black book and secured Sienna Reese to take Zach's secret slot.

Sienna who was a bigger star than Zach anyway, her last album having broken out and made her a mainstream superstar instead of an indie darling. With both street cred and now massive sales, she suited the CloudFest crowd to a tee. They had always walked a tightrope between interesting new up-and-comers and crowd-pleasing big names well enough that CloudFest remained cool and edgy and damn profitable.

But Sienna wasn't a Harper. And she definitely wasn't Faith's brother. So the victory of having pulled a rabbit out of the hat so to speak didn't really make Faith feel any less pissed off at Zach.

Not only had he bailed, but her opportunity to talk to him and Mina about Harper Inc. and her new idea for it had just evaporated. This weekend had been the one break in his schedule. Fringe Dweller was heading back out on tour next week, so it wasn't likely he'd be coming home any time soon. These days Mina wasn't exactly a fan of travel, and getting her off-island was nearly impossible, so it wasn't going to be easy to engineer another face-to-face meeting. A sensible person would have given in and decided to try and get Zach to Skype, but she really wanted to talk in person.

But he'd killed that by canceling on her.

Hence her current mood. Which had started off bad when Mina had relayed Zach's message and only worsened while they'd sat around and done the extra work to figure out how to get Sienna's setup onto the island and make all the other changes happen that rippled out from changing a performer at this late stage.

She'd been trying to keep everyone from seeing just how furious she was, but she was reaching her limit. Any minute now she was going to snap at someone.

Or, she thought as she rubbed the back of her neck

and stared at her staff, start throwing things. Ziggy, Theo, Ally who worked in the Harper offices, and Leah Santelli, who usually ran the Harper Inc. recording studio but pitched in with whatever needed to be done at this time of year, were still looking at her like she'd lost it.

Maybe she had. But none of them deserved to be snarled at or witness Faith having the tantrum she really wanted to throw. So she would reserve that for the next time she spoke to Zach and get everyone else out of the danger zone.

"I mean it. None of us are going to have any time to ourselves or much sleep for the next week. And I, for one, have had enough for today."

Ziggy lifted a shaggy eyebrow but apparently he knew better than to argue. He pushed back his chair and started packing up his stuff. The other three watched him for a moment then followed suit.

"We starting back at the usual time?" Theo asked as he slid his laptop into a battered leather messenger bag.

"Bright and early," Faith managed, through teeth that seriously wanted to grit. Or something. She wasn't sure that she knew exactly what gritted teeth were.

Behind Theo, Leah, who along with Ivy formed the other two of what Grey had liked to call the Unholy Trinity—aka Faith's best friends—mouthed "Everything okay?"

Faith nodded and made a little shooing gesture. Which earned her a narrowed look from Leah's big green eyes and no doubt would require an explanation in the morning, but for now apparently Leah was going to let her get away with it.

Five minutes later, she had locked up the offices and was driving Grey's truck the short distance back to the main house, only looking over her shoulder once to make sure that everybody else's cars were really heading down the drive and out through the gates and that no one was going to try to double back and check that she was okay.

But no one did and she parked the truck carelessly as she reached the house. Silence settled around her as she climbed out and stared up at the big white house in the moonlight. Usually it was a relief to come home to peace and quiet, but tonight the dark windows just reminded her how completely empty the place was.

She hadn't invited anyone to the island for CloudFest this year because she'd expected Zach and whoever he wanted to bring with him to be staying. It had been nearly a year since Zach had been home. She'd wanted some privacy for the little bit of time they might get to hang out.

So much for that.

The thought made her want to snarl all over again, and she padded toward the kitchen after she'd dumped her bag and keys. They'd ordered pizza for dinner at the office while they'd worked. It felt like a long time ago.

Maybe anger burned extra calories.

She yanked open the refrigerator but nothing on the well-stocked shelves appealed. It wasn't really possible to slam the door, but she gave it a good try before stalking over to the windows to scowl out at the empty grounds and the dark mass of ocean beyond.

The house seemed to close in around her with the darkness. Normally she liked being alone. It had been a rare enough thing in her childhood. Grey had almost always had guests when he'd been home and even when he hadn't—between three kids and three wives and the band and the housekeepers and the staff at the recording studios and the offices there'd almost always been someone around.

Not to mention there'd usually been half a dozen dogs and cats in residence at any time. Gray had been an inveterate gatherer of strays. Which was fine for him because he brought them home and dumped them on everyone else to deal with when Blacklight hit the road again. Not that Faith had minded. She liked animals, even if Gray had had a genius for choosing pets with issues of one kind or another. But she'd put the last of the cats he'd acquired to sleep about a year ago—a small gray and white girl who'd always followed Faith around like a fluffy shadow—and she hadn't yet been able to bring herself to start on the next generation of critters.

So there was just her and the house and the ever-present sound of the ocean just a few hundred yards away.

Usually that soothed her.

Tonight she just wanted—

Hell, she had no idea what she wanted.

Other than something that definitely wasn't here.

So maybe she needed not to be here either.

Fifteen minutes later she wheeled her bicycle up to the tiny side alley that ran the length of the Salt Devil distillery and propped it against the wall. Lights still shone through the frosted windows, which told her that Will and Stefan hadn't yet closed up for the night.

Good.

She pulled her hair free from the ponytail she'd tucked it into for the short ride and headed toward the entrance. There were only a couple of cars in the small parking lot. The distillery, which the Fraser brothers had opened five years ago, was off the beaten track—as much as anything on an island the size of Lansing could be called off the beaten track.

Cloud Bay was on the east side of the island, facing the California coastline. The land where Grey and the Blacklight boys had staked their claims was on the northern end of the west side where there was nothing between the ocean and the horizon and the beaches were wilder and less popular with the tourists. There were a few scattered businesses on this side of the island, a couple of small general stores, a gas station, and a bait and tackle shop along with a café and an art gallery. The distillery, and the bar that went with it, was the newest addition to the ventures that'd decided not to stay firmly within Cloud Bay's town limits.

But it wasn't a place the tourists tended to find as readily—most of the year at least. It would be frantic later in the week but the main barrage of festival attendees wouldn't arrive until tomorrow. They tended to stick to the bars in Cloud Bay for the first night or so before venturing further afield or stumbling across Salt Devil when they came to check out where the Blacklight members lived.

Faith had never been entirely sure why the Frasers hadn't gone for a property closer to Cloud Bay, if not in the town itself, where business would be steadier. Will had explained to her once—something about salt air and whiskey barrels and how that affected the taste of the whiskey he and Stefan would be making—but she hadn't really understood much of it. But the bar was close to home and she'd gotten in the habit of dropping in now and then.

In her current mood she'd rather stick a fork in her eye than deal with overeager festival goers in Cloud Bay, so the relative peace of Salt Devil was perfect.

Will was behind the old wooden bar, wiping glasses and setting them neatly back into racks. He smiled as he spotted her.

"Hey, Faith," he said easily as she slid onto one of the stools. "Didn't expect to see you here this time of year."

"Surprise." She made herself smile at him but couldn't quite keep the edge out of her voice. It was easy to smile at Will. He and his brother were both easy on the eyes. Tall and tanned and brown eyed. Easygoing. Will, who was the younger but taller than the two, wore his hair longish, its sun-streaked brown always looking slightly wavy as if the salt air made it want to curl. He'd stuck a yellow pencil behind one ear, taming some of the mane tonight.

His version of surfer-boy long hair looked far more natural than the Hollywood polished version Liam had sported earlier.

"The usual?" Will asked, reaching for a wine glass.

She shook her head. Will knew her. Knew that she tended to stick to a glass of wine if she drank at all. But tonight wine wasn't going to cut it. "What've you got that's good?" The Frasers were making their own whiskey on the island but were yet to decant—was that even the word?—any of it. If she was remembering right, they were planning to test part of their first batch next summer. Until then, they were importing whiskeys from around the world and sourcing Californian microbrews and doing arcane things with other liqueurs and barrels and stuff she'd never heard of to keep the drinkers of Lansing satisfied.

"Whiskey?" Will asked.

Another head shake. Whiskey had been Grey's drink. She didn't want to think of her family tonight.

Will tipped his head at her as he picked up a glass. "Everything okay?"

"It will be once you pour me a drink." She and Will weren't exactly friends but she'd spent enough nights here over the years that they knew each other well enough. He was a very good barman. Had that "tell me all your secrets" thing going on. She'd often had the feeling that he was one of the few people who saw through Faith Harper the rock star's daughter to Faith Harper the person. Unsettling.

But he never pushed and certainly never made a pass at her. She was fairly certain his taste in women ran more to the slim and quiet, like Mina. She'd caught him watching her sister a time or two but as far as she knew, he'd never made a pass at Mina either.

Not that Mina gave off anything like encouraging vibes these days.

"I'm fine, Will. Just don't feel like drinking wine tonight." Since she rarely drank anything more than a glass or two of white wine at any invite, that made his brow lift slightly again. But then he shrugged and nodded.

"I've got some aged rum that's pretty good. I'll make you something."

"Great." This time the smile came more naturally.

And when he slid a tall glass in front of her and she took a sip of something that was warm and spicy yet somehow sharp with a hint of . . . rosemary maybe, it eased another notch or too. She took another sip, closed her eyes to appreciate the taste as the warmth of the rum spread through her. "That's amazing."

It was. Delicious.

"Good, yes?" Will said.

She opened her eyes again, and nodded. "Perfect." Better than wine. Which she had never particularly liked. Precisely the reason she usually chose to drink it when she did indulge. She was never tempted to have too much.

There was no way she was going to let herself end up like Grey, a reformed alcoholic dead of liver cancer well before his time. But nor was she going to take Mina's route of never drinking either. Sometimes a little alcohol was just the thing and being able to nurse a glass made the regular social events that came with being the public face of CloudFest and Harper Inc. somewhat easier.

No one seemed to offer her the hard stuff when she had a wine glass in hand. No one ever noticed she mostly filled the glass with wine spritzers, which were about eighty percent club soda. And no one bothered to try giving her anything else—her reputation for not being the slightest bit interested in a high that came from anything other than booze was well established in the industry—so the wineglass was armor of a sort.

But every so often she'd let herself out to play a little and drink whiskey or tequila or rum or vodka. Which all tasted just that little bit too good to her. That was usually enough to send her back to the wine.

But tonight she'd sip Will's cocktail and hope it took the edge off her mood enough that she could pedal herself home again and actually manage to sleep.

"Will!" Stefan's voice bellowed from the kitchen beyond the bar, and Will made an apologetic noise and disappeared through the swinging doors to see what his brother wanted.

Which left Faith alone with her drink. Which was a third gone already.

So much for sipping.

So maybe it was time to look for another distraction. She turned on the stool and surveyed the mostly empty room. A couple were playing pool at the lone table and two older guys she thought might be part of the festival crew were seated at one of the few occupied tables. They were studying their check and obviously about to leave.

Maybe it was going to have to be a late-night session of silly banter with Will and Stefan after all. A thumping noise came from the kitchen and she heard Stefan swear.

Or maybe she'd just sit here and listen to the Mumford & Sons Will had playing softly in the background and enjoy some peace and quiet.

But then she looked past the older guys to the farthest table right up the far end of the floor-to-ceiling window that ran the length of the room on the ocean side and spotted the back of a blond head that looked far too familiar. Particularly when she matched it with the fact that Liam Sullivan was sitting opposite it.

Caleb White. Not who she'd expected to stumble over at Salt Devil. She took another slug of rum and studied him a moment, trying to figure out how she felt about him being here. Liam was staring out the window and talking on his phone while he sipped something clear over ice. Which left Faith free to appreciate the glory that was Caleb White's back in a tight dark T-shirt.

Lou was right. The man was mighty pretty.

So maybe what she needed to drive out her demons tonight was a little time spent admiring the pretty. Just looking couldn't hurt.

"Mind if I sit down?"

Caleb looked up at the words, startled. But surprise quickly turned to pleasure when he realized the woman standing at his elbow, drink in hand, was Faith Harper.

Faith who he'd been thinking about on and off all afternoon since she'd driven away in her beat-up red truck without so much as a backward glance.

He'd been very happy to discover she was just as gorgeous in person as she had been in those music videos.

More, in fact. Her face grown sharper now that she was older and her personality showing through those huge gray-green eyes instead of just looking music-video mysterious. Even dressed very casually, her cheeks flushed from the heat and her hair escaping the bun she'd piled it into, she'd been startlingly pretty.

And here she was again. Her hair was down now, falling over her shoulders in a mass of blonde and brown waves. Wearing what he was fairly sure were the same shorts she'd had on earlier. Though now she changed into a light cotton shirt in a greenish shade that made her eyes an even more interesting color than the beat up band T-shirt had. She looked tired, there were shadows under the big eyes. Tired, and maybe annoyed about something. But even tired and annoyed at the end of a long day, she was gorgeous.

Gorgeous, and standing next to him asking if she could sit with him.

So maybe his dorky attempt at getting her number—which she'd quite rightly shot down—hadn't completely turned her off him.

Not that he was here to hook up.

But he was here to be distracted from the mess waiting for him when he returned to the real world. Sponsors to be sorted out, media to deal with, not to mention all the people who made up his support team. And, beyond all of that, was the biggest freaking issue of them all, figuring out what the hell he was going to do with the rest of his life.

Thinking about it made him exhausted. He'd been about to suggest to Liam that they call it a night and try to bank at least one decent night's sleep ahead of what, according to Liam, promised to be a week of festival madness. So Faith appearing in the dimly lit bar seemed like the universe throwing him a lifeline.

Even if it was just a bit of harmless flirtation.

"Sure," he said and stood to pull the empty chair between him and Liam out for her. "Have a seat."

Her eyebrows lifted at that, but she smiled and sat, putting her drink down on one of the coasters emblazoned with the weird little piratical devil creature crouching on a barrel that seemed to be the bar's logo.

The logo might be weird but their booze was good and the burgers the kitchen had served up had been pretty damned good too, so he wasn't going to argue with their taste in graphic design.

"So," he said, picking up his own glass as Liam nodded at Faith and mouthed "Hello" before returning to his call, "do you come here often?"

Faith laughed at that, the sound low and throaty. Some of the fatigue in her face vanished, leaving her looking golden and carefree in the flickering light of the small lanterns that sat on each table, and his gut tightened with sudden heat.

As distractions went, she was one he was happy to have.

"Now and then," she said. "I like the view." She waved one hand at the window.

He knew the ocean was out there somewhere in the darkness. But what he could see in the window right now was their reflection. Her reflection, mostly. Which was no less alluring than the real thing.

"Me too," he agreed with a smile. He looked at the window version of Faith, who seemed to look back at him, her lips curving in the image. "It's kind of spectacular."

One side of her mouth quirked further in appreciation. Then her head turned toward Liam. Who was still listening intently to whoever was on the other end of the line. Caleb had assumed it was business at first—one of Liam's clients with some sort of crisis that had to be handled, in true Hollywood fashion this very second. But he was starting to think it must be some-one more interesting on the end of the line.

A girlfriend, maybe. Liam hadn't mentioned that he was seeing anyone seriously, but then Caleb had been away for a couple of months before Wimbledon and he'd been too busy with his own shit since he'd returned to get the latest from Liam. It was part of the reason he'd agreed to come to Lansing. Time to just hang out had become rare in both their schedules in the last few years.

Liam must have noticed them both watching, because he half-hitched a shoulder and then rose and walked away from the table, opening the sliding door in the glass that led out to a deck beyond the window and step-ping outside. He slid the door closed behind him, cut-ting them off from even his side of the conversation.

Caleb didn't know if Liam was giving Caleb space or whether he was just trying to keep his call private, but either way he wasn't going to argue.

Because now he was alone with Faith.

Faith, who sipped whatever it was in her drink and didn't say anything.

Seemed like getting a conversation going might be up to him.

Caleb had finished the second of two very good whis-keys that the guy at the bar—Will, that was it—had recommended before Faith had arrived. He'd had one night of drinking after he'd retired, but the resulting hangover—he didn't drink much when training and tended to get out of practice so to speak—had been bad enough that he wasn't planning to repeat the experience any time soon. Two had left him with just enough of a buzz to take the edge off the restless anxiety that had been dogging him since he'd announced his retirement. But it had also stolen his ability to think of an innocuous question to ask her.

The silence sat between them.

Faith put down her drink. "Did you find everything at the house?"

Caleb nodded. "Yes, thanks. Even found the grocery store. So we're all set." He didn't mention they'd basically loaded up with snacks and beer and breakfast foods. Since it was force of habit for him to eat healthy, he'd made sure not all the snacks were the junk Liam kept throwing into the cart. "It's a great house."

"Yes," she agreed. "Danny's into architecture. He's spent a fortune on that place."

"I like it. It's peaceful."

She smiled. "When Danny's not there, sure. When he's home, it gets a bit chaotic."

"Not settling down in his old age?" Caleb wasn't sure exactly how old Danny Ryan must be. Sixty-ish? It had been five, six, years since Grey Harper had died . . . that news had shocked the world . . . from liver cancer and he'd only been in his fifties. It was kind of crazy to think of the Blacklight guys being sixty but, as Grey had proven, being sixty was better than the alternative.

"Well, he's sober these days," Faith said. "Stopped drinking again a few years ago. But that doesn't mean he doesn't like company. Or has stopped pulling stunts. I think everyone always thought he did half the things he did because he was drunk or high. Turns out that doing crazy stuff for the heck of it is just the way he is." She sounded amused.

"Adrenalin junkie, maybe?" Caleb asked.

"I think all performers have a bit of that in their personalities," Faith agreed. "Once you get as famous as Blacklight, playing to crowds that size, it's definitely a rush. Hard to give up." She tilted her head at him. "You must know a little bit about that too?"

She hadn't mentioned the word tennis, he noted. Tactful.

"Yes." Though he'd always been more about the win than the fact there were people watching him win. Still, he couldn't deny that wanting the buzz that came with fighting his way to victory cheered on by nearly fifteen thousand fans wasn't part of what had driven him through years of training.

"Sorry," she said. "Do you mind talking about it?" There was curiosity in her tone

"It was my choice to retire," he said. "It's not a sore subject, if that's what you're asking." Not entirely true. There were people who were plenty sore at him. But he wasn't ready to talk to them. Nor did he want to explain his decision to the whole world yet. Not until he had his shit together.

But for some reason the idea of telling Faith was almost . . . comforting. She obviously knew all about living in the spotlight. He doubted she was going to run to anyone in the press and spill the beans about why Caleb White said he'd thrown in the towel.

"Okay. But we can talk about something else if you'd prefer." She took another sip of her drink. The level in the glass didn't decrease much. Maybe she wasn't much of a drinker either.

"Not much to talk about. I decided it was time. It was

starting to feel like hard work. And tennis has never been work to me." He didn't mention his shoulder.

She nodded, as if she knew what he meant. "Sounds sensible. Better to step back before you start to hate it."

"Yeah, I never wanted to be the guy trying to hang on too long. I guess I believe that everything has its time and once that time is over, you move on."

Her gaze sharpened a little as he said the words, a smile flickering over her face that he couldn't quite read.

"I'm not going to argue with that. Trying to make something happen when your heart's not in it or it's not meant to be is pretty toxic. You see that a lot in my business."

Her voice sounded slightly . . . wistful, and he wondered if she was talking about something more than watching plenty of bands wash out over the years.

But that felt like way too personal a question to ask someone he barely knew.

"Mine too."

She tilted the remains of her drink, the ice in her glass clinking softly. "The obvious question then, is what comes next. But you don't have to answer that."

"For now, I'm just playing hooky from life for a little while." He shrugged, looking back out the window for the moment where he could just see Liam leaning against the rail of the deck through Faith's reflection, phone still glued to his ear. "Seemed like the thing to do."

She made a noise that seemed like agreement but he wasn't sure.

"But that's enough about me for a while." He nodded toward the glass in her hand. "Should I ask about your day?"

Her mouth twisted into a grimace. "Let's just say it went downhill after I left Danny's."

"Something you want to talk about?"

"Not particularly. Just one of those days." Her eyes looked cooler.

Right. That was pretty clear. Whatever it was that was bugging her, she didn't want to talk about it. Time to pick something else to talk about. "Must be a lot of work to organize something like CloudFest."

"It is. But I have a great team and we've got a good system in place after so many years. And it's always worth it in the end." Her smile reappeared, her expression lightening.

"No playing hooky for you then?" he asked.

chapter five

Was that flirting? It felt like flirting. Caleb White was flirting with her. Or at least, throwing out the initial bait to see if she wanted to flirt back.

She considered it for a moment.

Rules or no rules, the thought of playing hooky with Caleb was tempting.

Very tempting.

Almost too tempting with the glow from Will's cocktail simmering in her blood. She'd forgotten how potent Will's concoctions could be. Right now, she was feeling more relaxed than she had in weeks.

But temptation or not, she still had a ton of work to do before the festival started.

"No playing hooky for me," she agreed, and was startled to feel a burn of resentment as she said it. Everyone else seemed to feel like they could skip out on their commitments. Maybe because she was always there to pick up the slack.

"At least," she amended, "not until Friday." There. That wasn't strictly flirting on her part, but she hadn't shut him down either. She wasn't entirely sure why not. Chalk it up to Will's magic rum and hope that she'd find her sanity again in the morning?

Caleb's brows lifted slightly at that. "Isn't that when the festival is in full swing?'

"Yes. But by that point, my role is mostly to hang out and talk to the bands and the VIPs and enjoy the shows. Unless there's a crisis, of course." Hopefully there wouldn't be anything else going wrong. Zach's little bombshell was enough of a wrench in the works. She had worked her butt off to fix that and she hoped like hell that everything would go smoothly from here on in.

They'd made changes in the wake of the accident last year, even if it hadn't been their fault. Gotten stricter on transport. Hired extra security. Limited the number of vendors on site selling alcohol and read them the extra-long version of the riot act to make it clear that anyone caught selling liquor to a minor or someone who had obviously had too much already would be dealing with the sheriff's department. And blacklisted.

She tapped her knuckles on the table softly. "Knock wood, of course. Don't want to jinx myself. And do not say anything like 'What could possibly go wrong?' Because the answer is 'a lot.'" Weather, illness, the inevitable minor injuries that happened with such a large crowd, not to mention wrangling something like a hundred acts to rotate through the four days the festival lasted. The number of variables involved was way too high to expect totally clear sailing. But little bumps in the road didn't require her intervention. Big ones did.

"I guess it's like a Grand Slam tournament in some ways," Caleb said.

"Probably. We probably have more gear to deal with. Speaker stacks are bigger than tennis rackets. But then, no broadcasters to wrangle. Your crowds are probably a bit more sedate too. And I'm assuming pro tennis players don't usually go on benders and pass out the night before a big match."

"Not very often, no," Caleb said with a smile. "You wouldn't get very far in the sport if you did that.

"Some of the younger players start out taking advantage of traveling the world to enjoy themselves but they soon learn that it takes a toll on their game. Besides which, most of the lower-ranked players need to save their money for travel and entry fees and coaching and gear. Once you get successful you can afford to party, but you don't want to pay the price in performance. Celebrations the night after a big win, sure. Maybe a couple of nights. But then it's back to the routine." He shrugged.

"My life would be easier if the same was true of musicians." Faith said. "And in their case, sometimes it's the opposite and the behavior gets worse as they get more successful."

"Well, I can't deny the circuit doesn't have a few divas of both sexes in terms of behavior. But generally it's not the getting-high and passing-out kind. The rules about drugs are strict and the testing is frequent. No one wants to be banned."

"No drug bans in music. Not until it's too late anyway." Which was a pity. If the studios and managers were willing to try and get bands to behave early on and cut off the access of some of the lowlifes who preyed on the perfect storm of youth, pressure, money and fame, then maybe Grey would still be alive. Or maybe not. After all, most people drink without becoming addicted. She frowned. Not exactly the train of thought she wanted to be having. She'd come here to shake her mood, not make it worse. "This conversation has gotten way too serious."

"Big money is always serious," Caleb said. He looked past her. "Looks like the pool table's free. Do you play?"

"I'm a rock star's daughter. I've spent a lot of time in bars and on the road in my misspent youth. Of course I play."

"In that case, do you want to show me how it's done?"

"What, Mr. Number One in the World Tennis Player doesn't know how to play pool?" Had he still been number one when he'd retired? She couldn't remember. He had definitely been number one for several years. Pretty impressive when you thought about it. It took a certain kind of single-minded dedication to get to that level. Grey had had that same drive.

She knew the costs that drive demanded.

What had Caleb given up to get where he was? Who had he left behind? She shoved the thought away. There was no reason for her to know. Or care. She wasn't getting involved.

"I know how," he said. "I just don't get to play very often. I've spent plenty of time on the road. But I tended to hang out on tennis courts rather than in pool halls." There was no judgment in his voice.

"Well, I guess that makes it my duty to continue your education, doesn't it?" she said. "What about Liam?"

Caleb's buddy was still out on the deck. She could just make out his silhouette near one of the lanterns that sat at intervals along the deck's railing. He still seemed to be engrossed in his phone call.

"Whoever he's talking to seems to have his full attention."

"You don't know?" She'd assumed it must be a girl-friend or something. The guy must have been out there for fifteen minutes or so already. That was either work or sex.

"He's a man of mystery," Caleb said. "Why, do you want his number?"

"I have his number," Faith said, letting her voice turn teasing in response. Dammit. She was slipping closer to the flirting line. She should stop.

But she kind of didn't want to. Flirting was harmless after all. Harmless and fun. "Danny sent it to me."

Caleb clapped a hand to his chest, looking faux wounded. "Now that's just rubbing it in. You take his number but you turned down mine." He let the wounded expression vanish and instead gave her a full-on mega-watt smile.

Faith leaned back in her chair, feeling her heart start to thump under the force of his attention. Pretty? Had she said he was pretty? The man was something beyond pretty. So she needed to tread carefully to keep this at fun level. "I didn't use his number though. Other than to send a security code."

"Does that mean you'd use mine?" His smile widened. "I'm happy to give it to you. You know, in case of emergencies."

She arched an eyebrow at him. No letting the man

see what that smile was doing to her nerve endings. He was good, but she had some pretty good flirting game herself when she chose. "Like what? Do you think you can solve CloudFest disasters?"

"I was thinking of something a little . . . close to home." His expression was hopeful.

"I'm sure you were. Tell me, Mr. White. Do you always flirt this hard with girls you hardly know?"

His face turned serious and he leaned in closer so that she got another breath of his scent. Spicy with a hint of the sea air. More intoxicating than Will's rum.

"Hardly ever." His blues eyes had turned darker.

Her breath caught suddenly. Damn. If that was a line, it was a good one. Really really good. "I see."

They stared at each other a moment too long. Butterflies—just the faintest flutter—moved through her stomach. Double damn. This guy was the real deal. Sexy. Sure of himself. Funny.

If they'd been anywhere else but Lansing and it had been any other time than now, maybe she'd have thrown caution to the winds and scooped him up. Because the look in those very blue eyes was reminding her that it had been more than six months since she'd had an orgasm that involved another person.

But tonight that wasn't what she wanted. When she slept with someone, she wanted it to be because she liked him and because she wanted sex. Not because she was more rattled than she cared to admit by all the balls she was trying to keep in the air and seeking a distraction. That didn't seem fair somehow.

Particularly not with someone like Caleb, who on a very short acquaintance seemed like a good guy. Of course, her douchebag radar could be completely off today too. Overloaded by her brother's behavior. But she didn't think so.

So tonight there would be flirting. But nothing more.

Across the table from her, Caleb leaned back suddenly. "Okay, there's way too much thinking going on behind those eyes of yours, Ms. Harper. Don't worry, I'm not going to push. A good player knows when to retreat to the baseline." He pushed his chair back. "So let's stick to pool tonight."

It was so exactly what she'd wanted him to say that she wondered for a moment if he was reading her mind. Then her brain caught up with the last part of his sentence. "Tonight." He'd said "tonight." Not "forever." Which, she was fairly certain, put the ball back in her court, so to speak. Another tick in the good-guy box for Caleb White. Unfortunately, that just made it harder to think of why she shouldn't follow through.

"Pool, it is," she said and went to choose a cue.

It turned out that Caleb wasn't quite so bad at pool as he'd made out. Or else he was a very quick study. She won the first game but then he won the second—just. At which point she pleaded thirst and headed over to the bar.

"Another?" Will said, emerging from the kitchen. He looked vaguely frazzled and there was a smudge of grease or something resembling grease on his cheek.

She shook her head. "One of those was enough. I have to get up early. I'll take some water, though. Sparkling."

"Me too," Caleb said, coming up beside her.

Will tipped his head at Faith, checking to see if she was okay with the company. She nodded slightly and Will smiled at Caleb.

"You two aren't doing anything for my profit margins, but sure. Two waters with fizz coming right up." He glanced at his wrist as he grabbed two glasses from the rack on the bar. "We'll be closing up in thirty minutes. You sure about the no more excellent alcohol thing? Last chance."

"Just water," Faith said firmly.

Will pretended to sigh and then wrangled ice, water, and lime slices into their glasses with lightning speed. Then he turned to the register and hit a few buttons. "Your check," he said to Caleb, putting the docket in front of him. "If you don't mind settling up now." He peered past them to the table they'd been sitting at. "Where's your friend?"

"Out on the deck making a phone call," Caleb said. He glanced at the check and then pulled a wallet from his back pocket. He pulled out a few bills and pushed them across to Will. "Keep the change. And tell your chef, great burgers. I'll be back before I go."

"You on the island long?"

"A week or so," Caleb said. He picked up his glass and drained half of it. "Faith, you want one more game?"

She nodded. She'd been ignoring the time but if Will was closing up that meant it was almost midnight. Time for Cinderella to go back home and face reality once more. But she could put that off for a little bit longer and stay here with Caleb. Who was close enough to a handsome prince for now.

At least as much of a prince as she could handle

today. "You didn't think I was going to let you get away without a chance to win back the title, did you?"

"Competitive, are you?"

"Sometimes."

Caleb grinned. "Okay. Set 'em up, pool shark. I'll go see if Liam's fallen off the deck, then we can play."

He disappeared across the room and Faith headed back to the pool table. Will followed her, collecting glasses off the few uncleared tables. Faith hadn't noticed that she and Caleb and Liam were the only ones left in the place.

"So how did you meet Caleb White?" Will asked as she started racking the balls.

"How did you know who he was?" she countered. Caleb had paid cash, no name on a credit card to give him away. She wondered if he used aliases when he traveled like Grey had had to.

"I recognized him," Will said. "Maybe you've missed it but he's been in the news a lot lately. And unlike you, I like sports. Being a man and all."

"God forbid you should lose your man card by lacking interest in watching people whacking balls around bits of grass."

"Exactly. So how did you meet him?"

"He's staying at Danny's place for the festival."

"Is Danny back?" Will asked. "I haven't seen him." He rested the tray of glasses on the edge of the table.

"No," Faith said. And there it was, reality invading her Cinderella moment. Dammit. She wanted a little bit longer with the fairy tale version of tonight. She wondered what was keeping Caleb. If he came back she could stay inside her little bubble of ignoring the outside world at least until midnight. "Hence the random people staying in his house."

"Does Danny know Caleb?"

"I think he knows his friend, Liam. Not sure how. You know Danny. Not big on details."

"True." Will shrugged and picked up his tray again just as Caleb stepped back through the sliding door. There was no sign of Liam.

"Where's your friend?" Will asked.

"He's heading back to the house. Something he needs to do apparently." He looked at Will. "What are the chances of getting a cab this time of night?" He picked up his water glass and drank what was left.

"With the festival crowd starting to hit Cloud Bay? Not great," Will said. He looked at Faith. "Did you drive?"

"Rode my bike," she admitted.

"So how were you going to get home?" Caleb asked.

"Ride my bike." She'd thought that was obvious.

"At this time of night?" Caleb put down his glass, frowning.

She shook her head right back at him. "This is Lansing Island. It's perfectly safe."

"Not with god only knows how many tourists here, it isn't. Particularly not if some of them are rabid fans of your dad." Caleb retorted.

Faith blinked at the vehemence in his tone. He looked—and sounded—genuinely concerned. But in his position, he'd have to be security conscious. But that didn't mean he wasn't overreacting. "You're more likely to get lost in the dark than I am to run into trouble riding a couple of miles home." She looked at Will. The few times she'd ended up here alone at closing time with no transport, he or Stefan had driven her home.

"I'd offer but our oven just decided to throw a fit. I need to help Stefan try to fix it. I really don't want to have to try and get a repair guy here this week. Tell you what, take Lulu. Stefan can drop me home. I'll swing by and grab the car in the morning. You can pick up your bike tomorrow. And you can drop Caleb here at Danny's on your way."

Will's use of Caleb's name was deliberate, Faith judged. Letting Caleb know that he knew exactly who he was if anything happened to her. Not that he could be that worried about anything happening to her if he'd made the suggestion. He always seemed to have a pretty good radar for jerks and assholes. Something you developed working behind a bar, he'd told her once. So if Will thought Caleb was okay, that was another tick in the good-guy column for him.

She nodded. "Okay. Thanks."

Will looked at his watch again, and Faith realized they'd been talking for nearly ten minutes. It wasn't fair to make Will stay open just for the two of them to play pool if he and Stefan needed to work on the oven. "Go get your keys," she said to him. "Caleb and I will get out of your hair. Rain check on the rematch." She aimed the last at Caleb, who nodded.

"Sure."

Will smiled gratefully. "Thanks. I'll be right back."

He took the tray through the doors into the kitchen, reappearing a minute or so later with the key. "She's parked in the usual spot."

"I'll take good care of your baby," Faith said. "And

if you or Stefan need a pass to anything this week, just let me or Theo know. No problem."

"That would be great," Will said. "But we'll have to see how slammed we get."

"The offer stands," she said. "Now go conquer that oven."

She led Caleb out of the bar and into the night. The warmth of the air was sea-scented and heavy after the air-conditioned bar. It seemed to close around them, making a bubble of just her and Caleb following the row of lights around to the back of the building to where Will's old Mustang was parked. Old but lovingly restored. It was painted a deep blue that seemed black under the light above the rear entrance into the bar.

Caleb let out a long low whistle. "Nice car."

The car was a 1967 convertible. But if Caleb knew about cars, he knew that already. And if he didn't, well, it wouldn't mean much to him. "Yes. Will's other obsession."

"Besides the whiskey?"

"Uh-huh." She unlocked the driver's side door. Lots of people didn't lock their cars on Lansing. After all, there was only one way to get a vehicle off the island if it got stolen, and the ferry operators knew most of the resident's cars by sight. Everyone knew Will's car. It was the only Mustang on the island. But Will wasn't an islander by birth and he didn't take any chances with his baby.

Caleb ran his hand along the side of the hood, admiration clear on his face.

Boys and their toys. She never really understood the obsession. Sure, some cars were mighty pretty, but in the end she was happy enough with one that got her from point A to point B in relative comfort. She climbed in then slid across the bench seat to unlock the passenger door from the inside, pushing it open.

"All aboard the pony express," she said.

Caleb laughed and climbed in. "Maybe I should take up car restoration as a hobby now I'm retired."

"Do you know anything about engines?"

"No, but I could learn."

"Sure," she agreed, easing the car into reverse. She doubted he was really that interested in learning how to pull apart a car. Grey had liked cars too but he'd been happy enough to pay other people to fix them up for him.

The area behind the bar wasn't huge and the car was a big beast but she was used to driving Grey's old truck. Though, right now, she was far more interested in what was inside the car than its size. As wide as the black leather bench seat was, she was all too aware that there wasn't much space between her and Caleb. And that they were all alone in the dark.

She wound down her window after navigating through the small parking lot out front of the bar and pointing the car toward the exit onto the road. It was tempting to put the roof down but she didn't want to risk Will's wrath if she messed it up somehow. So the window would have to do to give her an illusion of space and a reminder that there was a world outside the car. One where she and Caleb barely knew each other and she had a whole lot of responsibilities waiting for her in the morning.

That thought brought on a sudden odd urge to rebel.

To give her world the middle finger and do something crazy. Something Grey would have approved of.

So maybe that was the wrong thing to think about.

She steered the car through the familiar bends of the road from Salt Devil to Danny's place, not needing to really pay much attention to what she was doing. She could make the drive with a bag over her head. Could probably drive all around Lansing that way and never miss a beat.

Unlike her heart, which was bumping just that little bit too quickly to let her fool herself into thinking she didn't have a rapidly developing case of, to quote Ivy, "flaming panties," when it came to Caleb White.

Well, her panties were just going to have to cool it a little longer.

She let her left hand drift out the open window, fingers spread to catch the night air rushing against her skin so one part of her body had a chance to feel cool.

"My mom would tell you that's a terrible habit," Caleb said. His voice sounded lower in the darkness. Rumblier.

Sexier.

Engine vibrations. That was it. Blame it on the roar of whatever supercharged monster engine Will had put into the Mustang. That was what was making his voice sound so good.

Note to self: Drive the Prius if you ever have to share a car with this man again.

"I know this road. There's nothing I could possibly catch my hand on." She turned her head slightly to look at him for a second. He'd lowered his window too, his elbow resting on the window frame, his fingers gripped around the top. "And hello, pot, kettle, black. You do not have all limbs inside the vehicle, Mr. White."

"My hand isn't sticking out," he said.

"And what would your mom say about that response?"

"She'd tell me not to be a smart-ass."

"I think I like your mom. What does she do?"

"She's a doctor. I think she'd like you too."

Faith shook her head. Nope to him getting any kind of wrong idea. "I'm not really the kind of girl mothers approve of."

"Why not?"

"Rock star dad. Tattoos. Not interested in settling down."

"You have tattoos?" he said, sounding intrigued. "I hadn't noticed."

"That's because so far you haven't seen any parts of me where they're noticeable."

"I see." He sounded even more intrigued. "But they're somewhere a mom might see them?"

"I think it's more the alcoholic-rock-star–womanizing-dad thing than the tattoos. My family's reputation precedes me. They think I'm going to have my wicked way with their precious boys and break their hearts."

"Are you meeting these moms via time travel? That all sounds very nineteen fifties to me," he said. "And just so you know, I am on board with wicked ways."

She laughed at that. "In my experience, most men are."

"Maybe the men you meet are smarter than their moms."

"Oh no." She pulled her hand back in the window as

the approached the turn-off to Danny's drive. "The moms have my number. I'm not the marrying kind, as they used to say."

"Really?" He sounded skeptical.

"Trust me."

"I take it this is you telling me that if I ever get to sample your wicked ways, I should beware?"

She tried to ignore the way the rumble underscoring "wicked ways" made her want to invent some very wicked ways on the spot. Dammit. "Let's not get ahead of ourselves." She pulled into the drive, rolled the car to a stop outside the gate. "And, not to change the subject or anything, but we're here."

Caleb blinked. "So I see. Any point in me asking you in for a nightcap?"

As much as part of her wanted to say "hell yes," she shook her head. "Not tonight."

"Rain check on that too?"

"We'll see."

"All right," he said. He didn't sound that put out. She didn't know if that was good or whether she should be a little insulted. Caleb undid his seatbelt and turned to face her. "Then I'll say good night. And I'll tell you one more thing." He slid a little closer along the seat and leaned toward her. Not too close. Giving her plenty of time to tell him to back off. To say no.

She stayed right where she was. Pinned in place by the weight of that blue gaze and the pounding in her chest and the heat suddenly burning through her again. She tried to sound casual. "What's that?"

"The same thing I tell my mom when she's butting into my love life. That I'm a big boy and I can take care of myself." He leaned in close, until his mouth was hovering only a couple of inches from hers. "Also, that I believe that when you've beaten a girl at pool and hitched a lift with her in a Mustang that it's only polite to kiss her good night."

"Oh," was all she had time to say before he closed his mouth over hers.

She couldn't pretend she hadn't thought about what it might be like to kiss him over the last few hours. What sort of kiss it might be. Most of her first kisses had been the hot, fiery, let's-get-naked-fast kind.

Caleb White was undeniably hot but this kiss was . . . different. His mouth coaxed hers, gently, his hand cupping the back of her neck. Each tiny change in angle he made seemed to connect with a different nerve. First her lips were tingling, then hot, and then the heat spread out and down from there in a molten rush.

She opened her mouth and tasted him, tasted whiskey and man and heat. He groaned but he held her there, suspended with him in the dark, focused just on him and the places their bodies touched. She wanted more. Wanted closer.

But as she swayed toward him, tried to slide around in the seat so she could get nearer, he pulled back, leaving her startled by his sudden absence.

"Good night, Faith Harper," he said. And then he was out of the car walking away from her, vanishing into the night when he stepped beyond the reach of the headlights, leaving her wondering exactly what the hell had just happened.

chapter six

Faith's eyes opened before her alarm the next morning.
Unfair. She'd set her alarm at an appallingly early hour
after coming home, so why was her brain robbing her
of any of the few hours sleep she would get? She rolled
over in bed and groaned when the numbers on her
phone's screen showed just how early it was.

It had taken her an age to get to sleep, her body buzzing from that oh so brief brush of Caleb's lips. Too
brief, in retrospect. Lying in the dark in her big empty
bed, she'd spent way too long wondering why she hadn't
just given in and let him take the kiss further. And then
invited him home. Rules be damned.

But no. Last night she'd practically fled after he'd let
her go, almost shaken by the sudden surge of heat between them. It wasn't until she'd gone to bed that her
brain decided to regret that decision and keep her tossing and turning.

So she figured that the least her body could do would

be to come to the party and let her sleep as late as possible.

Apparently not. Now she was awake and her to-do list started running through her head. The sheer number of things she had to get done that day mingled with the memory of Caleb, filling her veins with nervous energy all over again.

She let out one last grumbling moan, then threw back the covers before climbing out of bed and into her running gear.

She needed to move. As much as she hated at least the first fifteen minutes of every single one of her morning runs with a passion, she did like the eventual burn that cleared her head and let her just be for the rest of the run.

Yawning and moving on autopilot, she left the house and headed down the path toward the headland. If Mina was awake, then her big goofy yellow Lab, Stewie, would be out. He was always happy to accompany Faith on her morning adventures, unlike Mina who preferred to swim, walk, or bike rather than run.

But Mina being awake was a big if at this time of day, her sister being a bit of a night owl like Faith and Zach, a tendency the three of them had inherited from Grey. But Mina's schedule was never really dependable because of the search-and-rescue thing, so it was worth a try. Stewie was big for a Lab, big enough to deter any tourists who might decide to brave the private end of the island's beaches and try to get a closer glimpse at the Harper house from that vantage point.

Her lungs started to ache a little as she quickened her pace, her body telling her this was a terrible idea as it always did. But she ignored its complaints and focused on where she was putting her feet on the gravel path. When she reached the white-painted picket fence that surrounded Mina's cottage, there was no sign of Stewie panting at the gate, waiting for her with his doggy grin as he always did when he heard her coming. She paused for a moment and waited, but the blinds in the cottage were down. That meant either Mina was still asleep or that she'd been called out during the night and hadn't made it home yet.

After a minute or so there was no sign of stirring inside the house. No barking either. Stewie must be either snoring at the end of Mina's bed or with her wherever she was.

So no silly Labrador antics to distract Faith during her torture session this morning. Oh well. It was so early—barely daylight—that she doubted anyone else was likely to have made the effort to be up and about. The beach should be empty.

If it wasn't, she could summon one of the security guys with a press of one of the apps on her phone. One of Ivy's inventions. A more subtle version of a panic button.

But she didn't want to think about security. She wanted to run.

She set off again and followed the path down to the beach before setting off along the hardened sand in her usual direction toward Danny's place.

The slap of the salt in the wind that hit her once she actually reached the beach started to wake her up, and she eased into the rhythm of the run and felt her mind start to go blank with relief.

She'd always loved the beach. Mina loved the water that surrounded the island and Zach had always been ready to leave but Faith loved the boundary of it all. Where the sand and the rocks and the water met. Where the wind stole your breath and the roar of the sea cleared your head.

Here, life felt simple. If only for thirty minutes a day.

She rounded the next curve in the bay, making her way up and over the rocks that scattered along the beach to avoid moving down toward the water. She knew her way over those rocks blindfolded. Yet, as she started to scramble down the other side, she almost stumbled when she spotted Caleb coming in the other direction. For a moment she contemplated turning around and trying to disappear before he spotted her, not quite ready to face the man she'd spent the night thinking about.

But then he lifted a hand and waved, and she moved back down onto the sand before she could think about it.

She jogged toward him, pulse thudding from more than the exercise. He wore a white T-shirt made of one of those complicated athletic fabrics and baggy red shorts, and the wind whistling in from the sea had rumpled his blond hair.

The way he moved across the sand, his stride sure and easy, made it clear he was an athlete. Someone in command of his body. Which looked even nicer in the clear morning light than it had yesterday. Maybe because she'd learned a little more about the man who occupied it last night at the bar.

"Hey," he said when they reached each other. He didn't even sound out of breath. Which was just annoying enough to break her out of the spell cast by the length by the play of muscle in his arms and legs as he moved and drop her back into reality. Sweaty, slightly out of breath reality.

He came to a near-halt next to her, jogging a little in place, looking like he could run for miles more. He probably could. He was, after all, a world champion.

She squinted at him through her sunglasses. As well as not being out of breath, he looked wide awake. Stubble darkened his jaw and his hair was rumpled, but there were no shadows under his eyes.

Unfair.

Especially when the rumpled look only made him look hotter. Made her think of beds and the scratch of whiskers across her skin. Sent a shiver of good old-fashioned want down her spine.

"Let me guess," she said. "You're a morning person."

He shrugged. "Force of habit. Twenty-odd years of getting up early to practice or train leaves a mark. So far my body hasn't gotten the memo that there's nothing to wake up at six a.m. for." He studied her a moment. "Though I could point out that I'm not the only one out running at god-early-o'clock."

"My father was a musician. I'm genetically incapable of being a morning person. In my case, it's too much to do and not enough time to do it." Not entirely true. She did like her morning runs and at this time of year, it was far cooler to do them early. But on non-running days, sleeping in was definitely her jam.

"Fair enough. Feel like some company?"

Running with him seemed easier than having any sort of discussion about the fact that he'd kissed her last night. Or the fact that so far he'd made no move to kiss her again this morning. Or the fact that she found both those facts so damn confusing. "Sure. I usually go round to Danny's and back. Sometimes a bit farther."

"Sounds good."

She hesitated. "You'll have to run back this way again if you finish up at my place."

"Not a problem. What is it? A couple of miles from here to Danny's?"

Because adding a couple of extra miles to his run was apparently not a big deal if you were Caleb White, superman. Gah. Maybe she shouldn't have agreed to running together. Did she really want him seeing her panting and sweaty?

Yes, we do, part of her brain suggested. But given that the type of panting and sweaty it seemed to be thinking of was something that she definitely wasn't ready to put on the agenda this morning, she ignored it. Maybe if she ran, endorphins would override all the dumb female hormones in her body that were feeling so very pro-Caleb this morning.

"Something like that," she said and set off again. Caleb fell into stride beside her, obviously slowing his pace. Just as well, given he was a good half a foot or so taller than her. She would never have kept up with him if he'd set the pace. She tried to focus back on her stride and the movement but all she could really think about was the man beside her. Good thing there was really only one way to go along the beach so that she couldn't wander off the path while distracted or something equally embarrassing.

After a couple of minutes, Caleb moved a little ahead of her and then turned so he was jogging backward.

She shook her head. "Now you're just showing off."

"Running backward is good for you," he said. "Uses different muscles."

"Yeah, well, I'll save it for the elliptical. I like my ankles unbroken." She did appreciate the view though. Then wondered whether he'd turned around so he could watch her.

Those very blue eyes were definitely fixed on hers as he continued to move backward. Until, before she knew what was happening, he stumbled slightly and fell on his butt. She was too slow to react and tripped over his feet, falling toward him. He apparently had better reflexes than hers because he managed to catch her and guide her down so she landed on the sand on her knees next to him rather than on top of him.

Though as she watched him flop back, laughing helplessly, she was forced to wonder if that was such a good thing. The fact that he found his fall so funny, that he obviously didn't take himself too seriously or care about making an idiot out of himself in front of her, was strangely appealing. And the thought of being pressed up against that long expanse of muscle and laughing man, and staying there until he kissed her again was a pretty good one. Good enough that she didn't make any effort to move from where she was, instead just sitting back on her heels and watching him. Eventually the sputters of laughter stopped and he pushed himself up.

"Well, that'll teach me to show off," he said as he brushed sand off his left calf. He looked up at her. "You okay?"

"Fine," she managed. "Nice catch." She dabbed at a

sandy patch on her own leg to distract herself from the urge to reach out and help him clean up his.

"A smarter man might have broken your fall a different way," he said.

She froze. Then lifted her head slowly.

Those eyes were waiting for her. And the friendly look in them had been stripped away by the same sudden heat that had caught her the night before.

"Is this where we talk about last night?" he asked.

"Is there something to talk about?"

"Faith, if you're telling me you've forgotten I kissed you, then I'm going to have to take that as proof that I didn't do it well enough and try again."

She couldn't immediately think of a reason why that was a bad idea. Until she remembered that they were in the middle of the beach. Sure, it was a private beach but private in this case meant "accessible by almost all her friends, family, and employees" at any given moment.

If she was going to change her mind about not allowing her love life onto the island, she didn't want to do it with an audience. She definitely didn't want Lou to know if she chose to . . . whatever . . . with Caleb. It would be unfair to get Lou's hopes up that Caleb White might become a regular fixture in their lives. Because he was headed back to his world after the festival and that was exactly how Faith wanted it. So no, no second kisses where everyone could see them.

"I remember," she said and wondered if he could see in her eyes what she could see in his. And if it made him feel hot and shivery like it did her.

"Good. Which brings me back to my original question."

She wasn't sure she remembered what his original question was. He was officially fogging her brain. Dammit. Who knew that a tennis player would turn out to be Faith catnip. The universe had a weird sense of humor.

What had he been asking? Something about . . . right. Whether or not she wanted to talk about last night's kiss. She didn't know the answer. "How about 'Yes, I want to talk about it, but I don't think it's a conversation that I want to have before I've had coffee and a shower?'" That at least bought her some time to think.

He nodded. "I can live with that." He pushed off the ground to stand, then reached down to help her up. His fingers were strong and warm and sandy where they curled around hers, the sand seeming to scrape against suddenly sensitive nerves, sending a spike of heat up her arm and down through her body as she stood.

Caleb White was definitely far too potent to be tangling with so early.

"Thanks," she said, trying not to protest when he let go of her hand. Or to offer help when he started brushing sand from his butt. "So how about we get this run finished?"

Caleb let Faith set the pace as he followed her along the beach. They'd run to Danny's in silence and then Faith had simply turned and headed back the way they'd come.

She'd obviously meant it when she said she wasn't ready to talk about the kiss until they'd had coffee. Which was fine. He could wait. Let her take the lead if that was what she needed.

And hey, if he was honest, hanging back gave him a very nice view. Faith had said she wasn't into sports, but she obviously worked out. Running on sand was hard work and he didn't know exactly how far the distance from her house to Danny's was but it felt like they'd run at least three miles so far and she was still moving easily.

He sucked in a lungful of the salty air and grinned as he ran. He tried to work out outside when he could but sometimes travel and schedules meant that it was just easier to hit the gym. He got plenty of time out on the court, of course, but that was different. Once he stepped onto a tennis court he was focused on the game and honing his skills and tactics.

He barely noticed anything other than the ball and the lines and the voice of his coach and the feel in his muscles as he tried to perfect each move.

Running with pale sand squeaking under his shoes with a view of the ocean on one side and grassy slopes interspersed with rocky patches on the other—not to mention the gorgeous woman in front of him—was a lot more fun. And the beach was deserted, which was even better. He had a house in Malibu but the beach was almost always crowded. If he wanted to run there he had to do it at sunrise. With a cap and sunglasses and always on the lookout for paparazzi lying in wait.

It was never exactly relaxing. But here, it felt like the only two people in the world were him and Faith.

From what Liam had told him, the Blacklight guys owned most of the ocean frontage around the northwest end of the island, and their beaches were private. It had been part of the reason he'd agreed to come.

He didn't know how strictly the Harpers and the other guys enforced the rules with the locals but so far this morning he hadn't seen a single person besides himself and Faith. And there was nowhere that paparazzi could really hide. The rocks that cropped up in random clumps along the beach weren't exactly gigantic and there were no dunes or big trees between the beach and the sand. The sand just kind of petered out and changed to grass and bushes and then the gardens beyond.

They were nearly at the lighthouse that sat on a small point at the far end of the beach. It looked kind of small to him, its tower painted white with pale blue shutters. Windows pierced the curved walls at intervals, and the tower blended into the little house built around the base of it. The whole thing sat in a tiny garden fenced off from the rest of the headland it stood on.

He jogged up next to Faith. She turned her head, slowed a little, and wiped her forehead with the back of her hand.

"Cool place. Does someone live there?"

She nodded. "My sister, Mina."

She had a sister? He didn't think he'd known that. "Mina? Is she older or younger? Don't think I ever saw her in one of Blacklight's videos."

"No, you wouldn't have. Mina doesn't like the spotlight. She's also not exactly musical. And she's younger, to answer your questions." Faith led the way up a path that skirted along the edge of the fence line. "Okay, long route or short route?"

"What's the short route?"

"We cut across the land up to the house. Long route,

back down onto the beach and around the bay a bit farther. It's only half a mile or so more." She lifted her arms
and stretched up onto her toes. In the early light, her face
pink from the run, she kind of glowed. And he really
wanted to kiss her again. But he'd said he wouldn't push,
so he wouldn't.

"You're the one who has to get to work today, so I'm
good with whatever you want to do." He did, after all,
still have to run back to Danny's. And while the distance
wasn't huge, he was definitely starting to feel the effect
of the run after not hitting the treadmill or playing any
tennis for over two weeks.

She studied him a moment. "You sure?"

"It's not like I'm in training or anything," he said.
"No one is clocking my miles any more." As he said the
words, he felt a weird surge of happiness. No one clocking his miles. No one riding him, telling him what to
do or where to be. He could lie on the sofa and eat pizza
all day if he chose.

Not that he'd managed to sit still for too long yet. He
and Liam had swum yesterday afternoon and then he'd
prowled around the house while Liam had read. Then
they'd headed to the bar. This morning he'd woken
wanting to run.

But now, with her, the nervous energy that had driven
him out of bed was easing. He'd told Faith that he was
playing hooky, but this was the first time since he'd announced his retirement that he really felt like that was
true.

Maybe there was something in the sea air.

He smiled at her. "C'mon, we should get going or
you'll stiffen up."

"Oh, the almighty Caleb White is immune from the effects of such a puny run?" she said, smiling at him.

"Well, probably not. I haven't really been hitting the gym for the last couple of weeks. But the almighty Caleb White is used to feeling sore from training. And also, as I mentioned earlier, the almighty Caleb White has nothing in particular to do today, so he can spend the day soaking in the almighty Danny Ryan's hot tub if he needs to. You, on the other hand, need to go out and run the world."

She snorted. "Lansing is hardly the world."

"Maybe not. But CloudFest is a big deal. And you seem to be the queen of that."

"If I'm queen, then where are all my minions to carry me around all day and fulfill my every whim?"

"Off organizing your festival at a guess," he said. Then he stepped toward her, arms outstretched. "Of course, the almighty Caleb White would be happy to carry your majesty around, if she so desires."

That earned him another snort. "I think the almighty Caleb White is just trying to cop a feel."

He laughed. "Can't blame a guy for trying."

"No," she said. "Who knows, play your cards right and I might even let you." She grinned at him evilly. "But only if you catch me first." She took off then, at almost a dead run, bolting down the path much faster than he'd expected based on their previous pace. He stood frozen for a moment, then what she'd said sank in. He took off after her.

His legs were longer, but Faith had a head start and the advantage of knowing the terrain. She used the trees and garden beds and benches like a pro so that every time he thought he was catching up to her, she'd change direction and gain a few feet.

When the garden finally ended, the house loomed up before them, surrounded by a paved sweep of drive. His couple of weeks out of training had started to catch up with him. He'd never been a sprinter. Tennis matches were marathons, after all.

Faith on the other hand, apparently had hare rather than tortoise in her background. Either that or she really didn't want to be caught. But as she bolted up the couple of steps that led to her front door and touched the brass knocker before turning round to grin at him in triumph, he didn't think that was actually the case.

"Damn," she said as he reached the bottom step a few paces behind her. "I really need my phone to immortalize this moment on film. I can't believe you didn't catch me."

"You had the home-court advantage," he retorted. "I demand a rematch."

"Sorry, no time this morning," she said. "But I can offer you some coffee."

He wasn't dumb enough to say no to an invitation inside. "The almighty Caleb White likes coffee."

She rolled her eyes. "The almighty Caleb White should stop talking about himself in the third person soon." She put her hand on a panel near the door and it opened inward.

"Hey, you started it," he said, then added, "nice gadget." He leaned in to look at the panel. He'd taken it for just a dark panel in the strip of frosted glass that ran down either side of the white door.

"Dad always believed in good security, and Ivy, who

looks after our computer systems, likes to play with the latest and greatest. Saves me having to take keys on my run." Faith paused in the doorway, tilting her head at him, gray-green eyes considering. "You understand that coffee in this case means actual coffee?"

"I didn't trip and hit my head between the beach and here," he replied. "No change to our deal."

She smiled at that and walked inside.

He'd been too focused on their race to pay much attention to the house itself. It was big and white. Danny's place was all glass and stone and wood. Edgy and modern. And mostly empty of the kinds of things that made a house a home. There was art but no personal photos. A well-stocked library but no books or magazines lying around on any of the tables or couches. The entertainment system Liam had spoken about was huge, as advertised, but everything was stored on a computer and accessed via remote. It felt like a large hotel, albeit a very sleek and cutting-edge one.

The impression he had of the Harper house was more traditional.

But stepping inside the door, he got the feeling he'd stepped into a whole other world. It was light and airy with polished wood floors and white walls. Through a doorway off the front hall he could see a massive living room filled with as many sleek gadgets as Danny had. But the clean lines of the place were blurred with color in the rugs and furniture and in the art and memorabilia that crowded the walls in a mishmash that shouldn't have worked but did. He wanted to stop and take a closer look, but that seemed kind of nosy.

"Nice place," he said drily.

"Thanks. We like it." Faith said, still walking.

"We? Someone living here with you?" She'd said her sister lived at the lighthouse. Was there another sister? He knew Grey had had a son and had a vague idea that he was a musician as well. Maybe he was back on the island for the festival?

Damn. If there were random family members wandering around, then having a conversation about their kiss might prove difficult. Which meant he'd just have to be patient.

"My brother and sister and I own the place together," Faith said. "Force of habit to use 'we.' "

"Your brother? Zach, is it?" he said pulling the name from some corner of his brain.

"That's him. You a Fringe Dweller fan then?"

"Fringe Dweller? The band? They're good. He's in that?"

"He's the guitarist."

"Not the lead singer?" Not following in their father's footsteps?

"He sings. But he didn't start the band. He stepped in when their guitarist quit after the first couple of years." She frowned, and he wondered what it was about that that bothered her.

"Is he home for the festival? I don't remember Liam mentioning them. He's a fan." Liam had sent Caleb a link to one of Fringe Dweller's songs a year or so ago.

Faith's frown deepened. "No. They had another commitment." She shoved open a door, held it open for him.

Hmmmm. Maybe Zach was a touchy subject?

"So you do live here alone, then?"

They'd reached a big sunny kitchen. Big enough to

feed a small army. Lots of white cabinets and a long well-used pine table standing next to a row of French doors overlooking the garden. The chairs around the tables were wood too, but he caught glimpses of color on their seats. A silver laptop sat on one end of the table next to a stack of file folders and a bright red leather notebook.

The floorboards were darker than the table. No rugs. Plants filled corners and hung from dark metal chains attached to the ceiling at intervals. On the wall at the end of the French doors, framed band posters hung in seemingly random order above a bright red upright piano. Above the frames, a battered acoustic guitar was suspended from the wall as well. The poster in the middle of the haphazard arrangement proclaimed SEX AND SAND AND ROCK 'N' ROLL in large letters.

He grinned and walked over to look closer. "Family motto?" he asked as he turned back to find Faith watching him.

"One of Grey's, maybe," Faith said. "That's the poster from the very first CloudFest." She did something to the complicated-looking coffee machine on the counter that made it hiss with steam.

"Your dad had a sense of humor."

"When he wanted to, yes. More to the point, he was always very good at attracting attention when he wanted it. It's what made him such a good front man." She paused in her coffee-making, looking distant for a moment.

Way to go. First he'd brought up her brother, who seemed to be a bit of a sore subject, and now he had managed to add her dead father to the mix. Smooth.

"He was an amazing performer. One of the greats," he said. It didn't chase the expression from her face. Which made him wonder exactly how great Grey Harper had been offstage. It couldn't be easy growing up with a dad that famous. And who must have been away a lot. But he'd only met Faith yesterday and it didn't really seem like the time to dig into her past.

He was more interested in her immediate future. Like when he would be able to see her again. "So," he said, "just how nuts is your schedule this week?"

chapter seven

Faith had been reaching for the coffee, but she stilled at Caleb's question, considering. "Imagine total mayhem and multiply it by about ten." She thought about it for a moment and reached for the extra-strong Colombian beans that she usually avoided if she wanted to sleep in the next eighteen hours. It was time to embrace caffeine wholeheartedly for the next week. "Maybe fifteen." It wasn't an exaggeration. And she needed Caleb to understand that.

His face fell. "Even today and tomorrow? Before the festival starts?"

"Today and tomorrow will probably be the busiest, in terms of the sheer amount of stuff I have to do." She slotted the portafilter into place and started making him an espresso. She hadn't asked what he wanted but she wasn't really in the mood to fool around with milk and the steamer this morning. She poured the coffee into a tiny cup and pushed it across the counter to him. "Sugar's in the canister." She pointed toward the skull-and-crossbones decorated tin.

"Black and plain is fine."

"It's strong."

"Even better." He lifted the cup, sipped cautiously. Blinked. Then sipped again. "Yeah, that's the good stuff. You missed your calling as a barista." He grinned then nodded at the machine. "Aren't you having one?"

She'd been distracted watching him. He was so big and blond and all-American looking he seemed out of place in this house. She was used to scruffy musicians, stubbled and bleary eyed, who didn't really come to life until well into the afternoon. All tattoos and piercings and bling and attitude.

As far as she could tell, Caleb was almost the complete opposite of that. Well, there was a little attitude. Though his was more a natural confidence than swagger. Which made her . . . nervous.

Ignoring the flutter in her stomach, she focused back on the machine. When she had her own coffee in hand she paused again. The polite thing to do would be to take him over to the table and sit and chat. But that felt . . . weird.

She shook her head briefly. Why was she so nervous around him? It wasn't as though she hadn't had flings before. She knew what to do, how to be, how to keep things casual. And yet, Caleb White kept throwing her off-balance.

"Dollar for your thoughts?"

"A dollar?"

"No one wants a penny anymore. Inflation."

"Can't buy much with a dollar these days either," she

pointed out. Then she took a mouthful of coffee to buy herself some time. There definitely wasn't going to be any telling Caleb she'd been thinking about the fact he made her nervous. That would be just plain odd. Not to mention totally awkward. Even picturing his face listening to her made her even more nervous. "Just thinking about what I have to do today." That wasn't going to win her any prizes for world-class small talk, but it would have to do.

"And what is that exactly?" Caleb straightened.

"Last-minute things. Making sure each act's gear is here and stowed away. Going over the final lists of all the transport to and from the site for the artists. That includes making sure the airfield has the schedule too. Checking that all the artists have been given the right information about where and when they need to be at any given time. Going through final security briefings. Getting around to all the performers who've arrived already—to say hi and see if they're happy with everything. Talking to food and beverage suppliers if I need to. Getting the latest reports from the stage crews. Sitting in on a sound check at each stage. Checking on the catering for the parties we throw." It was a little depressing how easily that list rolled off her tongue without her having to think about it. She'd been running Cloud-Fest for six years now and had worked with Grey and the team for a few years before that, not to mention watched how it all came together every summer for most of her life, and she knew it all by heart it seemed.

"Yep, that's a lot," Caleb said. He came around the counter, rinsed his espresso cup in the sink and then came back to stand beside her. He stood with one hip resting against the counter, facing her. There were only a few inches between them again. He wasn't crowding her, just standing a tiny bit farther inside her personal space than a stranger would have. Given she'd already kissed the man, she couldn't fault him for pushing that boundary a little.

She could fault herself for wanting to step in and close the gap between them.

Because that would only lead to shenanigans, as Mrs. Santos, the principal at her high school might have said. Hot and, no doubt, thoroughly enjoyable shenanigans.

"You're thinking again," Caleb said. "And this time I really want to know what you're thinking about."

"Why?"

"Because your expression went a little bit fuzzy there, Harper. Like maybe you were thinking dirty thoughts."

Heat flared into her cheeks even as her brain started to helpfully supply a whole series of dirty thoughts—the kind of things that Mrs. Santos would have not considered shenanigans but something much worse—to go with his words.

God. She wanted to kiss him.

"I don't tell men my dirty thoughts on the first date." Not always true. But she definitely wasn't telling them to this man.

"Last night was our first date."

"It was?"

"We had a drink, we played pool, you drove me home. I kissed you. That sounds like a date to me."

"Yeah, well, I'm not telling them to you on the second date either. Not that this is a second date." She held up a hand. "This is coffee after a run. That isn't a date."

"At this point I'm less interested in the definition of the date and more interested in the fact you're having dirty thoughts," he said.

Dammit. He was fogging her brain. At seven thirty in the morning. Bad man.

Bad in all the right ways. She felt herself sway toward him a little.

No!

"My thoughts are my business," she said, pulling back. "Though I will say that my dirty thoughts are worth more than a dollar."

"That I do not doubt," Caleb said. "And, you know, completely in the non-prostitute sense of the notion, I have a black Amex and am willing to use it."

She laughed. "Mr. White, I have plenty of money of my own."

"Then how can I bribe you to tell me your dirty thoughts?"

"I suggest you try and use your imagination."

"If I use my imagination about your dirty thoughts, I'm going to have to hope that Danny's showers run cold."

"He has a state of the art solar heating system, so probably not. The ocean can be pretty chilly on this side of the island though. Maybe you could swim home."

"Now that's just cruel." But he was laughing and she felt herself grinning back up at him, enjoying the back and forth of standing there flirting with him. Though she had a feeling what they were doing wasn't so much flirting anymore. More like actual verbal foreplay. The man had a good brain. And a good mouth.

The memory of how he'd tasted in the dark flooded back through her.

Make that a freaking fantastic mouth.

"I really do need to get going," she said. "My team is meeting at eight thirty."

"You're the boss, aren't you? You can be late. No one is going to fire you."

"I told you, this week I can't play hooky."

"Can't or won't?"

"Both, maybe. I'm sorry but this week, the CloudFest schedule rules all."

"What if I offered to fit in with your schedule? Be at your beck and call?"

Now that was an excellent idea. "Maybe."

"Sure I can't persuade you to be late?" He leaned in a little closer.

"I'm sure," she said. She didn't sound sure, even to her own ears. She was sure about one thing though. She wanted his mouth again. "But you know, I'm not sure that coffee entirely woke me up. Let's see if you work any better." She rose up on her toes and pressed her mouth to his.

This time, he wasn't so gentle. This time he was hungry. His hands came to her waist and he pulled her into him while his mouth fought with hers. The taste of him made her want to get even closer. She pushed her hips into his, felt him against her, hard and hot through the thin layers of their exercise clothes. Felt the spike of heat and longing and wanted to throw caution to the wind and start pulling his clothes off.

But then she heard her phone shrill to life in the

distance and knew she had to stick to her guns. "Duty calls," she managed, panting a little as she broke off the kiss.

"Duty stinks," he said.

"I can't entirely argue with that," she said. "But that doesn't change the fact I have to take this call."

"Fine," Caleb said. He looked both really turned on and a little cranky. She knew exactly how he felt. "I think I'll just go try that ocean thing you were talking about."

"Don't drown," she said. "If you drown I won't get to see you later." Then she picked up the phone and backed away from the renewed flash of heat in his eyes that was tempting her to forget all about CloudFest and being an adult.

When Caleb finally made it back to Danny's, sweaty and still feeling undeniably frustrated despite his decision to take Faith's advice and see if a dip in the ocean might make him feel better about her tossing him out, he found Liam sitting on the front step, car keys in hand.

"Going somewhere?" Caleb asked, easing off his damp sneakers. Dumb to run with wet shoes and sandy feet but he hadn't had much choice after his unplanned swim.

"Back to L.A."

"What? Why?"

"Something I need to sort out," Liam said. He tossed Caleb the keys. "Drive me to the ferry and I'll leave you the car."

"But what about the festival? And the house?" Danny

Ryan had loaned the house to Liam, not Caleb after all. Danny Ryan probably had no idea Caleb was even here. Unless Faith had told him. But no, he couldn't think about Faith right now.

"I'll try and be back Thursday. Friday at the latest."

"Aren't the ferries coming to the island booked up weeks in advance during the festival?"

"I know someone with a chopper. I'll twist his arm if I have to. And I called Danny. He's cool with you using the house. Said someone else might show up."

"Who?"

"He didn't say."

"That's not exactly useful information." Caleb shoved the keys into his pocket, then remembered his pocket was kind of wet and pulled them out again. He shook them out and pointed the fob at Liam accusingly. "We're supposed to hang out this week." The thought of rattling around this giant house alone for a few days didn't appeal. He wanted distraction, not time to think.

"I know. It's just a couple of days. Enjoy the peace and quiet. Go drink more of that great whiskey from last night. Then enjoy the festival. I'll be back." He said the last in what was possibly the worst *Terminator* impression Caleb had ever heard.

"You're not going to tell me what this is about? Is it work?"

Liam shook his head. "I'd tell you but then I'd have to kill you," he said. "C'mon, Tennis Boy, the next ferry leaves in thirty minutes."

"I was planning on taking a shower."

Liam looked at him as though he was only just noticing what Caleb was wearing. "Did you go for a run in the ocean rather than along the beach? That's kind of doing it wrong."

"I went for a run. I got warm. I decided to see what the water was like. You know. Having fun. Like I'm on vacation or something. The vacation you're bailing on."

"You're a big boy," Liam said. "I'm sure you'll find ways to entertain yourself. In fact, you looked like you were finding one okay last night. What time did you get home anyway?"

"About forty minutes after you, so get your mind out of the gutter." Caleb unlocked the car with a click of a button.

"Faith's hot."

"I'm not blind."

"I'm just saying." Liam tossed his case into the back of the SUV and came around to the passenger door.

"Not looking for advice on my love life from a guy who's running back to L.A. to fix something he screwed up with a girl."

Liam's face darkened as he climbed into the passenger seat and snapped his sunglasses into place. "Did I say it was a girl?"

"If it was work, you'd tell me."

"I believe in client confidentiality."

"You're also ruthless about going offline when you want to. So I'm guessing girl not work."

Liam didn't answer.

"Not answering means yes," Caleb said, enjoying channeling his frustration into needling Liam a little.

Liam's head turned and even through the dark lenses of his sunglasses Caleb could feel the burn of the death glare he was delivering. He grinned.

"So did you kiss Faith Harper last night?" Liam said after a few more seconds of staring.

"None of your business." Caleb steered the car through the gates that had opened automatically as they approached and then out onto the road, gunning the engine.

"That's not answering. Not answering means yes, doesn't it, Caleb?" Liam said, mimicking Caleb's tone earlier.

"No, it means none of your business." Caleb didn't believe in kissing and telling. There'd been a few girls over the years who'd decided to sleep with him and sell their story to the tabloids. He understood the appeal of making a quick buck but it had never been an enjoyable experience to be the one being used as a cash cow. So he kept his private life private wherever possible. Not that pro tennis left much time for a private life.

Which probably meant he should cut Liam some slack. "If you're serious about this girl, you could have mentioned her before."

"One, I'm not admitting there is a girl. And two, you haven't been around much the last few months, even if I had something to tell you."

"They have these things called phones now," Caleb retorted. "You know, that thing you had glued to your ear for hours last night?"

"Dude, if this is your mood after an early morning run, you need to take up a different form of exercise," Liam said, folding his arms and focusing his gaze back on the windshield.

As if on cue, Caleb's stomach rumbled. He laughed. "You may have a point." He could see the outskirts—

such as they were—of Cloud Bay in the distance. Maybe there'd be a bakery or café open this early. He had the feeling that eating wouldn't rid him of the edgy feeling he'd had ever since he'd left Faith's house, the one that had made him turn 'round several times during his run home, wanting to just reverse direction and head back to her. But if he was going to feel cranky, there was no point being hungry *and* cranky.

Six hours later, Faith was buried in paperwork, starving, and beginning to regret not just staying home with Caleb.

Her eyes blurred as she stared at the status report on all the stage prep that Ziggy had just e-mailed her, her brain refusing to take in even one more piece of information.

Time for food. And more caffeine. She'd already had three cups of coffee since she'd arrived at the office and her nerves were buzzing. But the way the day was going, she wasn't very likely to see her bed anytime before midnight, so she needed something to keep her going.

Oh to be eighteen again. She leaned back in her chair and stretched her arms out. Once upon a time she would have partied all night and worked all the next day no problem. But these days she had grown very fond of a good night's sleep.

A fact that would probably make Grey roll over in his grave in disgust.

But he wasn't here to make fun of her need for sleep any more. Nor had he ever really done the job that Faith was doing.

Sure, he had had the idea for the first CloudFest and

had worked to talk the other guys in the band into it, not to mention getting the acts for that first year. And he'd always been involved in choosing the acts who'd appeared each year, but he'd left the detailed logistics of the things to his manager and Ziggy and the rest of the team at Harper Inc. He'd said what he'd wanted and other people executed it.

Right now that sounded pretty damned good to Faith.

"Minion, fetch me a muffin," she said experimentally into the air.

"We're running short on minions today," Theo said, poking his head 'round into her small office. "But there are muffins downstairs. And sandwiches and stuff. In other words, lunch is served. And Lou's here. She asked if you have a minute."

"She did?" Lou rarely dropped in during business hours. At least, not this time of year. Faith's stomach rumbled, but she figured she might as well deal with her mom first. "Sure, tell her to come on up. And save me a muffin. And a sandwich or two."

"Okay," Theo said agreeably. He pushed his glasses back up his nose and withdrew. Two minutes later, Lou walked through the door with a plate of muffins in one hand and a mug in the other.

"Coffee?" Faith said hopefully.

"Herbal tea," Lou said firmly. "You drink too much coffee festival week."

"There's a reason for that," Faith said. She came around the desk to hug Lou and relieve her of a muffin.

"Humor your mother and drink something else. You can go fill up on coffee once I've left."

"If it makes you feel better," Faith said. She took the

mug in her free hand and sniffed experimentally. "Mint?"

"Spearmint and chamomile," Lou said. "Calming."

Calming and grass-flavored, Faith thought, but she took a sip before putting the mug down and focusing on the muffin. Which appeared to be banana chocolate chip. Her favorite. Much better than grass tea.

She took a huge bite, chewed, and swallowed while waving for Lou to take a seat.

"You could eat something healthier than muffins too," Lou said.

"You're the one who brought them up here," Faith protested. "I'm hungry. And I'll have a sandwich or whatever's downstairs too. But it never hurts to start with dessert."

Lou took a muffin for herself, breaking it neatly in half and then breaking off a smaller piece. "You have a point."

Faith ate more of her muffin at high speed while she shuffled some of the papers strewn over her desk into neater piles.

"Mina told me about Zach," Lou said. "I'm sorry."

"Zach is not your fault," Faith said. "Don't worry about it."

"I know you were looking forward to seeing him."

Faith sighed. "Mom, I really don't want to talk about Zach."

Lou gave her a that's-not-going-to-work look. "I'm not defending him, if that's what you think. He's putting you in a hard spot, canceling on you."

She looked annoyed. Zach was likely to get a phone call from his stepmom sometime soon. Faith couldn't help feeling amused by that. Lou was probably one of the few people who could put the fear of God into Zach. Quite frankly, Zach deserved a dose of displeased Lou. "I've found someone else," she said firmly.

Lou's worried expression eased. "Oh, good. Anyone I know?"

"Yes," Faith said. "I called Sienna Reese."

Lou smiled approvingly. "She's the one who recorded here a year ago?"

"Yes." Faith nodded. Sienna had recorded a couple of songs for her latest album at the Harper studio. The album had taken off, the first huge hit of her relatively new career. Not that that had much to do with where it was recorded, but she'd stayed with Faith for the week or so she was on the island and they'd hit it off.

"She seemed nice," Lou said.

"She is. Very. But I'm less concerned about nice than available at this point. Luckily she's that too." She took another bite of muffin. Then another mouthful of grass tea, avoiding the urge to look at her watch. She needed to be at the main stage in another hour or so and still had e-mails to answer and paperwork to sign off on before then. "What did you want to see me about?"

"Archive business," Lou said.

Faith groaned. "Mom, can't that wait until next week? I've kind of got a lot on my plate." She waved her hand at the papers stacked inches deep around her. "You know more about the archive than me anyway."

"Yes, dear but I'm not one of Grey's kids. Just the ex-wife. This is the sort of stuff you should be in the loop about."

"The lawyers have been working on this for a couple

of years. Another week isn't going to hurt." Lou had first floated the idea that Grey's papers needed to be collated and archived not long after he'd died. The lawyers handling the estate had backed her up. Said they needed the inventory of all Grey's belongings for probate anyway. But with one thing and another, all of the Harpers struggling with the loss, they'd dragged their heels on starting the project.

A year had passed. Then Mina had announced she was getting married at eighteen. By then Faith had been focused on finding her feet running Harper Inc., given that keeping the business of Grey Harper and Blacklight and the recording studio and the festival running seemed more immediately important than sorting through the mountain of stuff Grey had left behind. She'd been just coming up for air two years after that when Adam, Mina's husband, had been killed in a car accident.

All in all, it had only been about eighteen months ago that Lou's nagging, in concert with the lawyers, had finally gotten the archive project back on the table.

"What's turned up this time?" Faith asked.

The trouble with pulling the archive together was that Grey had been a complete pack rat. A secretive pack rat as it turned out. To start with, he had houses on three continents. Eight of them. All of them were full of things he'd collected in his travels, artworks and furniture mixed in with the little black notebooks he'd carried around to write lyrics in, the diaries he'd kept sporadically, notes he'd been apparently keeping for a biography that never happened, and all the other records of his life and career. Photos, demo tracks, videos. Miles of paper and multiple hard drives worth of electronic files. So far they'd turned up about ten laptops in various states of readability and twice that many back-up drives— not to mention more USBs than could be counted.

Adding to the problem was the fact that Grey had been perfectly happy asking his friends to look after a box or a suitcase or stashing stuff at a recording studio he'd worked in. Tracking it all down was taking forever. And then the storage units had started turning up. Grey had also apparently thought nothing of renting a storage unit anywhere in the world he was staying for a few weeks and filling that with stuff too. He'd left behind keys to those and statements of bank accounts he'd opened when he was bored and never bothered to tell anyone at Harper Inc. about. A complete maze of information.

Luckily the lawyers were managing the process of taking the first pass at sorting through whatever was found. They passed on everything that was personal or related to his music and were slowly sorting out the paper trail in relation to anything money or business related.

If something that they deemed urgent was discovered, they contacted Lou. She also got the monthly progress reports. Because she had volunteered to help Faith with wrangling this part of the estate, seeing as Faith had been getting busier and busier running the festival and Harper Inc. and the recording studio business. Who knew that Faith had no time for this sort of thing this week.

"Are you sure this isn't your way of trying to pump me for information about Caleb White?"

"Of course not," Lou said indignantly. Then, "Why, have you seen him again?" She smiled encouragingly.

Now there was a question she had no intention of answering. "Mom, you wanted to talk about the archive."

Lou's eyes narrowed. Faith met her gaze, willing her face to not give away anything about Caleb White or his damned kisses.

"The lawyers sent through the latest list. They think they've found a storage unit in New Jersey. Can you think of anyone Grey knew in Jersey?"

"Off the top of my head, no." Nor could she think of any extended time that he'd spent there. . . . Lou was from Nebraska and he'd met Zach's mom, Zoe, in Paris but she was originally from Chicago. Emmy, Mina's mom, had spent time in Manhattan but had been born in Hawaii. So no obvious relatives sprang to mind. But Grey made friends wherever he went and there was no way to know if he'd been to New Jersey or not. She hitched a shoulder. "I guess we'll find out when they track down the storage locker."

Some of the things they'd found in Grey's hoards, as they'd started calling them, had been interesting. A couple of his guitars. A few demo tapes. Lots of photos from life on the road that he'd taken before digital became a thing. But nothing that was important enough for her to worry about it now.

She'd been planning to talk about the estate and the archives and how close they were getting to wrapping it all up with Mina and Zach after CloudFest. But that was going to have to wait. It wasn't like any of them needed cash. Grey had set up trust funds for them when they'd been babies and they'd each gotten that money when they'd turned twenty-one. And Harper Inc. had a steady income stream that kept it operating smoothly.

But it would be nice to have it all over and done with. Closure. Finally. Then they could all move on. Maybe. Lou chewed her lip. "I guess."

Faith looked up. "Mom, let the lawyers deal with it. Dad's been gone for six years already. Anything that's waited this long can wait a little longer.

"I know. I just—"

She knew that expression. "Don't even think about it. Those masters are gone." The damned missing masters. The never-quite-dead legend of a solo album that Grey had made and never released. Grey swore he'd tossed them in the ocean when he'd decided he hated the record. But somehow Lou had never quite believed him. Every time the lawyers found another damned storage unit, Lou got the "maybe this time" look in her eyes. Faith had no idea why she was holding onto the idea for so long.

"So he always told us. But I don't know. It would be just like him to make an album and to stash it so it could come out after he'd gone."

"He knew he was dying long enough to have done something about that," Faith pointed out. "He didn't make any dramatic deathbed pronouncements about one last album or where to find them. I really think they're gone, Mom." She'd wanted to believe too, once upon a time.

And now, well now, it would be great to have the masters just to hear Grey's voice saying something she'd never heard before. She'd never told anybody that she still had the last few voicemails he'd ever left her. Or that she had hunted down as many Blacklight bootlegs as she could find in the months after his death, just to hear those moments of him talking between songs. But he was gone. And so were the masters. If indeed, they'd ever existed.

Lou sighed. "Okay. Sorry, I know you're busy."

"Never too busy to scoff muffins with my mom," Faith said with a smile.

"Or to drink lovingly prepared herbal tea?"

"Or that," she agreed and picked up the mug just to keep Lou happy.

chapter eight

It was close to seven when Theo reappeared in her doorway, looking distinctly rumpled. None of the Harper employees wore suits and ties to work but Theo usually managed to make khakis and polo shirts look formal. Tonight his dark brown hair stood up in spiky tufts like he'd run his hands though it one too many times and his pale blue shirt had a splash of something brown spilled across the pocket.

Which was a sign of exactly how busy they were. Normally a spill would send Theo home for a change of clothes. Or to the closet in his office where he kept spares. He must have gone through his stash already this week.

"Something up?" she asked as he dropped into her visitor's chair without so much a "Hey." Her stomach tightened as he grimaced in response. What now? She'd spent the day getting things squared away and had just started to feel like she was actually making progress and that the festival might actually start in twenty four hours as planned.

"Do you want the bad news or the bad news?"

Faith sat back in her chair, telling herself not to panic. Theo's expression was grim though. She was pretty sure panic was warranted. All the muscles in her neck tensed in sympathy with the knots in her stomach. "Define 'bad'? I'm-not-going-to-be-happy-about-something bad or hurricane-bearing-down-on-the-island-about-to-kill-us-all bad?"

"You're not going to be happy," he said. "Though the weather forecast isn't particularly good either."

She reached for the mug on her desk. "Is that one of the two things?" Trying to ease her nerves, she took a rapid mouthful only to realize she'd picked up the mug Lou had brought her earlier. Which was now half full of cold spearmint and chamomile tea. *Ugh.* Turned out cold herbal tea that she hadn't much liked in the first place wasn't terribly soothing.

"No."

"Then let's leave the weather gods out of the conversation for now." There wasn't much she could do about the weather. Unless there was torrential rain or an electrical storm, they'd go ahead. Torrential rain seemed unlikely given the current dry conditions.

"Okay." Theo took off his glasses and rubbed his forehead before sighing. "Well, the first thing is that somehow the news that Sienna is the secret guest got out."

Crap. "Somehow?" Faith had sworn Sienna and her team to secrecy. It was the one non-negotiable thing that anyone signing up to take the secret slot at CloudFest had to agree to.

"Someone tweeted it. We're still not sure how they got the news. Her manager swears it wasn't anyone they know. Someone at the transport company, they think. Someone who had a picture of gear with her name on it and a transport order for Lansing. Still, *who* is kind of a moot point. The news is out."

Faith fought the urge to just bang her head onto the desk. "Okay. Well. It's not going to affect ticket sales." They were already sold out. "But it does take the fun out of it for everyone. I guess there's no chance the tweet can be deleted or something?"

"By the time someone from Sienna's team saw it, it had already been re-tweeted twenty thousand times," Theo said. "And it's on all the other social media channels."

Well, there were worse things that could happen. But she would be tracking down Carl Ashton, Sienna's manager, and reminding him of the meaning of the word "confidential" and suggest he find a new transport company who also understood it.

"What's the other thing?" she asked.

"It's kind of good and bad," Theo said. "So try and stay calm."

"Theo, no one has ever felt more calm from being told to stay calm."

"It's like this. The news of Sienna performing leaked. But it turns out she can't be the secret guest anyway."

"What?" Faith yelled, hearing her voice leap several octaves. She sounded like a demented dolphin. Seriously? Sienna was going to screw her over as well? "I spent hours yesterday organizing this. She promised. And the news is out."

"All of which is true," Theo said. "But half an hour ago, she broke her wrist."

This time Faith did drop her head onto the desk. Guilt that she'd assumed Sienna would pull out warred with major "are you kidding me" rage. Was this really happening? Sienna was a singer, yes, but she was a singer who accompanied herself on the piano. Faith had spent enough time seated at a piano to know that you needed both hands to play the damn thing.

"I don't suppose she can sing while someone else plays for her?" she asked without lifting her head.

"She's probably having surgery tonight," Theo said. "There's no way she'd be allowed to travel. She'd be too hopped up on pain meds to perform even if she could get here."

"Plenty of people have played the CloudFest stage stoned," Faith muttered.

"Yeah but not someone who prides herself on her clean vegan teetotal lifestyle. I doubt she could pull it off even if she could find someone who knew all her songs at this late notice."

"So we now have to announce she's not the secret act, deal with the press that goes with that, *and* find a new secret act?" She wanted to cry. The list of people who were the kind of artist they needed to take the slot—the kind the crowd would be wowed by—was pretty short. She'd already asked about three quarters of them yesterday.

"That's about it," Theo said.

"You want me to call people, don't you?"

"Yep."

She thumped her head gently across the desk. "You

know what, I think we should take up a new gig. Something dull. Box making. Or insurance."

"No room for a box factory on the island."

"There could be. The CloudFest site is big and flat. Perfect for a factory."

"Faith."

She lifted her head reluctantly. "Let me sulk just for a minute."

He looked at his watch. "You have fifty-eight seconds."

"I hate you."

His mouth quirked. "No you don't."

"I hate musicians. Make sure you remind me to send Sienna flowers and stuff, but I hate musicians."

"For forty-five seconds more, you're allowed to hate musicians. Then you have to pretend you love them all and get back on the phone."

She glared at him. He looked down at his watch.

There was silence. She tried to breathe deeply and slowly. It didn't do much to make her feel any better. Extra oxygen apparently just fueled the fires of outrage. She tried to channel that energy into coming up with a new candidate to take the slot. Her mind stayed stubbornly blank. She put her head back down on the desk. It was tempting to just crawl underneath it and wash her hands of the whole mess.

"Time's up," Theo said.

She didn't move. "I have no idea who to call."

"You'll think of someone."

"It's kind of late notice, Theo." CloudFest kicked off on Thursday. It was Tuesday. Reluctantly, she straightened.

"It was late notice yesterday and you pulled that off." Theo was looking calmer now. Probably because he'd dumped the problem in her lap.

"Yesterday gave us an extra day to organize something. Now we only have forty-eight hours before the festival starts." In reality, there was more time than that. The secret act played on Sunday night. But still, it was no time at all when she had no idea who to ask. Fuck. "Right now, I hate you too. You know that, right?"

"I can cope." Theo stood. Then hesitated. "You know, maybe you could try Zach again."

"He has a gig."

"This is an emergency."

Faith shook her head. "I really don't think our emergencies mean much to Zach anymore. I'm sorry, Theo. I'll see who else I can come up with."

She really didn't want to make the call. Faith glared at the cell phone sitting on her desk, hoping it might spontaneously combust or vanish in a puff of smoke. Anything that would mean she couldn't make the call she was about to make. But the phone just sat there, red, blue, and shiny white in the silly Captain America case Mina had given her for Christmas. Unhelpful damned thing. Right now she needed a superhero to rescue her but apparently her phone case wasn't going to turn into Steve Rogers and save the day any time soon.

The phone and the contact list it contained had failed her. For two hours she'd been making calls, trying to find an act to replace Sienna. And for once, her mojo had failed her. She'd cajoled; she'd sweet-talked; she'd thrown the Harper name around, offered free recording time; offered, in one case, a guaranteed headline slot at next year's festival. Everyone had turned her down. Regretfully in most cases but, still, turned down was turned down.

Everyone was booked, out of the country, or apparently tied up in other obligations that couldn't be wriggled out of.

Which left her with either no surprise act and a lot of disappointed festival goers, or one last Hail Mary pass.

Calling Zach.

Seeing if, for once, she could guilt him into doing the right thing.

She didn't hold out a lot of hope. She hadn't managed to guilt Zach into anything much since he'd been maybe fifteen. It had been hard enough to guilt trip a big brother at the best of times. That had changed to nearly impossible once he'd left home.

But she had to try. For the festival's sake.

As much as she didn't want to.

No time like the present.

God, she hated that saying. People only used it when you had something truly sucky to do.

Hating it, however, didn't change the fact she had to make the damn call.

Sighing, she picked up the phone and thumbed through to Zach's number in her favorites, then waited for the call to connect.

To her surprise, it didn't go immediately to voicemail. Whether or not he'd take the call when he saw her number on his screen was another matter. She held the phone to her ear and started to gnaw on a fingernail before stopping herself. There was no time in her schedule for a manicure.

"Hello?" Zach's voice came over the line.

Oh god, was he going to pretend he didn't know who was calling? "Zach, it's me," she said.

"Faith?" he sounded wary. Which might be smart on his part after his stunt sending Mina to break the bad news to her yesterday.

"Yes. Your sister. The middle one. You remember me, right?"

"Yes." He sounded even more wary.

"Oh good. I was wondering. After you sent Mina to do your dirty work yesterday—that was pretty chicken shit, by the way." The words tumbled out of her mouth before she could stop herself and she bit her lip. She was trying to get him to do her a favor. Yelling at him was probably not the way to go.

Trouble was, now that she was talking to him, it was hard to remember anything but how pissed off with him she was.

Zach made an exasperated noise. "Maybe I just didn't want to have the conversation we're having now."

"Did you really think you'd avoid it?" Sometimes Zach's ability to ignore the fact he might be causing trouble was infuriating. One thing he'd inherited from Grey was a kind of cast-iron optimism that everything would work out in his favor no matter what. That the universe would shape itself around him to his satisfaction.

Maybe you needed that sort of personality to believe

that thousands and thousands of people would want to pay to hear you sing or play guitar.

If it was, that particular genetic gift had passed her by. She wasn't exactly a shrinking violet but she didn't assume she was always going to get her own way either. Of course, that could be Lou's influence. Maybe the fact that Zach hadn't had Lou in his life from the beginning was the difference between them. Either that or he'd gotten a double whammy of the confidence thing from Grey and Zoe, who had also been ferocious about going after what she wanted.

Even when it meant leaving her only child behind.

But apparently Zach hadn't learned anything from the damage his parents had left in their wake as they chased their dreams.

"No," he said. "Is there something you wanted? Is everyone okay?"

"Everyone's fine," she said. "And we can argue about you calling Mina instead of me another time." She was letting him off the hook. Just for now. Because now she had more important stuff to deal with. "But I did call for a reason."

"Which is?"

He was keeping it short. Not even a "How are you?" or "How's the festival planning going?" She couldn't deny the sting of it.

She rubbed her chest, clutching the phone harder, trying to push down the bubble of anger again. "Well, it's like this. Sienna Reese was going to step in and take your spot.' She paused, giving him time to absorb that information. She didn't know how he felt about Sienna, but she did know her brother. He was a competitive creature. Even though he was the one who'd pulled out, the news that she'd replaced him with someone who was arguably doing better than Fringe Dweller would annoy him. "But now Sienna's broken her wrist so she can't."

"That's too bad," he said, not sounding sad about it at all. "But I don't see how that's my problem."

Faith gritted her teeth. Conciliatory, she had to be conciliatory. "I was hoping you'd reconsider," she said, trying to sound reasonable rather than infuriated. "I've been calling around but there's no one who can do it at this short notice. Seeing as you're the one who kind of put me in this spot, I thought maybe you might change your mind."

"Didn't Mina tell you about the gig?"

"She did. And I know it's a big deal for the band. But it's for a couple of nights right?" She'd checked the dates earlier. "Surely you could miss one. They could get someone else in. I'll even charter you a plane. You can be here, do the gig, and then be back in New York in less than a day."

"Actually they can't just 'get someone else in,' " Zach said, sounding annoyed now. "I'm part of the band, I'm not just a fill-in guitarist."

Ah. She'd hit a sore spot. Dammit. Zach had started with Fringe Dweller as exactly that. A fill-in guitarist, meant to be temporary. But he'd stuck. "I know you are. But doesn't that mean that you also have some say in what you do? I mean, you're writing for them now. They need you. Can't they give you one night off? Hell, Ryder could play the guitar parts if he wanted to."

"Ryder has enough to do."

Zach sounded even more pissed off now. Faith wondered if he and Ryder were getting on each other's nerves again. Truth was, Ryder Lange was a great guitarist in his own right. But he had chosen to focus on his vocals. Take the lead singer role, which meant more often than not he didn't play onstage.

But there was no doubt he could cover for Zach if he had to for a night. But the question was whether or not Zach wanted to admit it. Or maybe, whether he wanted Ryder to realize that for himself. But fuck it, Zach had been with the band for years now. They'd only started having success after he'd joined. They were hardly going to ditch him.

He and Ryder were the ones with the talent and both of them weren't exactly hard on the eyes—Zach might be Faith's brother but that didn't mean she didn't see that he'd been blessed with very good genes from the combination of Grey and Zoe's DNA.

He'd always been stupidly pretty for a boy as a kid, the kind of child that women stopped to coo over in the streets and that little girls had always wanted to play with. But then, when he'd hit puberty, the pretty had been replaced by something harder. Something no less attractive, judging by the sheer number of girls who'd vied to be Zach's whatever-the-hell-he-wanted-them-to-be in high school and ever since. Fringe Dweller had a massive female fan base compared to some of the other bands who played their brand of hard-edged indie rock. Ryder and the other guys weren't going to alienate all those fans that had Zach's picture on their phones or Pinterest boards.

"Zach, I really need your help. You know what these

surprise gigs mean to the fans. They love it. It's the reason Dad started putting them into the mix." She didn't want to break the tradition. Didn't want to be the one letting down all the people who came to the festival each year.

"I know," Zach said. "But Dad's not here any more."

"So you'd do it for him but not for me?" she said. Her voice cracked a little and she bit her lip.

"Faith—"

"No, don't 'Faith' me," she snapped. "You know what, Zach, I've put up with a lot of your shit since Dad died. Since before Dad died, really. So has Mina. You've run off and played rock star while I held things together here. Mina's husband died and I'm the one who's been here for her. You left us behind. Fine. But I've always helped you and the band out where I could. So I'm asking you to give something back for a change. It's one day. One gig. One lousy day, Zach. I really need you to do this."

"Try and see it from my point of view—"

"No," she said flatly. "Screw your point of view. Too many damn people in your life spend time bending over backward to accommodate the Zach Harper point of view. Giving you your own way. Letting you be a self-absorbed rock god, just like Dad was. You remember Dad, right? I remember him. I also remember you saying you wanted to do music like he did but you didn't want to do the rest of your life that way too. So don't. Do the unselfish thing for once. Help me out."

There was silence on the other end of the line.

"Are you kidding me?" she said, unwilling to believe he was really going to say no. "I'm practically begging you here and you won't do it?"

"I'm sorry." His voice was terse.

"No, you're not," she said. "But I am. Sorry that my brother has turned into just another rock star who believes his own hype and doesn't give a shit about anyone but himself. Sorry that I actually thought you might not let me down this time. But I was wrong. And you know what, Zach? I'm done being wrong about you. If this is how you want things to be—if you don't care about me or Mina and what we're doing—then fine. That's the way it will be. Just don't expect us to be there if your perfect little rock bubble comes crashing down around your ears." She felt her breath catch, her eyes start to prickle. Dammit. She was not going to let Zach hear anything close to tears from her.

"Faith—" he began.

"Screw you, Zach," she said. She hit the end button on her phone so hard she thought she might have cracked the screen. Then she picked up her notebook in a rage, and tossed it at the wall.

It hit with a solid *thud*. Thirty seconds later the door opened and Theo stuck his head into the room.

"Everything okay?"

"No." She looked around the room for something else that was safe to throw.

"I take it things aren't going well. Did you talk to Zach?"

"Screw Zach." She stood up, knocking her chair over. She didn't know exactly where she wanted to be but she knew she didn't want to here at Harper one second longer.

Theo's brows flew up. "Faith?"

She grabbed her purse and shoved her phone and

wallet into it haphazardly. "I'm done. You can all find someone else."

"But we—"

"No." She held up a hand. "I've had it. I don't even know why I'm doing this right now when no other Harper gives a damn about CloudFest." Not to mention Danny or Billy or Shane.

"But *you* give a damn about it," Theo said, sounding alarmed.

Faith bared her teeth at him and slung the purse over her shoulder. "Not right now I don't. I'm out of here. You can all sort out another act yourselves. Leah's got just as many names in her contact book from the studio as I do. Or ask Sal. Or Ziggy." Between them, Leah's dad, Sal, and Ziggy probably knew ninety percent of people in the industry.

"You can't just leave."

"Yes, I can. Because you know what? This is my damned company and my damned festival and if I want to walk out on the whole damned thing I will and there's nothing you can do to stop me. Now get out of my way, Theo."

She pushed past him, heading for the front door. Leah looked up from her desk as Faith stormed past, just as startled as Theo, but Faith was in no mood to stop and offer explanations so she just kept walking.

It wasn't until she was sitting in her car, keys in hand, that she knew where she wanted to go.

chapter nine

"Mind if I come in?"

Caleb blinked at Faith. He hadn't expected to find her on his doorstep any time soon. She'd made it fairly clear she didn't have much time to spare for the next few days. But he wasn't stupid enough to look a gift horse in the mouth, so he got out of her way. "Be my guest."

"Thanks," Faith said, the words more snarl than anything else. She stalked into the house, the heels of her ankle boots tapping on the floorboards like gunshots.

He closed the door and followed her, watching her stride into the living room and head for the bank of cabinets behind the TV. Her hair was loose, bouncing in time with each step.

Pissed off, in his judgment.

A judgment confirmed when she stopped in front of one of the cabinets built into the walls of the living room, flung open the door, and pulled out a bottle of vodka. Her knuckles where her hand was wrapped around the neck of the bottle were white. Much like the teeth she bared in a grin that looked more savage than happy.

Right. Whatever had happened today hadn't been good. And now she was here on his doorstep. So what the hell did that mean?

"Where's Liam?" she asked, on the move again, this time headed for the kitchen. The vodka in the bottle sloshed in time with the tapping heels.

"He had to go back to L.A. for a day or so," Caleb said. He caught up to Faith at the refrigerator door.

"Good," Faith said. She yanked the freezer open. She reached in, and her hand emerged gripping another bottle of vodka.

Two bottles? That seemed excessive. But, as he watched, she slid the one she'd taken out of the cabinet into the freezer, keeping the cold one in her hand.

"Good?" he asked. He knew where the glasses were, so he reached up to the cabinet and took down two.

But before he could hand one to Faith, she opened the bottle and took a swig.

"Good," she said. "Because here's how I thought tonight could go." She held the bottle out to him. He took it, more out of reflex than anything else. Though he was starting to think that maybe keeping Faith away from the booze until he could figure out what the hell was going on might be a good idea.

Faith's eyes, fixed on his, were fiercely green.

A dangerous shade. A "watch out world, I'm spoiling for a fight" shade.

Which was just as well. Because of the two most obvious things that might drive someone to swigging vodka straight from the bottle, being full-on furious about something was a better option than someone being dead.

Right now all that sea-washed green fury was directed at him but he didn't think she was actually pissed off with him. He couldn't, off the top of his head, think of anything he could have possibly done in the last twelve hours that could have made her so angry. Not when his day had involved a drive into Cloud Bay to take Liam to the ferry, picking up bagels and a coffee for his breakfast, and then a lazy drive around the island before he'd come back to the big empty house for an equally lazy afternoon of lying poolside and alternating napping with laps.

But whoever had pissed her off, he was glad not to be them. Because she looked like she wanted to bite something. Hard.

Tipping the bottle up to his mouth, he tried not to think of Faith sinking her teeth into him while he moved inside her.

Now there was a hell of a thought. One that would probably require the whole bottle of vodka to drown out. But right now he needed to keep his wits about him. So he only took a small mouthful. Faith didn't seem to notice.

"You were saying?" he prompted as the vodka hit his stomach, burning outward.

Those eyes were nearly a feral shade now. And all that intensity focused on him. He took another swig. The heat of the vodka suddenly paled in comparison with the heat those eyes stirred up.

"I was thinking we could have a couple of drinks and

then I'd take you to bed and have my wicked way with you."

Caleb almost choked on the vodka. He sputtered slightly, managed to swallow, and coughed once more as vodka seared its way down to his throat. He wiped his mouth. "Excuse me?"

"You know, sex? The hot and sweaty kind." She tilted her head, still looking more pissed than turned on. "That was what was behind those kisses, wasn't it? The idea we'd sleep together? A good old-fashioned one-night stand? Or a good old-fashioned however-many-nights-you're-here stand?"

"I—" He wasn't sure exactly how to respond. "Hell yes!" seemed kind of . . . inappropriate. But then again, she was the one propositioning him. So maybe it was polite.

"You can say yes, Caleb," she said with a little jerk of her chin. "It's okay. You. Me. There's a buzz there. And I for one am in favor of taking advantage of that fact." She reached for the vodka but her eyes kept watching him. The green was still bright, but he got the feeling the heat in them wasn't all anger any more.

He held the bottle up out of reach, stalling. "Have you been drinking? Before you got here?"

Her eyes moved to the vodka as she stood on tiptoe and made a grab for it. He lifted his arm higher. Faith wasn't short for a girl, but at six five he had the advantage.

"Give me that."

"Not until we finish this conversation. Have you been drinking?"

"Why do you care?"

"Because I don't sleep with women who are only propositioning me because they're drunk. I'm not a prick."

"I know you're not a prick," she said. "I wouldn't be here if you were a prick." She paused a moment. "Well, maybe that's not true. I can't say I haven't slept with an asshole or two in my time. But I don't think you're one."

"Good. But that doesn't answer my question." He kept the vodka out of reach. Saw her glance up at it again as if considering her options. A wrestling match over alcohol was not the kind of wrestling match he wanted with Faith. Opening one of the cabinets, he put the bottle up on the highest shelf he could reach. Then closed the door and turned back to her.

Those eyes were stormy now. "You know, I might reassess my opinion of you if you won't give me back my vodka."

"It's Danny's vodka."

"Danny would want me to have it."

"I doubt that." He had no idea what Danny would want actually. The guy was a rock star. Maybe he believed in free-flowing vodka at all hours of the day. Though he remembered that Faith had said he'd quit drinking. But the fact he kept his liquor cabinet so well stocked suggested he had no problems with anyone else drinking. Still, he doubted anyone who cared about Faith wanted her drinking her problems away. "Answer the question."

"No, Mr. Concerned Man, I haven't been drinking. Unless you count coffee. Or herbal tea."

He grinned at her. "Nope. Last time I checked those didn't cloud your judgment."

"You think my judgment has to be clouded for me to want to sleep with you?" She suddenly looked amused.

"No," he said. "Believe me, I am all in favor of that part of your proposal." He tried to ignore just how true that fact was. His body had roared into a "let's do this *now*" mode as soon as she'd used the words "bed" and "wicked ways" in the same sentence. But he wasn't about to give in to all those caveman instincts until he knew that was what Faith really wanted. "Just establishing that, you know, it's not the booze talking."

"You and vodka," she said. "Number one and two priorities on my list right now." She stepped a little closer to him. The simple cotton dress wrapped around her body was a deceptive shade. Deep moody gray like the sea when it got mean. The neckline was scooped and from his current angle he could see straight down to the silvery gray lace of her bra. Which kind of made him lose track of exactly what they'd been talking about. Because she had excellent breasts and he really wanted to see more of them.

"Now that look is the one I'm after," Faith said.

He snapped out of his lingerie fog. "What look?"

"The one that says you're thinking about how to get me out of my clothes. Here's a tip, give me back the vodka, pour me a drink, and I'll help you do it. You'll get to see all my tattoos."

The slant of her head and the glint in her eyes combined to create pure temptation. And damn, he wanted to know what tattoos hid beneath that dress, marking that golden skin. What parts of her they pointed to.

He had a sudden vivid picture of playing join the dots

on her body with his mouth tracing a path across her skin while she urged him on.

Fuck. His hands clenched against the need to grab her and carry her to his bed.

He summoned the last shreds of willpower he possessed and shook his head. He wanted to sleep with her. Wanted to be inside her. Wanted to make her moan under his touch. He was crystal clear on that point. He hadn't been expecting to do it tonight, but he wasn't fool enough to turn down her offer.

If it was what she really wanted. "Faith, I'm more than happy to let you use me for sex." He was rock hard, the ache of it proof of just how willing he was. "But if you want something to make you forget whatever it is that's pissed you off so badly, you have to choose. Me or the booze. Pick your poison." He reached out and ran his thumb along the curve of her lip, half-expecting her to pull away. Instead she opened her mouth and pressed her teeth into the flesh of his thumb. Just hard enough.

Heat ran up his arm, and he saw her eyes go wide and dark.

"Trust me," he said. "I'm better than vodka." He pulled his thumb away, the scrape of her teeth over her skin making him harder still.

She smiled up at him then, the expression savage. "Prove it."

Caleb apparently wasn't a man who needed to be asked twice.

He moved forward and his hands went to her ass and he lifted her as though she weighed nothing.

Damn. Strong. She had to remember that. But right

now, as she wrapped her legs around his waist and twined her arms around his neck, it wasn't the most immediate thing on her mind. Not when the taste of his skin was in her mouth and his hands were gripping her like he'd never let her go.

Nope. Right now. She wanted his mouth. Wanted him to kiss her and make everything go away except the good stuff. She wriggled a little and smiled when his eyes went dark.

"There's that look I like again," she said and tried to pull his head down.

"Hang on," he said.

"I already am," she pointed out, squeezing her legs a little tighter to make her point clear. "What we're aiming for here is the hot and heavy, no-talking kind of sex. So kiss me already."

"Logistics," Caleb said, clutching her tighter.

It felt damned good. He smelled damned good so close. She kind of wanted to climb inside him and not come up for days. Which meant she had to make him stop talking by dealing with the details. She got the hesitation. This wasn't his house after all—or hers—and while Danny's house was full of all sorts of tempting squishy sofas and counters and even a hot tub, it didn't seem quite right to avail herself of them. So, that was one thing decided. "Bed," she said. "Condoms. My last physical was thorough and I'm all good. I'm on the pill, but still condoms. If you don't have any, then Danny keeps them in the guest bathrooms."

"I have them," Caleb said.

She smiled approvingly. "I like a man who prepares before he comes."

That earned her a grin before his expression turned focused again. "Bed. Condoms. Anything else?"

"The rest we can figure out as we go along," she said. "So kiss me already."

"You got it," he said and his mouth lowered again.

No more messing around, it seemed. This kiss was different from the one they'd shared in Will's Mustang. Hungrier. Urgent. Clearly Caleb meant business.

She would have smiled at the thought but she was too busy kissing him back.

It was a take-no-prisoners kind of kiss. And with each move of his mouth on hers, it was clear that this was the kind of battle both of them could win.

Faith threaded the fingers of her right hand through Caleb's hair, and gave herself up to him.

Her focus narrowed to Caleb. To the solid muscle of him pressed against her thighs, to the warmth of him burning into her skin. To the taste of him filling her mouth and her senses and the scent of man and night and good old-fashioned want rising around her.

The thudding of her heart was so loud in her ears—a pounding beat like a driving bass line—that for a moment she thought someone had turned on the sound system.

She rode the rhythm down. Down to the place where it was dark and hot and needy. Where the man and the moment were all that mattered. Until she was jolted back to awareness by the thump of her back hitting the wall and her eyes flew open.

Caleb pulled his mouth away. "Sorry," he muttered.

Her brain reengaged enough to realize that he'd carried her across the room and she was now resting against the wall nearest to the bottom of the staircase that led to the second floor. She hadn't even noticed them moving.

"Let me guess, you picked an upstairs bedroom?"

"Yup."

"If you put me down, I could walk."

"Not gonna happen." His right arm tightened around her. His left was braced against the wall.

So he wanted to be all caveman, did he? Carry her up to his room and drag her into his bed? She wasn't opposed to that notion. Hell, if she was going to sleep with a world-class athlete, she might as well make the most of it.

Caleb took a step toward the stairs.

"Wait," Faith said. She twisted a little. Found the panel of the wall that controlled the various systems Ivy had loaded the house up with. Lights, down. Air-con, who cared? If she had her way they were going to be getting sweaty no matter what. She pushed another button, bringing up the sound system. Hit another few keys and smiled as drums and wailing guitars issued from the speakers that were positioned at intervals all around the house. A beat to match the pulse in her throat and between her legs.

"You know," she said, "beds are overrated." She wriggled against him again, pressing into him harder. Felt him grow harder in response. "We could make this work."

Even as she said it, the thought of it made her head swim. She could hear the slide of his zipper, feel the slow slide of him into her while her back pushed into the wall. She swallowed. God. If the anticipation was this good, what was the real thing going to be like?

Caleb shook his head. "Bed." He swung her around so that her back was to the staircase. And started up the stairs as though he was carrying nothing at all. His mouth found the side of her neck as he walked and nerves sparked into life that drove any thought of protest out of her head. Beds were good. Beds had scope for . . . exploration.

Exploring Caleb was going to be . . . well, some word she couldn't actually think of right now. They'd reached one of the guest bedrooms, and Caleb shoved the door— already slightly ajar—open with his foot and kept moving. He didn't stop until suddenly Faith was lying on the end of the bed, legs hanging over the edge of the mattress, and he was leaning over her, all his weight on the arms that he'd placed on either side of her.

Surrounded.

In the best way.

Heat radiated from him and she had the crazy thought that the pulse she could just see beating in his throat in the moonlight flooding through the windows was moving in time with the music that was pounding around them.

She pushed up on her elbows. Wanting to taste his skin at the exact spot where his blood was beating so hard. To see if she could feel that beat against her tongue. See if she could make it go even faster.

Caleb made a noise somewhere deep in his throat as she pressed teeth and tongue to his skin, a sound that vibrated through her lips as much as her ears.

A very good sound.

One that made her shiver.

"Faith," he muttered. "Christ." Then he pulled free,

hands coming to her waist, moving her further up the bed, following her as she went. She didn't particularly have time to think before he'd yanked down one of the straps on her dress, tugging cotton and lace out of the way before his mouth closed over her nipple.

Her turn to make noise it seemed. God. So good.

He knew how to use his mouth, and she twisted beneath him, wanting more.

Needing it.

She started to reach for his hand, to guide it down to where she really wanted him to touch her, but he was a step ahead of her. Fingers slid up her thigh, heat blooming in their wake. His mouth moved to her other breast as those same clever fingers slid under the elastic of her underwear like it wasn't there and found her clit with one sure stroke that had her arching off the bed with his name on her lips.

She could feel his mouth stretch into a grin against her skin, and she sank her fingers back into his hair to pull him back up to kiss her again.

He tasted even better now, but even the kiss couldn't distract her from the feel of his fingers sliding against her, sliding into her. Good. So good. But not enough.

Not that she was quite ready to give up the sensation to tell him that.

Because. Damn.

She knew musicians were meant to be good with their hands. But from her limited experience of the species, she was forced to admit that tennis players had them beat.

Maybe it was all in the wrist muscles or something. Because each time his hand flexed it felt glorious, and she slid deeper into the delight of him. Letting him give her what she wanted. But not quite enough.

She wanted to know what other games he could play.

With a reluctant gasp, she tore her mouth free of his. "Condom?" she managed to say. Two syllables were about all she was capable of. Of course, the two syllables she really wanted to say were actually "Fuck me." But she was trying to keep a small grip on reality here.

Caleb moved his hand away—which she didn't approve of at all—and rolled to the right of the bed. Danny's guest beds ran to large and Caleb felt suddenly way too far away.

She distracted herself by wriggling out of her dress. Then losing her underwear. She tossed her bra toward Caleb to remind him where she was. He was busy losing his own clothes, and she momentarily lost her train of thought when the T-shirt came free of his head and she got a glimpse of back muscles that might as well have been sculpted by someone with a supreme appreciation for the male body.

A view that only improved when he rolled onto his back to push his jeans down, revealing abs that made her mouth go dry.

Dear lord.

She hadn't thought that men really had bodies like that. She's slept with men who'd taken working out seriously before, but there was working out and then there was being the world's number-one tennis player apparently.

He was all lean muscle, abs carved like hills and valleys. Only lightly covered with hair that led her eyes down to where the two muscles that angled across his hips joined the party, like little signposts to heaven.

Which didn't seem to be little at all.

Nope. The erection that was clearly stretching the capacity of his boxer briefs was just as impressive as the rest of the man.

She may have moaned then, and before she knew what she was doing she moved toward him, hand sliding under the overworked cotton to close around him.

His head dropped back and he made another one of those noises.

"Good?"

He nodded. He shoved the briefs down, so she had better access. Under her palm, he was heat and slide, growing harder with every move she made. His head fell back, the heartfelt groan of appreciation echoing through the room.

Which made her want him more. Too much to keep up with what she was doing, much as she had definite plans for making him lie back and let her do what she wanted with him later on. But right now, she wanted more.

"Condom," she said again, the words somewhat breathless.

It took him a moment to open his eyes and when he did, his expression was pleasingly foggy. Good to know she wasn't the only one.

"Condom," she repeated. "*Now.*"

That seemed to break through. He reached out a hand and then somehow they were rolling back toward the middle of the bed. She blinked, trying to work out exactly what had happened. She heard foil tear and before

she'd really caught her breath again, Caleb was over her
once more. His hand gripped her thigh, coaxing her leg
up over his hip.

She was only too happy to comply. And as she felt
him settle against her, all that heat and hardness sliding
across the places where she was aching, she didn't need
any more coaxing to wrap her other leg into place, so
she could pull him closer.

And then he wasn't sliding over her, he was sliding
into her, slow and steady, seemingly finding every place
inside her that was most sensitive until he was all the way
home, and she was pinned there, frozen under the weight
of him, sunk in the sensation, eyes locked on his.

Time stretched in that gaze. Too long. And not long
enough. She wanted to feel him like this for some endless time but also wanted to feel more.

Wanted him to move. To give her that slide and
stretch and oh, god, now he was.

His mouth came down on hers and his hips started
to flex, and she stopped thinking altogether.

There was only Caleb and darkness and the pleasure
of him around her and inside her. He moved like a machine, sure of himself, sure of what she needed. As
though he could read her mind. Or her body, at least.

It felt better than she'd imagined. Better than anything she'd ever imagined.

She moved with him as the need and the pleasure
twisted and spiraled its way through her, until she was
sure she had to be actually glowing with it.

It was too good, almost, too much.

Like he'd laid more than her body bare beneath him.
Like he knew her secrets.

At least the ones she only thought about alone in the dark.

She wasn't sure she was ready for him to know more. But she didn't want to stop either, didn't want him to stop the rhythm of it, the strength of him moving into her.

He kissed her then, deep and hard, adding an extra layer of sensation that was almost too much. She made a sound that was almost a sob, needing . . . hell, she had no idea any more.

Caleb was breathing fast but he didn't falter. He lifted his head, drove deeper still so she cried out his name as she arched up into him wildly, digging her fingers into the muscles of his back as she fought to . . . well, she didn't know that either.

Her eyes closed, and Caleb laughed softly. "Look at me," he said as he increased his pace again. He was all there was now and she did as he said. Found those blue eyes, that were near black in the moonlight, showing her she wasn't alone in whatever this was. That the heat flooding her was burning through him as well.

"Faith, let go," he said. "I've got you." And she couldn't fight it any more and gave in as the orgasm tore through her and sent everything away completely.

chapter ten

"Do you want to talk about it?" Caleb asked, sometime past dawn when she was lying against him, her head resting on his chest.

"Talk about what?" Faith asked, brain thoroughly melted by excellent orgasms and lack of sleep. She'd been half-dozing, lulled by the sound of the ocean drifting through the window and the steady thump of Caleb's heartbeat beneath her ear.

"Whatever it was that brought you to my doorstep wanting vodka and, well, this."

Her pleasant fog started to disperse a little. Dislike. She didn't want to think about reality. "Are you complaining?"

He chuckled, the noise vibrating through the side of her head. "Do I look like I'm complaining?"

She twisted onto her stomach, so she could prop herself up to study him. Lounging against the pillows, sleepy eyed and satisfied, she couldn't say that he looked upset about how the night had turned out.

"No," she said. "Which is just as well," she added, with a smile. "I put a lot of effort into last night."

"I remember. I appreciate it." One of his hands skimmed over her shoulder, his thumb moving slowly to the topmost point of her tattoos. "I like these." His hand moved lower. "All these little musical notes floating down your back. And the other ones."

She shivered despite herself, remembering how he'd used his mouth on every part of her marked by ink, then batted the memory away. He'd done some marking of his own. She was pleasurably sore in quite a few places. "You cannot possibly be ready for round . . ." She paused. "Okay, I've lost track. But more than you can possibly be ready for." Indeed she was feeling the effects of hours wrapped around Caleb. Muscles were not the only part of her feeling slightly tender this morning.

"You know, some men would take that as a challenge."

"Oh god, don't tell me I've awakened your competitive spirit."

"Nope. You've worn me out. For now. But that doesn't mean I don't like touching you still."

She ignored the "for now" part. That implied there was going to be another night. She hadn't yet decided if she was ready for that. The night had been hot and wild, yes. Caleb knew exactly what he was doing with every inch of his body. But somewhere in the early hours, somehow, each time they'd reached for each other again, hot and wild had turned a little more . . . something else. Something slower. Something more . . . intense. Intense meant emotion. Something she didn't want to get caught up in.

This was a festival fling.

She'd thought she'd been clear enough but now she wanted to make sure Caleb wasn't going to get the wrong idea. Awkward.

"Are you ignoring my question on purpose?" Caleb asked.

Dammit. The man had a mind like a steel trap. She'd gone off on a lust-fogged, sleep-deprived tangent and he was still on target, sitting there waiting for the answer to whatever he'd asked her to begin with. What was that again? Something about talking about why she'd turned up on his doorstep.

That was a no. Talking about Zach and why her brother was an asshole was in the same territory as feelings. Too big a can of worms for morning-after talk.

But now that Caleb had brought up the subject, she found herself thinking about Zach and the festival despite her good intentions. She groaned and rolled away, pulling the pillow over her face. The thought of leaving Caleb's bed and going in to face the final day of preparations was about as appealing as the idea of stabbing her eyes out with a dull fork.

"Is that a no?"

"Yes," she said, voice muffled by the pillow. "No talking about it."

"Right." The pillow suddenly disappeared, tugged out from her arms, and she found herself looking up at Caleb's face. His eyes, so very blue in the sunrise light that turned the rest of him to gold, looked concerned. "Did I ruin the mood?"

She sighed. "Maybe."

"Sorry."

"Not your fault. You're not the one who's pissing me off."

He smiled at that. Half-smiled, at least. "Good to know. I won't ask you who, seeing as though you don't want to talk about it. Anything I can do?"

She glanced at the clock on the bedside table. Thought about everything that waited for her at the Harper offices. But there were a few more hours before she had to get out of bed and face any of that. She reached up to hook a hand around the back of his neck. "Yes. Come back down here and distract me some more."

"I thought you said you didn't want another round?"

"Yeah, well, I changed my mind. I'm fickle." She batted her eyelashes at him. "Why don't we just fool around for a little while and maybe you'll talk me into something more."

He shifted then, moving so he was on top of her. His hips on hers. His weight bearing her down into the bed. And she had to give him props, because she could feel more than his hips. This sleeping-with-an-athlete thing had turned out to be a very good idea. Because the man had world-class stamina.

She wriggled a little, heard him groan softly as she moved and smiled up at him, heart starting to beat faster again at the feel of him against her. Even though there was a little pain mixed in with the pleasure of it. He smelled like sleepy, sexy man. The whole room smelled like sex. She breathed it in happily, letting the sensation pull her under into that place where she didn't have to think again.

Caleb pressed his hips more firmly against her and bent his head to press his mouth against the place in the curve of her neck that always made her go weak at the knees. Just as well she was already lying down.

"You're going to be the death of me, Faith Harper."

That made her laugh. "I doubt it. But hey, at least you'd die happy." She tipped her head back to give him better access.

"Can't argue with that," Caleb said. "How about you?" His lips grazed her ear, the words a quiet sexy rumble that made her want to purr.

"Would I die happy?" She considered the matter. "Keep doing that and, yeah, maybe."

"Maybe?" He lifted his head. "Just maybe?"

"Stop fishing for compliments," she said. "It's just I'd be kind of pissed off to miss the festival after working my butt off all year."

Caleb shook his head. "Anyone ever tell you that you're a workaholic?"

"Says the guy who was number one in the world. You get to that spot by taking it easy?"

"No. But I did know when to take a break when I needed to."

"You think I don't?"

One side of his mouth lifted. "If I had to put money on it, I'd guess you're already thinking that you have to be work in, what, less than two hours if your schedule yesterday was any indication."

"I like what I do."

"What you do was pissing you off last night."

She couldn't argue with *that*. "I thought we already covered that I don't want to talk about it."

"We did. And I don't need the details. I'm just saying that maybe it wouldn't kill you to play hooky."

"And we already talked about that. CloudFest is a multimillion dollar business, Caleb. It starts tomorrow."

"Which must mean that all the preparation must be nearly done. So, tell me, would the world end if you stayed in bed with me today? Took some time to do something only for you?" He did something with his hips that pushed her deeper into the mattress and set off tiny bursts of fireworks in all the right places. "Don't you deserve that?"

God. She really did. And he was making it really hard to remember that there were rational arguments about why it didn't matter what she deserved.

Not this week, at least. "Anybody ever tell you you're a bad influence?" she said. Her words came out more than half sigh as his hand found her breast.

"Occasionally," he said with a wicked grin. "Not often enough." He pushed against her again, all hard beautiful man. "Play hooky with me, Faith. Just for a little while. Have your wicked way with me and to hell with everyone else."

His words were more intoxicating than Danny's vodka. Combined with what he was doing with every slow pulse of his body against hers, the rush of sheer *wanting* that rolled through her, it was a nearly irresistible combination.

What was she so worried about anyway? Caleb was right. CloudFest was about to happen and everything left to do could be done by someone else.

Part of her mind chimed in with a reminder that they still didn't have someone to replace Sienna. But she'd put that problem in Theo's court last night. She was the boss after all. No one else was stepping up to take the job. And if being Grey's daughter had taught her anything, it was that if you were the big dog, you decided what you wanted and everyone else had to deal with it.

She had no desire to turn into a diva and she knew how to step up and take charge when the situation required it. But she'd spent a large part of the last six years or more of her life scrambling to keep up and keep things afloat since Grey had first been diagnosed.

Maybe she didn't have to hang on to the reins quite so hard.

Maybe, she thought hazily, as Caleb's mouth moved down her body, she could hang onto someone else for a few hours. Let him take charge.

Her stomach quivered under his lips, the sensation of his slightly stubbled chin on her skin delicious. She sighed and let her head drop back onto the pillow.

"Is that a yes?" Caleb said, stopping what he was doing.

Stopping was bad. She wanted that mouth. So she had to answer the question. Could she really do it? Was it as simple as saying yes?

She was about to open her mouth and say just that when she remembered the party. The one she was supposed to be hosting that night. Grey had always had everyone involved in the festival, artists, and crew over to their house the night before the festival started. A welcome to the island, break a leg, let's do this type thing to kick CloudFest off.

BBQ. Music. Beer. The odd bit of mayhem.

A way to blow off some of the pre-festival nerves

and get everyone into a "we're all in this together" frame of mind. Grey said it made things run more smoothly, and from what she'd seen over the years, he was right about that.

After Grey's death, she'd kept up the tradition but moved the location to the VIP tents that formed a small canvas village in the staging area behind the main arena. It had felt too weird having all the people at their house with Grey no longer there to hold center stage. But there was no way she could miss the party. Not without having every single person whose path she crossed for the rest of the festival ask her where she'd been.

And she might have broken her not-on-the-island rule but she wasn't ready to let everybody else know that. "Crap."

"What?" Caleb asked.

She explained the party to him.

When she finished he shrugged. "Okay, so play hooky for most of the day. You must have a team and hordes of caterers and that sort of thing running this party, right? You don't have to actually cook the BBQ yourself?"

She laughed at that. "No, I leave the BBQ to the experts. I just eat it."

"Then I don't see the problem."

It sounded so simple when he said it. So maybe she should just let it be simple. Give in.

"Okay," she said. She started to put her hands on his head, to encourage him to continue what he'd started, when she had another thought. "But I need my phone."

"Your phone?" He sounded suspicious.

"Trust me, if I just don't turn up at the office this morning and nobody can find me, then everybody is going to leap to the wrong conclusion and assume a crazed fan has kidnapped me or something." She tried to keep her voice light but it wasn't a scenario she took lightly.

"Ah. Right. Of course." Caleb rolled off her, which made her curse her practical side. "Where exactly is your phone?"

"In my purse downstairs." The fact that he hadn't blinked about her mentioning a security issue threw her for a second. Until she remembered he probably lived with a certain amount of it himself.

"Stay right there," he said and clambered off the bed.

Now that it was light, she had a better view of the tattoos inked on his back. She'd noticed them last night but had been too busy with other things—more enjoyable things—to try and work out what they were in the dark. Five neat columns along his right shoulder blade. Each column three deep with small pointed symbols she'd thought were maybe stars but could see now were compass roses. North firmly pointing up. Fifteen of them in all inked in black and deep blue and red. Fifteen. That must have some significance. Maybe if she knew more about his career, she'd know the answer. It seemed a little embarrassing to ask. So, stick to the topic at hand. Her phone. And why Caleb was the one climbing out of Danny's very comfortable bed to retrieve it. "You don't have to get it for me."

He shot her a grin over his shoulder.

"I'm not letting you out of my bed one second earlier than I have to. I will fetch the phone. You stay right there." He didn't wait for an answer, just padded across the room—which gave her a near-perfect view of his perfect butt flexing as he moved—and vanished out the door.

She took advantage of his absence to dash to the bathroom, swishing water around her mouth and taking care of other needs. It was tempting to climb under the shower, but if she did that, she was fairly sure that Caleb would join her. Which she was in favor of, but she was also fairly sure she'd forget all about making phone calls if she got her hands on wet slippery Caleb.

She just made it back to the bed when Caleb reappeared, phone in hand.

"Make it quick," he mock-growled as he tossed it to her. He knelt at the end of the bed, started crawling up to her. When he reached her feet, he tugged the sheet away and started kissing her ankle. It made it difficult to concentrate on what she had to do. She bit her lip and opened her message app.

Nothing's wrong but I'm not going to be around until . . . she hesitated. A sensible woman would say "two." But she felt nothing resembling sense as Caleb's mouth started moving up her leg.

. . . three or four. Note no code word. I'm fine but the phone will be off. See you at the site.

Hopefully they'd believe her. She and her siblings, and Lou, all had a code word they were meant to use in any situation where they were in trouble. Use that word, and the security team would swing into action. Which was exactly what she didn't need happening here. She sent the message to Theo, Ivy, Leah, and Ziggy, then turned the phone off. She dropped it over the edge of the bed as

Caleb's lips reached her thigh and his hands started pushing her legs apart.

"Now," he murmured as she sucked in a breath, anticipation and lust shooting through her limbs, "where were we?"

chapter twelve

It was near midday when Faith woke again, Caleb's arm curved around her. She sighed for a moment, tempted to close her eyes and let sleep pull her down into oblivion again. Then her stomach growled noisily and she realized she was starving. She and Caleb hadn't had breakfast, and the dinner she'd eaten at her desk back at Harper the night before was a very distant memory.

Food.

Now.

Also caffeine.

As much as Caleb made it very tempting to stay in bed, the fact was that woman could not survive on super hot sex alone.

She lifted his arm off her waist. He made a sleepy protesting noise but didn't open his eyes as she slid out of bed.

She'd worn him out. Pleasing thought.

The least she could do was cook the man lunch.

Thanks to his skills in bed, she was feeling more relaxed than she had in weeks. So she'd enjoy that feeling for a little while longer while she cooked. And then she'd have to leave. She really didn't want to think about that. Not yet.

Moving quietly, she gathered her dress and under-wear from the floor and slipped into the bathroom. Danny didn't just stock robes for his guests. She knew there'd be spare toothbrushes and shampoo and soap. All things she needed. Sweaty sex was awesome, but there was a point when sweaty turned into stinky and she didn't want to reach it.

Caleb was still asleep when she came out of the bath-room. He was on his stomach, one arm tucked under the pillow, blond hair spiking in all directions. The white cotton sheets only half-covered him, draping the big body enticingly, making his skin look even more golden. Like something out of a magazine.

Maybe that was what he could do next. Sell expen-sive bed linen. Women would be lining up if you put the image of him, just as he was, in an ad. Which begged the question why she wasn't climbing right back into bed with him.

Her stomach rumbled again, as if in answer. Right. Food. She made a beeline for the door before her will-power evaporated like sea spray.

The house was quiet when she came downstairs. Phew. No sign of Leon. She called up music on the house system, in the mood for something cheerful.

She kept the volume low and set the speakers to play only in the kitchen, then bopped around singing to

Katy Perry and Rihanna while she investigated the contents of the fridge and pantry. Caleb had mentioned something about the grocery store and apparently he'd been telling the truth. And apparently he ate more than the steady diet of junk most guys she knew would have chosen on vacation. The fridge held eggs and cheese and milk and actual honest-to-god vegetables. She piled those onto the counter, then turned back to grab the juice and the open packet of ground coffee. If she remembered correctly, Danny had a French press some-where. Not quite as good as her espresso machine, but it would do.

The kettle went on to boil as she dug into the cabi-nets to find first the French press and then a glass so she could at least have juice to fill the void in her stomach while she made omelets.

"Something wrong with the beds at your place?" Danny's voice almost gave Faith a heart attack. She only just avoided dropping the glass in her hand as she whirled. Danny stood a few feet inside the kitchen door, looking amused and a little surprised. His black hair was pulled back into a short ponytail. He'd shaved off the salt-and-pepper goatee he'd been sporting for the last few years, though there was a glint of silver stubble on his chin. Which couldn't hide his famous dimples. Not when he was grinning at her like he'd just caught her with her hand in the cookie jar.

Though, right that minute, she was more concerned with what the hell he was doing here than with his mood. "Would you believe yes?" she asked, stalling. She didn't know why she was stalling. She seemed to be fairly comprehensively busted.

"That house has seven bedrooms. And you have guesthouses. So unless there was an earthquake I haven't heard about and the whole tip of the island fell into the ocean, probably not." Danny yawned, rubbing his chin. "Plus I see two glass, two mugs, two plates. Want to try again?"

Definitely busted. She poured juice, still stalling, willing her face not to blush.

This, this right here, was why she had a not-on-the-island rule to start with. No embarrassing encounters between people she cared about and the men she slept with. Who were never going to be around long enough to have a need to meet the people she cared about. Thank god she'd pulled her clothes on before coming downstairs.

She'd been thinking of the possibility that Liam might be back from L.A. or that Leon might be doing his thing in the garden. Finding Danny here had never entered her mind as likely. But Danny finding her here in his house on a day where he knew damned well she should be at Harper taking care of all those pesky last-minute CloudFest details was one thing, Danny finding her in his house wearing only a sheet or one of Caleb's T-shirts or something else that screamed "Why, yes, I did spend the night having wild sex" at midday was a whole other level of embarrassing.

"I stayed over," she said, closing the carton of juice. No point beating around the bush. Danny was not the kind of guy who made judgments about anyone's sex life. That would be the ultimate pot calling the kettle black scenario.

"You sleeping with Liam Sullivan?" Danny cocked his head at her.

"Liam went back to L.A. for a day or two. Some sort of work emergency. I'm sleeping with his friend."

Danny's brown eyes sharpened. "His friend got a name?"

"That was probably a question you should have asked before you loaned out your house to them," Faith said. "One of these days one of your guests is going to clean you out."

Danny shrugged. "Nothing important here any more. It's all replaceable."

Faith hid her wince. Once upon a time this house had been Danny's home. "I'm sure your insurance company is thrilled with that attitude."

"The amount I probably pay them, they can just shut up and pay up if something happens," Danny said. "So what's the mystery man's name?"

"What are you even doing here?" Faith asked.

"Don't change the subject."

"My subject is more interesting than your subject." The kettle was boiling and she leaned over to switch it off. Coffee could wait.

"My house, I get to pick the topic of conversation." Danny crossed his arms over his broad chest. The tattoos on his forearms rippled to the beat he tapped with his fingers as he waited for her answer. Katy had moved onto singing about waking up in Vegas. Just a little too close to the bone right now.

Well, it could've been Pink's "Walk of Shame" instead.

She lifted her chin, giving in. She couldn't think of any way of keeping Caleb out of this. He was staying in Danny's house. So if she just told Danny what he wanted to know, they could get back to her question. As in what the hell Danny was doing on Lansing. "His name is Caleb White."

"Caleb White?" Danny frowned, and then his face cleared. "You mean the tennis dude?"

chapter eleven

"That's me." Caleb walked in through the other door to the kitchen. The one that opened out to the stairs and the bedrooms. He wore jeans and a T-shirt but his feet were bare. His hair still stood up every which way and he needed a shave even more than Danny did. It was blatantly obvious he'd just rolled out of bed. But he didn't look particularly concerned that Danny had appeared out of nowhere. Just kept walking across the room until he was a couple of feet from Danny, and then held out his hand. "Danny Ryan, I presume? Nice to meet you."

Danny looked amused. "Kid, you're staying in my house. You should know who I am."

Caleb shrugged and didn't move his hand. "I do. I was being polite."

Danny studied him a moment then reached out and shook his hand.

Faith let out the breath she'd been holding. "There. Now, everyone knows everyone."

"Well," Danny said, "Caleb and I just met. Seems like the two of you know each other a little better than that. Never knew you had a thing for jocks, Faithy."

"Don't call me Faithy," she retorted. "And who I sleep with is my business."

Beside Danny, Caleb's eyebrows hitched upward, as he watched the two of them.

"If you're done trying to freak Caleb out, how about I make some breakfast—er—lunch and you can tell me why you're here?"

Danny folded his arms again. "Who said I was done trying to freak him out?"

"Me," she said firmly. "This is not a topic for discussion."

"Where's your friend? The Sullivan kid," Danny said to Caleb.

"He had to go back to L.A. for a couple of days. Something came up." Caleb said. "He said you didn't mind me staying here alone. If you do, I can make other arrangements."

Faith wondered if he realized exactly how scarce accommodation on the island was during CloudFest.

Danny shook his head. "No. It's not a problem. It's good for the house to be used."

"Which brings me back to the subject of why you're here," Faith said. "Lou said you weren't coming to CloudFest. The fact that you loaned your place to Liam and Caleb kind of backed that up. What changed your mind?"

"That would be you," Danny said. He walked over to the fridge and pulled out a bottle of water.

Faith was confused. "Me?"

"Theo called me. Said you were having a problem with getting someone to do the secret gig. Said Zach screwed you a little. Might have used the phrase 'major freak out.' So I thought I'd come on over and solve a few problems." He looked her up and down. "I guess the fact that you're here with him"—he jerked his head at Caleb, who was frowning a little, listening to this exchange—"instead of at the office means Theo was right about you freaking out."

Faith ignored that part. "Exactly what problems are you going to fix?" Danny's methods for solving problems—once he decided he was going to weigh in on something—could be a little unconventional.

"Well, for one thing, I can take care of your issue with the secret gig."

Caleb looked kind of confused at this. Right. She still hadn't told him about yesterday's dramas. And she didn't intend to. No point dragging him into family politics.

"Unless you think the fans don't want to see an old dude like me play anymore?" Danny said with a smirk that said he was confident they did.

He wasn't wrong about that. The fans would lose their collective shit at the sight of one of the Blacklight members stepping onto the stage. None of them had played at CloudFest for years. But she didn't say it. Because she was too busy trying to adjust to the fact that Danny had come home to help her out.

For a moment the rush of sheer gratitude and happiness overwhelmed her and she had to toy with the canister of coffee for a moment to make sure she wasn't going to cry.

Crying would freak both Danny and Caleb out. Instead she leaned over and planted a kiss on Danny's cheek. "Welcome home."

One side of his mouth quirked and he snaked an arm around her waist and hugged her close before letting her go. "It's good to see you, Faithy."

She let the nickname slide this time. "You too, old dude." She nudged him out of the way and picked up a knife. "Who's hungry?"

"Me," Caleb said.

"I could eat," Danny said. He moved to Faith's side, reached for a bowl. He was a great cook when he bothered to do it. Though she wasn't sure whether him helping out right now was a nice gesture or some weird male thing where he was making a point to Caleb that he was part of Faith's family.

She was too hungry to try and work it out. She started chopping vegetables.

"So, Caleb," Danny said, "how do you like your eggs?"

After they'd finished eating—and Caleb couldn't remember when he'd had a meal that felt quite so awkward—Faith pushed her chair back from the table, gathered up the plates, and disappeared into the house. Leaving Caleb and Danny sitting on the deck overlooking the ocean. Caleb turned to glance after Faith. Nearly an hour had passed since he'd come down to the kitchen. Then he'd been full of plans to see if he could coax Faith back to bed one more time before she had to leave.

That wasn't going to be happening now. Faith didn't seem particularly perturbed that Danny had found her in his house with Caleb, but Caleb got the feeling that she was going to make her exit earlier than planned. Which sucked.

He was only on the island for a week. And Faith was going to be working all hours of the day for most of that time if what she'd told him was true. He'd been hoping for a little more time with her.

"So, Caleb," Danny said, "how are you enjoying it here so far?"

Caleb turned back to face him. There was no mistaking the slightly proprietary tone in Danny's voice. It wasn't the island he was asking about. It was Faith. Just the question he wanted to hear from a man he'd only just met. Particularly when that man was practically family to the woman he'd just started sleeping with. So he was going to pretend like hell he thought Danny was just asking about Lansing. "So far it seems like a nice place." He waved an arm toward the ocean. "It's definitely pretty."

"It is that," Danny agreed, dark eyes firmly fixed on Caleb. Now that Faith had gone, those eyes weren't so friendly.

"But you don't live here full time?"

Danny tipped his head. "I travel a lot. You know something about how that works, I suspect."

Caleb nodded. "Yes. Up until a few weeks ago, at least."

"Right. You quit. And what comes after tennis?"

He didn't correct him on the difference between retiring and quitting. It didn't really matter, even though something about the way Danny said it didn't sit easily. "That's what I'm figuring out."

Danny drummed his fingers of one hand on the table briefly, tugging at one of the silver rings in his ear with the other hand. "I get that. But let me offer you some advice."

Caleb stiffened. "All right," he said, keeping his tone noncommittal.

"I've known Faith all her life." Danny scrubbed a hand over the silvery stubble on his chin. A fading tattoo of a hammer flexed across the back of his left hand with the motion. The handle ran up his wrist joined up to a chain that snaked its way up Danny's arm to disappear under the edge of the plain white T-shirt he wore.

Caleb nodded, acknowledging this. He watched Danny, trying to get a read on exactly where this conversation was going. The other man was leaning back in his chair, the very picture of casual. Caleb might have been convinced without that watchful gaze. Danny looked like a rock star, with the tattoos and the slicked-back black hair—which came from a bottle judging by the gray in his eyebrows and stubble. But without those, he wouldn't have picked Danny as a musician. He was a little too . . . intense. He would have guessed he did something with his hands. Danny's tanned forearms and hands were strong. Muscled in a way that was familiar to Caleb. Not exactly the same as a tennis player's arms but the arms of a man who'd built muscle and strength over years of doing something physical.

Years he'd also spent watching Faith grow up.

And right now, Caleb, who'd spent years learning to read the subtle shifts in a man's arms or legs or the line of his body in order to know what might be coming over the net at him, was reading tension in every move Danny made.

"You seem to like her."

Another nod. No point denying it, given how Danny had found them.

He stared back at Danny. Was he about to get the rock star equivalent of the "what are your intentions" speech? "I've only known her a couple of days, but yes, I do." He braced himself, wondering what was coming next.

Danny seemed to be wondering himself because he didn't immediately respond. Instead, he scratched his chin again, and then blew out a breath, his shoulders relaxing a little. "Look, kid. I'm the last one to try and give anyone advice on their love life. Or make judgments when it comes to sex."

"It seems like there's a 'but' at the end of that sentence."

Danny smiled wryly. "Yeah. I'm gonna break my own rule. Because this is Faith and she means a lot to me. Never had kids of my own, so I like to keep an eye on Grey's bunch now he's not here to do it."

Caleb nodded. "I'm sure in your position, I'd want to do the same." He hesitated then added. "You must miss him."

"Every day. Losing a friend like that—hell, Grey was more like a brother—it's not something you get over. Grey wasn't perfect but he was family." Danny paused. "Which is why I'm going to say, just be careful with Faith, okay? She puts on a good show, but she's lost a lot over the years."

"I'm not going to hurt her. She and I are pretty clear where things stand. And, she was the one who propositioned me, not the other way round." He said the words and wondered if it was TMI. But Danny grinned, looking almost proud.

"That's my girl." Then he frowned. "She's a pretty private person. I don't want to hear you mouthing off about this."

Caleb held up his hands. "Trust me, I am planning on flying under the radar as much as possible from here on in. I'm not giving the press any reason to pay more attention to me. I've had quite enough time in the spotlight. I just want to get on with my life."

Danny nodded. "Sounds reasonable. You think you can?"

"Can what?"

"Give up the spotlight. It's a hell of an addictive feeling, in my experience."

Caleb shook his head. "Tennis isn't like music. I always knew there'd be an expiration date."

One gray eyebrow lifted. "Which is why you have what you're going to do now you're out of the game all planned out? Knowing a thing is going to happen in your head is different from accepting it in here." He thumped his chest.

Note to self. Do not underestimate Danny Ryan. For someone who had a reputation as a party boy and wild child for decades, he seemed to have a little too much insight into some of the worries that ran through Caleb's head when he least wanted them too. "I'll be fine," Caleb said. He stood, not really wanting to be under the

Danny microscope any longer. "Now, you'll have to excuse me but I'm going to go help Faith clean up."

"He wasn't giving you the third degree, was he?" Faith asked when Caleb came back into the kitchen, looking vaguely harassed. Guilt pinged. She should have gone back out there and run interference except she hadn't really wanted to get Danny's third degree either.

Caleb shook his head. "No, he seems like a good guy."

She wasn't entirely sure she believed him. Danny was curious about people at the best of times, always wanting to find out what made them tick. He always managed to draw people out wherever he went, finding out their life stories and worries effortlessly. He'd turned some of those stories into the songs he wrote. So he was always on the lookout for more. Couple that with the fact he now knew she was sleeping with Caleb and she found it hard to believe that he hadn't at least mildly interrogated Caleb.

But maybe man-to-man talks weren't something you then told the girl in question about. It was a point of relationship etiquette she wasn't entirely clear on. One that hadn't really come up since her high school boyfriend. She knew he'd been intimidated by Grey. She couldn't blame an eighteen-year-old for that. No teen boy could be expected to be cool, calm, and collected in the face of a girlfriend's father who was stupidly rich, came with a security detail, and was a rock god worshipped by teen boys.

Plus, she'd been full of plans to leave Lansing at that point, so she had always known in the back of her mind she'd be leaving Scott behind. Since then her relationships had been like Ricky. Out of sight. No family involved. So she'd never had to deal with Grey putting the fear of God into another guy. In fact, he'd often ribbed her about when she was going to bring a guy home so he could do just that. They'd never really talked about it but she got the feeling he'd wanted to see her settled after he knew he was sick.

She'd always figured that was the reason he hadn't raised holy hell when Mina had gotten so serious so fast with Adam even though they'd both still been teenagers.

But relationships had hardly been high on her priority list. In fact, they were pretty high on her anti-priority list, if there was such a thing.

She didn't need—or want—the trouble.

Not that what she and Caleb had was a relationship. More like a three-day acquaintance with hot sex. She wasn't entirely sure how she felt about that yet.

The sex had been amazing, yes. She was all in favor of amazing sex.

She just still wasn't quite clear on why Caleb had been the guy who'd made her break her rule. Was it him, or was it just that he'd been there when she'd been so pissed off with Zach and in need of distraction? It probably wouldn't be a good idea to go back for round two until she had figured that much out. No matter how much her girl parts were currently sulking because they weren't going to get at least one more round with Caleb before she had to return to reality.

She was going to have to take a cold shower when she get home and hope that might drive the memories of last night from her head before she got to the party. She'd lost track of the conversation over lunch several times, when something Caleb had said or done had triggered a flashback of his hands on her or the way it had felt when he'd moved against her.

Sex flashbacks.

Who knew there was even such a thing?

Or that thinking about them could trigger one.

She pushed the thoughts of Caleb and all the very good things he'd done to her last night back out of her head. Dwelling on them wasn't going to make the rest of the day any easier.

She finished rinsing the dish in her hand and stacked it in the dishwasher. The cleanup hadn't taken long, she'd stretched it out because she'd needed a little time to catch her breath. And now, her clock was rapidly approaching midnight so to speak. She dried her hands on the dishtowel and looked around to see if she'd missed anything, not quite sure how this conversation should go.

She looked up at Caleb. Damn. He was gorgeous, the sunlight streaming through the windows, turning him golden and glorious. She swallowed. "I—"

"You have to go," Caleb said softly. "I know." He moved closer, snaked a hand around her waist and pulled her close, tipping his head down to lean his forehead against hers for a moment.

The simple gesture nearly undid her resolve. She'd been expecting a kiss perhaps, but this—standing there, just leaning into him, breathing in time—felt far more intimate than a kiss. His fingers stroked her waist lightly, little rippling touches that made her hot all over again.

"I had a good time last night," he said. "I liked that I

know all those tattoos you're hiding from all those moms now." His fingers drifted down her back, following the line of the flight of notes inked there as if he'd memorized them.

She nodded, swaying toward him a little, unable to talk past the lump suddenly in her throat.

"Christ," Caleb muttered as he stepped back. "Okay, you need to go. Or I'm going to carry you back up those stairs, Danny Ryan or no bloody Danny Ryan."

That made her laugh. "Not such a good idea. After all, you're the one who has to live with him for the next week."

Caleb groaned. "Maybe I should look for somewhere else to stay."

"Every square inch of the island that's available for accommodation over the next week has been booked solid for months," Faith said. "Including campgrounds, couches, and anything else that's even slightly habitable. The locals make a lot of money out of CloudFest."

"Damn. Liam better come back soon. It's kind of weird when I don't even know Danny."

"We have a guesthouse," Faith blurted before she could stop herself. "In fact, we have a couple."

"You don't have anyone staying in them for Cloud-Fest?"

She shook her head, not knowing whether or not she should be appalled at herself for mentioning it. Her and her big mouth. But she could hardly take it back. "Sometimes we host a couple of the acts, but my brother was supposed to be coming home this year and I wanted it to be just us."

"Was?" Caleb said. "Did something happen?"

"Long story." She definitely didn't want to talk about Zach. "But the short version is, if you and Liam think it's awkward here with Danny here, then you can use one of them. I won't be around much, but text me or whatever and I'll organize the security guys to let you in." She hoped that was casual enough. And clear enough that it wasn't an invitation for anything more than accommodation. Time to make a graceful exit before she did anything else stupid.

Like kissing him.

"Thanks. I might just take you up on that."

Caleb White living in her guesthouse. Right there. Next to her house. And her bedroom. Her girl parts started to get rowdy again.

Time to go. "I really should get going," she said. "Or I'll be late."

Caleb nodded. "It was nice playing hooky with you, Faith Harper."

"Thanks. You too." She stared at him a moment, wondering why the hell she was leaving. Party. Festival. Real life. Okay.

Exit, stage right, Faith Harper. Reluctantly.

chapter twelve

The party was in full swing before Faith felt like she'd found her balance again. Caleb had tilted her world a little. Just enough to throw her off her game. She'd spent the afternoon trying to work and then get ready but kept losing her train of thought. She'd found herself humming or singing at odd moments, or smiling for no good reason. Caleb had left an impression. A very fond one.

The cold shower hadn't really helped at all.

It would wear off, she hoped. This effect he was having on her.

It had to. He'd be leaving.

Still, the post-sex happy bubble had carried her through the stack of e-mails that had been waiting for her after she'd showered—even if it had taken her a little longer than normal. It hadn't even burst when she'd spoken with Theo, who clearly wanted to know where she'd been but was avoiding asking.

He'd been kind of wary, actually, which had made her

feel vaguely guilty about the tantrum she'd thrown the night before. She didn't feel bad about the result, though. After all, it had brought Danny back to Lansing. And it had brought her to Caleb. But she did feel bad that Theo had borne the brunt of her temper.

She'd apologize at the party.

She'd changed, picking one of her favorite dresses. White splashed with red poppies, in a vaguely fifties style, with a fitted bodice and a skirt that belled out around her knees. It was cool enough in the heat but still looked like she'd made a bit more of an effort than just throwing on a sundress or shorts and a tee. After all, the party signaled the real start of the festival.

For the next five days or so, she was Faith Harper—Grey Harper's daughter, keeper of the Blacklight flame, rock child, public figure. She'd slicked on red lipstick, smudged her eyes up a little, and piled her hair high, donning her armor. Stacked red and white and silver bangles and bracelets on one arm, and slipped on more rings than the few she habitually wore. Replaced the silver hoops in her ears with something more sparkly.

She hadn't balked until she'd looked at the heels in her wardrobe but couldn't quite face the torture of anything too high. Instead she'd slipped on a pair of ballet flats the same flaming shade of red as the poppies on her dress.

And then, public Faith firmly in place, she'd driven to the festival site and begun to work. First making sure everything was just as it should be, and then, as the musicians and crew started to drift in from wherever they were staying—which for some of them was only as far as their tour buses, the Lansing Ferry being just large enough to take a vehicle that size—she'd snapped into hostess mode, chatting to everybody, pointing them to drinks and food.

She'd managed a couple of mouthfuls of BBQ herself while she'd done her rounds, working the room, catching up with people she hadn't seen for months—longer in some cases—and keeping the party bubbling away at just the right combination of mellow and fun.

After an hour or so, Ziggy had joined her, introducing her to a couple of the acts she hadn't met before. When he broke away for a moment to talk about something with Rob Duncan, who ran the sound crew, Leah and Ivy had appeared at her side. They'd made polite noises at the people she'd been talking to and then dragged her off to a quieter spot.

"Where were you today?" Ivy asked quietly. Her brown eyes were half concern, half curiosity as she sipped the club soda in her hand—Ivy didn't drink at any event she considered work. And despite the little black dress she was wearing—paired with shiny black Doc Martens—this was definitely work for Ivy. The expression in her eyes was mirrored in Leah's.

"I took the morning off," Faith said. "It's not a crime."

"No, but it is unusual," Leah said, toying with one of the strands of hair falling down from the loose bun she'd tamed her mass of dark curly hair into. "Are you okay? We were worried." The hand not tugging at her hair held a beer. Leah could drink most guys under the table when she chose to. The green glass of the bottle matched the color of the silky shirt she wore over a short black leather skirt.

"I was pissed off at Zach," Faith said. She could admit that much to these two. "I needed a little time to calm down."

"And are you calm now?" Ivy asked.

The question brought Caleb to mind, and Faith had to fight not to let another one of those goofy grins steal across her face. "Yes," she managed. "I'm all good."

"Your face looks weird," Leah said, frowning. "Why does your face look weird?"

"My face does not look weird," Faith protested. She took a mouthful of the very weak wine spritzer she was nursing, both to avoid saying anything more and to try to chase away whatever it was on her face that was pinging Leah's spidey sense.

Leah had always been able to sniff out a crush at fifty paces. In high school, she'd always known who was pining for whom or were newly dating. All while managing to keep her own love life out of the spotlight. Until she'd announced she was engaged to Joey Nelson, one of the local teachers, a few years ago and married him exactly three months later. Six months ago she'd divorced him. And while the divorce had made her quieter than usual, apparently it hadn't dulled her interest in anyone else's romance.

Not that Faith was having a romance with Caleb. No, sirree.

"Did you throw yourself a pity party?" Ivy said. "You weren't drinking alone?" She studied Faith, rising on her toes to peer at her face. "You look way too good if you're hungover."

"I'm not hungover." Still having sex flashbacks, sure, but not hungover. Sex hangovers were not a thing. "And

I'm fine. No mystery to be solved here. I just needed a little sanity break before the real crazy started. And given I'm the boss, I decided to be nice to myself and give me some time off."

Leah and Ivy both looked suspicious. Faith felt guilty again. Both for the lie and for the fact that the two of them had been working just as hard as she had for the last few months. Leah ran the recording studio, was its chief sound engineer now that her father, Sal, was mostly retired, even stepped in as producer sometimes. And she always kept all those balls in the air with minimal fuss and helped out with CloudFest admin every year. Ivy, too, had mastered the juggling act. She had other clients on the island and on the mainland besides Harper Inc. The security crew who looked after the festival weren't her staff, but she consulted with CloudFest. After all, she managed the systems on all of the Blacklight guys' houses, and Faith's and Mina's places. Lou's too, not to mention a growing list of other Lansing residents. She was the one who knew Lansing like the back of her hand. She liaised with festival security teams and any personal security staff the artists brought with them, to make sure everyone was on the same page. With the island flooding with fans, that was a lot of work.

"Okay," Leah said eventually, sounding reluctant. "But you'd tell us if something was wrong, right?"

"Of course," Faith said. "You two are my first port of call. Well, maybe after Lou."

"Is Lou here?" Ivy asked.

"She has an invite," Faith said. Like Danny, Lou had a wide-ranging circle of friends, which overlapped the music world. "I haven't seen her yet. Why?"

"Just wanted to see how her trip went," Ivy said.

"She said it was great," Faith said. "I'm sure she'll tell you all about it."

Ivy was another one of the stray chicks Lou had gathered under her wing when they'd been growing up. "Hey, Danny's here," she said. A sudden smile flashed over her face. "I didn't think he was coming."

"He's doing the secret gig," Leah said after checking that no one could hear them. Then she turned and looked where Ivy was looking. "More to the point, who is that with—holy crap, that's Caleb White."

Faith nearly choked on her drink.

What the hell was Caleb doing here? Luckily neither Leah or Ivy were paying any attention to her, They were both staring across the room at Caleb. She coughed once, then recovered her composure before they turned back to her.

"That is definitely Caleb White," Ivy agreed. "Damn. That man is gorgeous."

Leah made definite agreement noises.

"Good grief, you're as bad as Lou," Faith said. "He's a tennis player, not God." Ivy and Leah, like Lou, had met with enough famous people over the years not to be easily dazzled. Yet the Caleb magic seemed to be working on them too.

Leah swiveled back, pivoting on the chunky green velvet heels she wore. "When did Lou meet Caleb White?"

"More to the point, does this mean you've met Caleb White?" Ivy chimed in, turning back to nail Faith with a curious look.

"He's staying at Danny's with a friend. Danny loaned them the place. But now Danny's here, I guess he's staying with Danny. I met him Monday when I took them the keys. Lou went all fangirly. That never happens."

"You didn't mention that," Ivy said disapprovingly. "And Lou is perfectly justified. That man is worth a squee or two."

"Or three," Leah added.

"I didn't mention it because I haven't talked to you," Faith pointed out. "We've been kind of busy."

"You've talked to me," Leah objected. "Could've given me the heads-up."

Faith frowned at her. "I met the man for all of ten minutes. It's not exactly my place to start pimping him out to my friends. Besides which, he's not exactly your type." Leah had, once upon a time, a definite thing for musicians. Before she married a teacher. Joey had been a jock at school. Faith doubted Leah would be dating another athlete any time soon.

"For that man, I could make an exception," Leah said. She and Ivy both turned back to stare at Caleb.

Reluctantly, Faith did too. Otherwise she'd have to explain why she wasn't. Caleb stood next to Danny, the pair of them looked like a study in opposites. Caleb, tall, blond and gorgeous in a white shirt and dark gray trousers. Danny in his habitual black, with silver in his ears and covering his hands. All-American versus rock star. They were already being surrounded by a crowd of admiring women.

She turned back, not liking the little tug of jealousy that flared in her gut at the sight. "Looks like you might have to get in line," she said, a little more sharply than she'd intended.

Ivy and Leah both turned 'round again. The thin gold hoops in Leah's ears swung back and forth while she shook her head at Faith. "That was an . . . interesting tone."

Ivy, too, was tilting her head at Faith, considering her.

Faith swished the straw in her spritzer and tried to look like she had no idea who Caleb White was, let alone any idea about how he kissed. Or did other things.

Ivy looked at Leah. "I think *Faith* might like to be in that line."

"I don't do island," Faith said automatically.

"He's not island." Leah retorted.

"He's *on* the island," Faith said.

"Temporarily, I assume, " Leah said. "Which would make him exactly your type. No strings."

"That's beside the point if I'm not interested."

"We need to get her eyes tested," Ivy said. "She's gone blind."

"I can see the man is pretty," Faith said. "I'm just not planning to sleep with him." And that was a total white lie. She wasn't *planning* to sleep with Caleb. She hadn't planned to sleep with him the night before. But if it just kind of happened . . . wait. No. She wasn't supposed to be thinking about doing that again. She was supposed to be keeping this party running smoothly.

"I should make the rounds again," she said to Ivy and Leah.

"Chicken," Leah said.

Ivy grinned, nodded, and made a clucking sound.

"Why are we even friends?" Faith muttered. "I'm

working. You two go join the Caleb White appreciation society if you want. I have to mingle."

After another hour or so of making small talk with her guests and taking complicated routes through the room to avoid coming anywhere near Caleb, Faith decided she'd earned a break. She ducked out of the biggest of the marquees and wove her way through the tents to the main stage.

Luckily, no one else seemed to have had the same idea. The backstage area was dark and empty. Embracing the breathing space, she made her way onto the stage itself, following the dim glow of the safety lighting.

From the stage the sounds of the party were still audible but only as a background hum. She heaved a little sigh of relief and walked to the edge of the stage, gazing out at the walled-off space, transformed from empty field to mini arena.

The darkened space was kind of eerie, the shapes of the speaker rigs and the sound stage looking like weird robots waiting to come to life. She closed her eyes a moment, imagining the crowds there tomorrow.

"Good evening, Cloud Bay!" She threw her arms in the air, mouthing the words. Mimicking the stance she'd seen Grey take a thousand times.

Then she grinned, lowering her arms, imagining the music and the energy and the joy that always seemed to fill the air.

People and music. Celebrating what they loved.

She opened her eyes, looked out over it all once more.

She'd done this.

She'd pulled it off once again. Brought it all together.

Given the CloudFest experience to all the people who'd start flooding though the gates tomorrow at noon.

That wasn't such a bad job to have. Achieving something that would give thousands of people four days of happiness.

Not bad at all.

Grey would be happy.

And that thought made her sad. She shook off the feeling. Focus on the good, not the might have been.

She held out her hands then, humming softly, soothing herself back into the place where she could just enjoy the accomplishment again.

Behind the happiness, a tiny familiar thread of wistfulness that it wasn't her that they were cheering snaked through her. She shrugged it away. In a way it would be her the crowd cheered for. Without her, none of the musicians back there at the party would be soaking up the love from their fans over the next few days.

Without her, CloudFest would probably have died with Grey.

And that would have been a damn shame.

Footsteps sounded behind her and she turned, expecting to see Ziggy or Danny. Instead, the man moving through the shadows, turned to silver rather than gold in the moonlight, was Caleb.

Of course it was.

"Doing your pre-game?" he said softly when he reached her side.

"Pre-game?"

His mouth quirked, the white of his teeth bright in the silvery light. "Sorry, jock talk. I always used to try and get some time alone on any court before I played a match on it. Get the feel for it. How the surface felt beneath my feet. How the air moved."

"I've been doing this a while," she pointed out. "I know how it feels."

"I guess you do," he said.

She nodded. "Besides, I won't be the one standing up here." She nodded back toward the rear of the stage and the marquees beyond. "I do all my work back there. So I don't need to pre-game or whatever." That was a lie. But she still was unsettled at the fact that he was here at the party. Even though he'd kept his distance up until now, having Caleb standing on her stage felt a little too much like two worlds colliding when she wasn't sure she wanted them to.

"You never wanted to be the one up here? Follow in your dad's footsteps?"

Did he know? That she had tried to make a go of it with Zach? That she'd failed? It seemed like a mean question if he did and Caleb had, so far, not struck her as having a mean bone in his body. So she gave him the benefit of the doubt. And decided to keep things simple by shaking her head. "Not sure anyone can follow in Grey's footsteps. He was one of a kind. Very big shoes to fill."

"That's not necessarily a reason not to try," Caleb said. "If you wanted to."

She looked back out at the arena, not wanting him to read anything on her face. It wasn't a story she wanted to tell him just yet. It wasn't the sort of thing you told someone who wasn't going to stick around. "There are other reasons."

Caleb nodded. "Fair enough." He studied her a moment. "You must miss him, this time of year."

God. Such simple words. But they stripped her bare. He saw her too clearly, this man. She blinked against the sudden prickle of tears. Not just for Grey. For the sudden sweet sensation that Caleb was someone she could trust. Who'd take some of the load if she asked him to. Who didn't just see Faith the ringmaster of the CloudFest circus, but Faith who had to lock away all the bittersweet memories to play that role.

"Sorry," he said. "Didn't mean to hit a sore spot."

She shook her head. "No. It's good. I don't want to forget him." Sometimes it seemed like everyone else was busy trying to move on. To fill up the hole. Maybe there was supposed to be a hole. A space for Grey to stay with them.

"What was he like?"

She laughed. It sounded like an easy question. It wasn't. "Wonderful. Terrible." She took a step closer to the edge of the stage, gestured out at the darkness. "He was my dad. I loved him. I still do. But this right here is what always had the truest part of him. It was the thing he was always running back to. The music. The fans. He loved us and he tried to be a good dad, mostly, but he could never give us all of his heart. And sometimes, I hated him for that. That and the drinking. I was so mad when he got sick." She turned back to Caleb, shrugged helplessly. "I wanted more of him than I got. I'd still give anything to have him back, even if I still had to share him with all of this."

"Faith . . ." Caleb's voice was soft. Gentle, not pitying. "I'm guessing you had more of his heart than you knew."

"Maybe." She smiled at him. "I wouldn't change it. Like I said, he was my dad. And, on the whole, I guess the good stuff outweighed the bad. He gave me a lot. This place, for a start. Lansing. I love it here."

It was true. Despite the fact that living in a small town drove her crazy sometimes, as did her family and running Harper Inc., she felt happiest when she was standing on this small lump of rock surrounded by the ocean. Whenever she left, even though she enjoyed traveling, she found herself getting itchy for the unique smell of the air and the unbroken view of her familiar chunk of ocean rolling out to the horizon.

"Can't blame you for that. From what I've seen so far, it's a very nice part of the world," Caleb said.

"Where did you grow up?" she asked. Enough about Grey. Or she probably would cry. She didn't want that. Not tonight.

"Oakland. Well, the outskirts of."

"California boy, huh?"

"You got a problem with that, California girl?"

"Nope. Though I'm pretty sure I'm required to think all mainlanders are inferior or I'll get kicked off the island." She grinned up at him.

"I doubt they'll be voting you off the island any time soon. Every one I meet here sings your praises."

She felt her smile slip, wondering just who he'd been talking to. And suddenly reminded where she was supposed to be right now. She glanced back. "I should get back to the party."

Caleb stepped closer, shaking his head. "Everyone back there is having a good time. They've got booze and BBQ and people were starting to pull out instruments when I came looking for you." As if to prove his point, the sound of a guitar suddenly drifted across the air.

Someone playing a random sequence of notes and chords. Letting their fingers get warm.

Nice sound. Who was playing? Not Danny, she'd recognize his style blindfolded. But someone who knew what they were doing, as they continued to coax notes out of the guitar until the randomness resolved and reformed and turned into the opening riff of "Hotel California." Not the most original choice, but it was the perfect song for this perfect California night. A chorus of voices started singing, the harmony a little ragged at first before it resolved into something gorgeous that made her want to sing too. Her toe started to tap.

"See," Caleb said. "No one's going to miss you if you stay here with me for awhile." He moved a little closer. So close she could feel the warmth of him on her skin. So close and yet all she wanted to do was move closer still.

"Me, on the other hand, well, I've been missing you all afternoon."

His voice had dropped a little, getting that rumbly edge that did such good things to her nerve endings.

"Caleb—" she said. She wanted him. But he scared her a little. How much of her would he see if she kept letting him get close?

"Faith," he mimicked. "No one's going to come looking for you."

"You came looking for me."

"I'm kind of hoping no one else back there has the same motivation as me to come find you tonight." He paused, eyes searching her face. They weren't so blue under the moonlight but they were still intense. "Or do they?"

The smart thing to do in this situation would be to

say yes. To pretend there was someone else out there who'd spent time in her bed.

Someone who didn't make her want as much as the man standing before her did. That might make him want her less. If he thought there was someone else. He was the kind of guy who wouldn't cross lines. But she couldn't do it. Didn't want to hurt him. Which was dumb when she barely knew the man. "No. No, they don't," she said. There. Truth told. Her reward was the sight of a smile breaking across his face.

"Good," he said. He moved a little closer still and she put a hand out, palm to his chest to keep him where he was.

"That doesn't mean I'm going to fool around with you or whatever it was that you had in mind here."

"Why not?" he asked. "I'm here, you're here. It's a beautiful night."

"I'm working," she said. Her hand was hot where it rested on the muscles of his chest and her fingers tingled. She had to fight the urge to close them, to crumple his shirt in between them and pull him closer. Closer was madness. Closer was all the things she didn't want.

Wasn't it?

"I thought we'd already established that everyone back there is perfectly well taken care of without you."

"You're not supposed to be here," she said.

"Take that up with Danny. He offered. I said yes."

"Why?"

He shook his head slightly, eyes fixed on hers. "Because I wanted to see you again. Even if all I got to do was look at you from across the room."

"Does that line work?" It should have been cheesy.

But she had to confess that it made her smile. Gave her a happy glow somewhere deep inside. Caleb White pining for her after just one night. It was good for her ego.

"You tell me," Caleb said. His shrug made the muscles under her palm shift, and she pressed a little harder.

Her hand was hotter. Her fingers flexed involuntarily, curling just fractionally as though she could draw him into her. "It's not . . . terrible," she admitted.

"What about you? Didn't you miss me this afternoon?"

Yes. But she wasn't going to tell him that. That would be foolish. "I was busy." She didn't look up. He'd see she was lying if she looked up.

"Ouch," Caleb said. "Obviously I need to try harder to make an impression."

If he made any more of an impression, she would probably burst into flames. "There will be no impression making."

"Never?" he asked.

God. She should say yes. Send him on his way. Then her life would go back to normal and she could focus on the festival and then getting back to her routine once it was done. But right now, in this moment, no more Caleb sounded like a terrible idea.

"Maybe not never," she said.

"Try not to overwhelm me with your enthusiasm. I'll get a swelled head."

"I'm sure you have enough women falling over themselves to demonstrate enthusiasm," she said. "Not to mention I'm sure there's a fan club or something."

"There is. But it's not like I founded it."

"You have a fan club?" She couldn't help the giggle

that rose. "What do they call themselves? No, let me guess. White's Wenches or . . . no, the Calebettes."

"Close. The Calebrigade. More unisex."

That made her laugh out loud. "I guess I don't have to worry about me being the cause of your swelled head then." For some reason the thought of him having a fan club was oddly comforting. A reminder that he had a life waiting for him. That he'd be leaving.

That maybe he wasn't as complicated as she feared. Which meant that maybe she should just let herself enjoy him while he was here.

"I didn't come back here to talk about my fan club," he muttered.

"But Mr. White," she said, batting her eyelashes at him, still amused. He looked kind of sheepish about the whole thing. Which was sweet. Sweet and weirdly hot. "I'm your number one fan."

That drove the sheepish look off his face. It was replaced by an intent expression that she recognized all too well. Her stomach curled in response, heat starting to burn there and spread down.

"Is that so?" Caleb asked.

"Do I get a T-shirt or a badge?" Her hand slid down his chest, elbow bending, so she could move closer. Any semblance of holding him at arms-length disappeared.

"You get something better."

"What?"

"This." And he bent, hand threading through her hair and his mouth finding hers with an unerring instinct.

chapter thirteen

Caleb's skills had been wasted on tennis. If there was such a thing as a ranking of kissers, then he would be the number one seed. She tipped her head back, let him show her just how good he was.

What was it about him that made his kisses so addictive? His lips slid against hers, the action so simple. So basic. Just skin to skin, but she melted against him. Her mouth opened and let him in automatically.

Like she'd been wanting exactly this.

Maybe she had.

Okay, she definitely had. Ever since she'd seen him standing next to Danny. But she shouldn't want it.

She knew that.

Or she wanted to believe she knew it.

Right now with Caleb kissing her, it was impossible to believe anything other than this was how things were supposed to be.

This man. This moment.

That mouth.

She twined her hands around his neck and pulled him closer. In response, his hands came around her waist and pressed together. Body to body. Warmth and skin and softness meeting hardness.

She wanted more and made a small protesting noise as her hands, drifting down his back now, found shirt, not skin.

Caleb seemed to share the feeling and he lifted her, so she wrapped her legs around him.

That was becoming a habit.

One that she couldn't bring herself to complain about. There was something about the fact he could lift her so easily that made her swoony. And she was just going to embrace her inner cavewoman and revel in it.

"Where can we go?" Caleb said and she came back to reality for a minute.

"What?"

"As much as I like the idea of doing this right here on the stage—because I'm dying here, Faith—I'm thinking it's a little exposed."

She tried to think. It was hard. Because he was hard, and hard against her.

"Put me down," she said.

His arms tightened. "No."

"There's a room under the stage," she explained. "But there are cables and stuff everywhere and I'd rather not kill us both because you trip while carrying me."

"I'm nimble," Caleb said.

"Good to know." She smiled at him. "But we can argue about this or you can put me down and we can go do something more fun."

It was insane, she knew. There were a couple of hundred people just fifty feet or so away under the marquees. And she was going to take Caleb downstairs and . . . "Put me down," she repeated. "And tell me you have a condom."

"I have a condom," Caleb said.

"Optimistic."

"You seemed to appreciate preparedness last night."

"I did. I do. Let's go."

He put her down then and they kissed again and then she led him back across the stage and down into the depths below. She'd never been entirely sure why the rooms down here were necessary—the bands and musicians playing at CloudFest could use a couple of the tents as green rooms and dressing rooms. But Ziggy had given her some explanation about structural integrity, and she'd accepted that. She was no engineer.

Now she was definitely in favor.

The journey took longer than she'd thought because Caleb kept stopping and kissing her, each time a little wilder, a little more hungry.

By the time they stumbled into the storeroom she'd been aiming for and closed and locked the door, she was starving for him.

She couldn't find the light switch. She didn't care. She knew where he was and that was all that mattered. He apparently felt the same way because he picked her up again and her back hit the wall with a gentle thud as she wrapped herself around him. She heard the slide of a zipper and the crinkle of foil, and then his fingers found her. Pulling her skirts up—thank god for dresses—sliding up her thigh and inside her underwear. She was wet, and moaned when his fingers slid inside her, first one then two. Working her urgently, his thumb brushing her clit until she bucked against him.

That was all the encouragement he needed. His hand disappeared and then she felt him. Thick and hard, nudging her. Pinned against the door, staring into the darkness, only vaguely able to make out the shape of his body, it was like her other senses had sharpened to make up for the lack of sight. She'd never felt anything so good, and the sound he made as he slid further into her was like a match to a flame.

"Good?" he whispered.

"Yes. More." She didn't want words. She wanted him.

She got him. Caleb began to move. Slowly at first, finding the angle. Letting her adjust. But then, as she moaned at the sensation and tried to find his mouth again in the darkness, faster. Harder. The fact he was holding her suspended against a door didn't seem to bother him. He was like a rock. Solid. Strong. Unmovable.

She knew he'd never drop her. Knew he had one focus right this second and that focus was making her feel good. He wouldn't stop until she did. Wouldn't let her go. She could trust him.

So she let herself be there, let herself take him in and give herself up to him. Let herself drown in each thrust and slide, to meet him and match him until he carried her over the edge, and she let herself fall, the sound of his name on her lips muffled by his mouth.

Afterward they were still, other than their heaving breaths. When her pulse had slowed enough that it wasn't pounding quite so loudly in her head, she smiled in the darkness. God. That had been good.

She wanted nothing so much than to do it all over again. But now that the roar of Caleb in her blood had receded a little, she could hear the music behind them again and knew she had to get back to the party.

Caleb slid free of her, adjusting his clothes before he put her down. Now that she could think again, she remembered where the light switch was. She turned it on and they were both bathed in stark white light. When she saw his face, she couldn't help the giggle that bubbled up. Red lipstick, it seemed, wasn't the best choice for frantic backstage sex. Caleb's lips were smeared with it and she imagined her own face looked no better.

"We need to clean up a little," she said. She looked around the room. There was a first aid kit in here somewhere, and this being CloudFest it would be stocked with more than just your basic first aid supplies.

The first year she'd taken over the festival, one of the women performing had tripped coming up the stairs and ripped her dress and her tights and then ruined her makeup crying. The delay in getting her back to the green room tent, finding what was needed to get her cleaned up, calmed down, and back on stage had been fifteen minutes of the crowd chanting its impatience that Faith had never forgotten.

Since then she'd made sure that there were emergency kits backstage that included supplies to deal with all sorts of emergency. Face wipes, pantyhose in a vast array of sizes and colors. Deodorant. Sewing supplies. Duct tape and Hollywood tape and staplers for when there was no time for sewing supplies. Breath mints. Deodorant. Lip balm. Baby powder. Various makeup items. Tampons. Hair products. Herbal drops that were supposed to calm people down. Throat lozenges.

She found the kit and extracted the wipes. She came back to Caleb, who'd put himself back together clothes wise, and got rid of the evidence on his face. His lips looked slightly pinker than usual when she was done, but she doubted anyone else would notice. She cleaned her own mouth up and then packed everything away. "I need to get back."

Caleb looked disappointed but he didn't argue with her.

She shook her head, watching him.

"What?" he asked, sounding as satisfied as she felt.

"I wasn't going to do this again," she said.

That made him frown. "You weren't? Just as well I didn't know that." He smiled briefly, looking down at her. "Can I ask why not?"

"Complications," she said. "And my avoidance of."

"Sometimes a little complication is a good thing."

"You're not so little."

He snorted. "I'll take that as a compliment."

"I wasn't talking about that."

"Pity. It would be good for my ego."

"I would think your ego would be just fine after what we just did."

"It was, until you told me you were going to give me the old 'let's pretend this never happened' treatment. Though, you could make it up to me." He steeped closer and she retreated.

"No! I have to get back to the party."

"I'm more fun than a party."

"That may be true. But that doesn't mean I can ignore my responsibilities."

"I get the feeling my 'how to play hooky' lessons haven't really sunk home yet."

"Maybe my 'this is the busiest week of my year' lessons haven't sunk in with you," she retorted.

"Does that mean you're about to avoid me for the rest of the week?"

"I think we just proved that my willpower is nonexistent when it comes to avoiding you. But that doesn't change the fact I'm going to be busy this week. And I have to work. And I don't want to be the subject of any ex citing tabloid stories, so we have to play it cool in public."

"So basically you're saying you want me to be your secret booty call?" He paused a moment, then grinned. "I am okay with that."

She'd expected him to argue. "You are?"

"Sure. This trip is me playing hooky, after all. And I think you're a pretty good way to do exactly that."

She ignored the tiny twinge of regret that registered that his playing hooky wasn't going to last that long. If she was going to keep doing this, she had to be clear about that from the outset. Caleb, like all the other guys she'd slept with, wasn't a forever thing. She didn't want a forever thing. "Okay. Then we have a plan." She patted her hair, tucking stray strands back into her bun. "Have you heard from Liam? Is he coming back?"

"Got a text earlier. He'll be here tomorrow afternoon."

Should she repeat her offer for them to use the guesthouse? Would that make flying under the radar easier or harder? On one hand, Caleb would be right there. On the other, lots of other people would be there over the course of the festival. Perhaps it would be better to just wait and see if Caleb asked. "That's good. So I'll call you when I'm free?"

"I look forward to it," Caleb said. He nodded at the door. "Do you want to leave first or should I?"

She hadn't thought about that. They couldn't just walk out together. Should she be worried that he had thought about it? No. That was dumb. He was famous. He knew about being discreet. And she wanted him to be discreet. It was all good.

"I'll go," she said and slipped out the door.

Faith was halfway back to the main tent when Danny loomed out of the darkness. To her credit, the squeak of surprise she made was only a small one.

"Are you training to be a ninja or something?" she said, trying to calm her heartbeat and look innocent at the same time. "I think I'm going to buy you some clothes that aren't black. At least that way I'll see you coming."

Danny shook his head at her. "Ziggy was looking for you. I noticed you weren't around and neither was Tennis Boy. So I thought maybe it would be better if I came and found you before Ziggy did."

Her cheeks were hot. Thank god it was mostly dark. "Oh. Okay, thanks."

He tipped his head at her. "If I keep walking, am I going to find Tennis Boy?"

She lifted her chin. "No comment."

"Fair enough." He studied her a moment. "You need to fix your lipstick."

"Excuse me?"

"You were wearing red lipstick. Now you're not."

"Lipstick wears off."

"You've hardly eaten anything and you only ever sip your drinks. There's a difference between worn off and wiped clean, Faithy. And if I know that and can notice it, you can bet that other people will too."

Dammit. Mental note. Nude lip-gloss for the rest of the week. Less noticeable. She should have thought about the need to reapply. The wipes had removed the smeared lipstick but she hadn't thought what people might think if her lips were suddenly bare. Just as well Danny had appeared. He was probably an expert on helping women look put together after sneaky sex. "Thanks for the advice. You can go back to the party now."

"You sure about that?" He looked past her and she hoped that Caleb had either taken a different route or had heard them talking before he'd reached them and was staying out of sight.

"I can walk to the security station where I left my purse and get my lipstick by myself, Danny."

"If you say so."

"I do. So, you can go back to party. Maybe you'll find Caleb. After all, you brought him with you, you should make sure he's having a good time." Yeah, not letting him off scot-free for that one. She didn't know if he was trying to mess with her a little or whether he'd taken it upon himself to play matchmaker, but either way, hopefully he'd get the message that he should butt out.

"Seemed kind of rude to leave him sitting in my house while I went to a party."

"I'm sure he could have found ways to entertain himself. And I have to go get my lipstick now." Because she really wasn't going to have a conversation with Danny about all the ways Caleb might entertain himself. She turned on her heels and started walking away.

She ignored the sound of Danny's stage-whispered "I'm sure he has" that floated after her.

The first people Faith ran into when she got back to the party were Seth Rigger and Lou. Of course. Because if she was sneaking back into a party after shagging Caleb White backstage and hoping that fresh lipstick and perfume were enough to hide that fact, the people she really wanted to run into were her mother and the man Faith was fairly sure wanted to be her stepfather.

Or Lou's husband at least.

She had no idea how Seth felt about taking on the Harper kids but he wasn't an idiot, so presumably he knew that Lou was a package deal. No way would she let anyone into her life who couldn't get along with her family. Lou had spent the last thirty years or so making sure Faith and Zach and Mina knew that they were her priority and that she had their backs. Faith couldn't imagine any scenario where Lou would stop mothering all of them.

But Seth had at least, unlike his daughter, always been friendly to Faith. Of course, whether or not he wanted to be with Lou or what sort of relationship he wanted with the three of them was purely a hypothetical until Lou actually decided to acknowledge that there was anything between the two of them other than friendship.

Lou was laughing at something that Seth had said when Faith came through the doorway and her face lit up.

"Faith, honey. I haven't talked to you all night." She pulled Faith into a hug, which made Faith really hope the perfume covered any scent of Caleb. Usually she was happy to let her mom hug her as long as she wanted, but today she wriggled free after a few seconds.

"Hey, Mom. You look pretty." Lou was wearing her favorite shade of deep blue. The silk shirt had a scooped neck and flowing sleeves. It made her silver hair and blue eyes and the beautiful fair skin that Faith always wished she'd inherited—rather than her freckled version—glow. Or maybe that was the company. And the margarita in Lou's hand.

Faith nodded at Seth over Lou's head. "Hi, Seth, you having a good time?"

"Yes," he said, with a half smile. "You always know how to throw a good party."

"Did Angie come?" She'd made sure that Theo had sent Angie an invite. No need to make things any more difficult between them than they already were.

"She decided to host a dinner for the press people," Seth said. "Booked out half of Bette's."

"Oh," Faith said. "That's a good idea, actually." Though really, she wasn't sure if she wanted Angie buttering up the press. But Grey had always had a strict no-press rule for his night-before parties. He'd wanted everyone to be able to relax. Faith had kept the tradition even through she knew that it drove some of the photographers and reporters who had good relationships with the bands crazy. If Angie had carted them all off to Bette's, which, despite the plain name, was the nicest restaurant on Lansing, that made things easier.

Bette Wilson had moved to Lansing about ten years

ago with her partner, Agnes, and together they'd taken over what had been a beachfront fish-shack type restaurant and turned it into a place where people lined up to eat at.

Bette had worked at several famous New York and Los Angeles restaurants before she'd decided to open her place, and whatever they'd taught her had stuck. Her food was ambrosia. She used fish caught that day by the locals and did things to it that could only be chalked up to witchcraft in the kitchen. Agnes was a pastry goddess. Between the two of them, hopefully the press would all be in too much of a happy food coma to get cranky about the fact they were once again locked out of Faith's party.

"Did you see that Caleb White came with Danny?" Lou said. "I haven't seen him yet." She smiled up at Seth. "We met him at Danny's house the other day. Such a nice young man. Very handsome." She looked meaningfully at Faith.

Right. Time to cut that off at the pass. She didn't want Lou thinking there was anything between her and Caleb. She'd only be upset when he did the inevitable and left the island. "Mom has a crush on Caleb White, Seth," she said. "You might have to take some extra lessons. She's going for the top seeds these days."

Seth grinned at her while Lou turned a little pinker in the cheeks than she already was. Interesting. Was she blushing because of Caleb or because of Seth?

"I could pull out my old letter jacket," Seth said. "I was number one in my high school. That'll show him." He grinned at Faith.

"You played tennis in high school?" Faith asked.

Now that she though about it, Seth had a similar build to Caleb. Long arms and legs. Strong shoulders. He was fit for a guy his age, only the silver streaks in his brown hair and the deep lines in the corners of his brown eyes revealed that he was closer to sixty than forty.

"I'm surrounded by tennis tragics," Faith said with a huge faked sigh. "There you go, Mom. You and Seth can talk tennis with Caleb to your hearts' content when you find him." She stood on tiptoe to look for Caleb. Lou was only about five foot four even in the two-inch heels she wore and could never see over a crowd. Faith pretended to scan the room. Well, mostly pretended. She actually did have her eyes peeled for Caleb's golden head. She hadn't seen him come back yet. Maybe he'd gone to one of the other tents this party was sprawled across. Or out to where they were serving the food.

And she really had to stop thinking about what he might be doing.

"Can't see him," she said, lowering her heels. "But I'm sure you'll run into him. Now, I really need to get back to work. Seth, did Theo give you your passes?"

"Yes, thank you. Looking forward to it."

"It wouldn't be CloudFest without you." Seth always claimed his singing voice made the dogs run for the hills, but he was a music lover. He'd come to the very first CloudFest and every year since. He was probably more friendly with Shane and Billy than he had been with Grey, but she knew that Grey had liked and trusted him enough to hire him for legal stuff. He was a good guy.

Pity his daughter seemed to have fallen so far from the tree.

She watched Seth smiling down at Lou. Lou was

smiling back, sipping her drink. Would she ever admit how she felt about Seth? Faith had no idea. She hoped so. She didn't relish the idea of having Angie as part of the family, but she'd deal with that if she had to. Angie would just have to deal too.

Lou giggled at something Seth said and Faith wanted to hug him. He made Lou happy and that was good enough for her.

How would Grey have felt if he'd lived to see Seth fall for his ex-wife? She liked to think he'd be okay with it. After all, Grey was the one who'd fucked things up with Lou. And she deserved a good solid guy after all the shit she'd put up with from Grey over the years. Alcohol and touring and fame had hardly made him the easiest person to share parenting responsibilities with. He'd done his part financially but Lou was the one left raising three kids, two of whom weren't even hers.

But that had been Lou's decision. One Faith was very grateful for. She couldn't imagine what it might have been like if Zoe and Emmy had taken Zach and Mina with them when they'd left Grey and she'd grown up seeing her siblings only a few times a year.

Despite how pissed she might be with Zach right now, he'd been a good big brother. And Mina, well, Mina was the best sister Faith could have asked for even though they were almost polar opposites. In every way except the part where they just loved each other.

So Faith smiled at Lou and kissed her cheek, then kissed Seth's too, and then went to be Faith Harper for a few more hours until the party wound up.

chapter fourteen

Caleb had lost his appetite for the party by the time he'd made it back to the tents. The only people he knew, apart from Faith, were Lou and Danny. Having just had sex with Faith that had been both outstandingly hot and kind of stupidly reckless, he didn't want to deal with either her mom or the guy who was probably the closest thing she had to an uncle.

But he didn't really want to make polite "nice to meet you" noises with a bunch of strangers either. Even if some of the faces he'd spotted were people whose music he loved.

What he really wanted was to be somewhere alone with Faith. Instead he was going to get an awkward ride back to the house with Danny later on followed, he imagined, by a restless night in a bed that would be sadly lacking in Faith.

Maybe he should have taken Faith up on that offer to use one of her guesthouses. If he'd done that then maybe there would have been more outstandingly hot sex later rather than a "let's pretend neither of us know what's going on here" drive back to Danny's house. He'd heard Danny's voice and Faith's as he'd walked back from the arena. Luckily he'd recognized them early enough that he'd been able to stay out of sight. But he'd heard enough to know that Danny had kind of busted them.

Hopefully that wasn't enough to make Faith retreat back into her "maybe we shouldn't" position.

Because he wasn't ready to stop any time soon.

All he had to do was convince her not to stop either.

He grabbed a beer out of a tub of ice that sat on a stand near one of the food tables. Faith knew how to throw a party, that was for sure. There'd been no stinting on food or booze. The ice cold bottle had an unfamiliar label, but he'd had one earlier and it had been good. Maybe a local brew? He'd skimmed through the slim *Guide to Lansing* Liam had picked up with their groceries but he didn't remember any mention of a microbrewery. That didn't mean there wasn't one. After all, you'd hardly expect to find a whiskey distillery on an island the size of Lansing. Or a world-renowned music festival. The place was full of surprises.

Including Faith Harper. So far she'd been the biggest surprise of all. And all he really wanted right now was to be alone somewhere with her. Making small talk with a bunch of people he didn't know was not even close to a good substitute. He was no stranger to parties like these. Between sponsor events, tour events, tour parties in various cities, and hell, just having enough fame to get invites to all sorts of openings and charity fundraisers and other nonsense, he'd done more than his share of this kind of thing. Admittedly most of them had been much more formal than beer and BBQ in a bunch of tents, but as beer and BBQ went, this was a cut above the ordinary. Faith knew what she was doing. The food was awesome, the beer likewise, and the mood was relaxed.

But he still didn't want to be there. Not if he couldn't be with her. He knew exactly where she was, he'd spotted her as soon as he'd entered the tent. The red flowers splashed all over the dress she wore stood out. But he wasn't going to join her because he knew she wouldn't want him to. And he knew he probably wouldn't be able to hide just how much he wanted to peel that delectable white and red dress off her body and take her back to his bed.

He flipped the top of the bottle and took a couple of swallows, evaluating his options. One, grit his teeth, put on his public Caleb face, and ride the rest of the party out. Two, find Faith and convince her to ditch the party and take him home. He snorted to himself. That option was about as likely as his shoulder magically being one hundred percent again and him getting back to number one. The final option was to find another way home. He could probably navigate his way back to Danny's.

The festival site was far enough away from the Blacklight houses that the proximity wouldn't encourage people to try and overflow onto their properties, but if the last few days had taught him anything it was that nowhere on Lansing was terribly far away from anywhere else. Still, he didn't know exactly how far it was back to Danny's and it was—

"You're Caleb White." A woman's voice interrupted his train of thought.

He blinked and focused. The woman who stood in

front of him had dark hair piled up on her head, a beer in one hand, and an assessing look on her face. The vivid green shirt she wore made the eyes doing the assessing several shades darker green than they possibly were.

"I am," he said. "And you are?"

She smiled at him. Her mouth was wide and full. "I'm Leah. Leah Santelli. I work for Harper Inc. Friend of Faith's."

"Another island girl," he said, lifting his beer in a "nice to meet you" gesture. Friend? Should that be 'best friend'? That would explain the look. Faith's best friend. He needed to be careful what he said.

She clinked her beer against his. "Something like that. Are you enjoying your time in Cloud Bay?"

"So far," he said. "I'm looking forward to the music."

The smile thawed a little, he thought. But he got the feeling he was being sized up. Had Faith told Leah that they'd slept together? Or had she used that weird best-friend telepathy that women seemed to share and nosed out that Faith liked him? Or was she working up to hitting on him herself? Of the three options, none was great but he really hoped it wasn't the third.

"Danny mentioned you were staying with him?"

"Yes. He loaned his house to my friend, Liam, and I tagged along. Had some spare time on my hands."

"Right. You retired."

She didn't beat around the bush, this girl. "Yes. It was time."

"So now you're footloose and fancy free?"

"Now I'm taking a break," he said, carefully. He still wasn't sure what her endgame was. "I don't think I'm the kind of guy who'd do very well just lying around not doing much for the rest of my life, so it's just a break. How about you, what do you do?"

"I'm a sound engineer. I run Harper's recording studio. And this time of year, well, it's all CloudFest all the time," she said.

"I can see how that would keep you busy." He gestured at the party moving around them. "Lots of balls in the air."

"This is just the calm before the storm," she said. "Though it might get a little rowdy later on. People working off their pre-show nerves."

"I should have been a musician instead of a tennis player," he said. "We had to work off our nerves with exercise and sports psychology and early nights. This seems more fun."

"You looking for fun?"

He put the beer down. "Is that a pass?"

Leah shook her head hard. "God, no. You're not my type."

"Okay." He was relieved but still wary. "Then I'll have to admit, I'm not entirely sure why you're giving me the third degree."

"Like I said, I'm Faith's friend. You've met Faith, right?"

"Yes. She brought Liam the keys to Danny's place." He wasn't admitting to any subsequent encounters. Faith might have told Leah everything, but he wasn't going to confirm or deny until he'd heard that from Faith herself. He wasn't going to be the one to out them and give her a reason to call the whole thing to a screeching halt.

"It's just you came up in conversation earlier and Faith had . . . a look."

This was straying into dangerous territory. He should change the subject. But he couldn't quite bring himself to. "A look?"

"A look I haven't seen very often." Leah arched her eyebrows. "A smitten kind of look."

Smitten? Who the heck talked like that?

"You get to the point, don't you?" He tilted his head at her. "Does Faith know you're over here, telling me all about her smitten looks?"

Leah shook her head again, the gold hoops in her ears swaying back and forth. "No. She'd probably kill me."

"Then in that case, I think I'm a little old for passing notes. Faith strikes me as the kind of woman who's perfectly capable of telling me that she's interested. That always makes things simpler."

"I guess you don't lack for candidates." Her eyes narrowed at him.

It was tempting to tell her it was none of her business. But it was never a good idea to get on the wrong side of the best friend. And the longer this conversation went on, the more certain he was growing that Leah was, indeed, Faith's best friend.

"I've dated a bit. But despite what the press would like you to think, I don't spend all my time screwing my way around the world."

"Good," she said.

This conversation was very weird. "Good?"

"I'm just trying to get the lay of the land. You know." She waved her hand in the air vaguely.

"I really don't."

"Faith needs a good guy. Her dad . . . well, Grey Harper wasn't Dad of the Year."

"Leah, this is all very fascinating, but I don't think her family history is any of my business."

Her lips stretched into a pleased smile. "Well, that's a point in your favor. And does that mean if she was interested you'd be interested?"

"I think I'm going with 'that's none of your business.'" Maybe it was an island thing. Everyone used to knowing what everyone else was up to. Which maybe meant it wasn't odd to try and set up your friend with someone you'd barely met. But island or no island, he wasn't going to give the game away.

She laughed. "You know, I think I like you, Caleb White. But I've taken up enough of your time. So, I'll let you get back to the party." She clinked her beer against his again. "Enjoy." Then she walked away.

Caleb watched her for a minute or so, mostly making sure she wasn't making a beeline for Faith but no, Leah joined a group of three consisting of Theo King, a tall black guy who Danny had introduced him too earlier who was apparently the Chief Operating Officer of Harper Inc.; a short woman wearing Doc Martens with a blunt-cut black bob who Caleb hadn't met but who, judging by her outfit, might be a musician; and a man with a mane of wild brown hair and a wilder beard who held a bright red ukulele in one hand.

Which left Caleb once again alone with no one to talk to. And this time he was going to do the smart thing and leave before anyone else in Faith's orbit decided to interrogate him.

Apparently when it came to Caleb, her willpower lasted less than twenty-four hours. Because at eight p.m., with a couple of hours still to go on the first night of Cloud-Fest, she found herself unable to concentrate on the music. Instead, the weight of her phone, tucked into the back pocket of her jeans, was like a sleek black rectangle of temptation, whispering *"All it would take is a text."*

She'd seen Caleb earlier, heading into one of the tents in the VIP area. Dressed in dark blue shorts and a red T-shirt with some sort of graphic on it that she couldn't quite make out, and with all those very well-muscled limbs on display along with the blue and white VIP passes hanging from the lanyard around his neck, he'd looked completely in his element. And completely edible.

It had taken a lot of willpower to turn around and walk in the other direction and focus back on the business of keeping CloudFest on the rails for the next four days. Still, maybe she'd used up her day's supply of willpower because she'd seen him again, at the front of the crowd at the main stage, singing along with a goofy grin on his face just a few minutes ago. Despite a day mingling with the crowds and the crazy, he'd still been looking very very good. And she'd suddenly wanted him very very badly. So badly she'd had to hold onto one of the steel supports at the side of the stage where she stood to stop herself from making a beeline for him.

She succeeded in staying put, but her hands still itched to reach for her phone.

Just one little text.

One little text and he'd be all hers for the night. Not that she really had any business doing anything with her night other than trying to get some sleep. There were still three more days of CloudFest left. But apparently her hormones were determined to write some checks that her body would just have to deal with cashing later on. And, after all, there was always caffeine.

So there really was no good reason not to text Caleb. Today's closing act would be done in an hour and even though she could go to the inevitable impromptu after-party that would spring up somewhere, she really didn't want to. Not when there was a much more appealing alternative on offer.

Caleb felt his phone vibrate in his pocket as he and Liam were working their way through the crowd, heading back to the relative sanity of the VIP area. He stopped as someone thrust an arm straight across his field of vision. There was a sharpie in the hand at one end of the arm and a guy wearing a hipsterish plaid shirt and corduroy shorts in an ugly shade of yellow at the other.

Caleb put on his polite face. He'd managed to get around without being hassled by fans for most of the day. He'd heard his name called a few times and had signed a few things for a group of giggling young girls who'd been with their moms, but mostly the crowd had been happy to leave him alone. Or maybe just more interested in the movie stars, TV stars, and musicians also in the crowd. It was a nice change from the last large crowd he'd been in at Wimbledon where he hadn't been able to go anywhere without his security team and people screaming his name.

"Sign my arm," the guy demanded. He looked half drunk, his words slurring a little, blue eyes bloodshot above the straggly beard.

He hated the rude ones. He usually tried to stop and sign for anyone who asked nicely, but the ones who just shoved things in his face like he was some sort of performing monkey pissed him off. But the guy was swaying slightly, his expression belligerent. Caleb knew the type. Ready to make a scene to prove his fucking manhood or something if Caleb didn't play along. Easier to just sign and move on. He reached for the pen.

"What's your name?"

"Tyson."

Short. Good. Because the guy's beer breath stank. Caleb wrote To Tyson and then scribbled his name quickly before handing the pen back. "There you go."

Tyson squinted at his arm. "Looks like a squiggle."

"That's my signature, dude, take it or leave it." The phone vibrated again and he turned back to Liam who was waiting patiently a few steps away.

"Too busy to talk to your fans?" Tyson grabbed his arm.

Caleb shook him off, trying to ignore the sudden flare of anger in his gut. "Just trying to enjoy the music, like everyone else. And I have somewhere to be."

"Think you're too good for us, do you?" Tyson muttered, stepping closer.

"No, but I think you're drunk." Caleb gritted his teeth.

"What the hell would you know?" Tyler shoved him.

Caleb shoved back and the guy fell back a few feet before his expression turned mulish and he squared his shoulders. Caleb braced himself, suddenly not caring if it was a bad idea to give in to his temper. Punching this dick in the face might just be what—

"Hey." Liam stepped up beside him. Put a hand on his arm.

"Dude, chill."

Caleb wasn't sure if that was directed at him or Tyson. But Tyson apparently thought it was for him.

"Who the fuck are you?"

"Someone who will quite happily shut your mouth for you if you don't back the hell off," Liam said. Caleb bared his teeth at Tyson, all for this idea.

Tyson looked from Caleb to Liam—who was only an inch shorter than Caleb—and apparently decided that two against one was bad odds. He scowled but turned away, shouldering his way back into the crowd.

Liam let out a breath and let go of Caleb's arm. "Let's go before he finds his friends. Guys like that always have equally dumb drunk friends."

Caleb nodded, trying to shake off the dull burn of anger in his gut. No point letting one idiot ruin the day.

When they reached the VIP area and the security guys had let them through, he remembered the vibrating phone and pulled it out of his pocket.

My place. One hour.

He smiled. His day had just gotten better, Tyson or no Tyson.

"Who's the text from?" Liam asked

Caleb shook his head. "That's classified"

Liam grinned. "Dude, did you hook up while I was off the island? Fast work, I'm impressed."

Caleb rolled his eyes.

"Who's the lucky girl?"

"If there was a girl, why would I tell you when you won't tell me who your mystery girl is?"

Liam had remained tightlipped about what exactly he'd been doing in L.A. when Caleb had picked him up at the tiny Lansing Island airfield at midday.

Liam gave him a disgusted look over the top of his aviators. "Okay, you have your mysteries and I'll have mine. But would I be able to make an educated guess based on my knowledge of the women you've met on the island while I was around?"

"I don't know, would you?" Caleb said. "All you need to know is I may be late back to Danny's."

When Faith got home, Caleb was sitting on the front doorstep, talking on his cell phone. He didn't look entirely happy. When he saw her, he ended the call and tucked the phone away into his shorts.

"Took you long enough," he said as she made her way across to him, feet crunching on the gravel. She was tired and pretty sure she smelled like she'd spent the day with a crowd of sweaty strangers, but the smile lighting his face made her feel beautiful.

"Got caught up, sorry. Who were you talking to?"

"My manager," Caleb said, the happy look fading a little.

"Everything okay?"

He nodded and made a little gesture like hitting a tennis ball with an invisible racquet. "Nothing I can't handle. Some legal stuff going on. But we're not here to talk about lawyers, I hope."

Whatever it was, he didn't want to talk about it. That much was clear. And while part of her thought maybe she should push, part of her just wanted to keep things simple right now. Simple won. "Really? Because I was looking forward to a deep discussion on contract law," she said with a smile.

"In that case, perhaps I should go back to the festival, find some people who have a better idea of fun than you."

"Oh, I think you'll like my idea of fun just fine," she said. "I'll make it up to you for keeping you waiting.

That brought a smile to his face. The force of it made her stop for a moment. Damn. She should be getting used to him by now. But the effect he had on her was growing, not fading.

"I'm going to hold you to that." He gestured toward the garden. Which smelled like sea air and flowers in the warm night. "Not such a bad place to wait. And your security guys let me in without any hassle, which was nice. Not exactly easy to just drive around the block a few times while I'm waiting around here." He stood and came down the steps to meet her.

"Yeah, I told them you were coming. Festival week, they can get a little . . . enthusiastic . . . if anyone unexpected turns up."

"It's okay. I understand security." He reached out and pulled her close. "At least you don't have guard dogs."

"Well, my sister's Lab might lick you to death if he comes across you, so be warned." She put her arms around his neck as she settled against him.

He laughed. "I'll try to stay out of his way." His hands tightened on her waist, thumbs sliding under the waistband of the tank top she wore. As his skin brushed hers, she shivered and his expression turned intent.

"Hello." His thumb slid along the line of skin above

the button on her jeans and heat spread downward like his hand was made of gasoline. She arched into him.

"Hello," she managed. "I was thinking of maybe taking a shower. Care to join me?"

"I thought you'd never ask," he said and bent to kiss her.

It was going to take a while to ever get used to his kisses. She closed her eyes and tasted his mouth on hers, pleasure sinking through her and light spiraling across her closed eyelids. She just wanted to stay there and let him kiss her. Then she remembered the shower part.

Standing here in the warm night air kissing Caleb was good. Standing with him naked under her shower would be even better.

"Inside," she said and took his hand, tugging him toward the door. It took way too long for her liking for them to stumble inside, and upstairs to her room, with a pause only to find a condom. Too long, but at the same time no time at all, as she shed clothes and dragged him into the shower stall, thanking God for her father's sybaritic taste in bathrooms. All the showers in the house were big enough to throw a party in, with multiple jets and other features that might as well have been custom-designed for enjoying yourself with someone else.

As Caleb lifted her and her back hit the steamy tile—the cool sensation of it startling against the heat of him and the water pouring down on them—she wondered why she'd waited so long to do just that.

Then Caleb's hand found her clit and he thrust inside her and she stopped thinking at all.

The water and the heat and the man assaulted her

senses, her skin slippery and sensitive to each move, each slide, each time they came back together after he pulled back and thrust again. She wanted to drown in him, to sink into his kisses and his touch, and not come up for air again. But her body had other ideas. And breathing was necessary to gasp for air as the pleasure took her inward, rising and falling and building until she came, clinging to him like he was the only safe place in the world.

He stilled a moment, muttered something in her ear as she spasmed around him, and then he started again. Harder now. Wilder. Unrestrained in his need now that she'd had her turn. There was nothing to do but hang on and meet him again and feel the new pleasure hit the aftershocks and merge and combine in a second wave of sensation that was close to pain but also so damned good that by the time he groaned and came, she was falling all over again.

"Every time I eat midnight snacks, I half-expect my mom to come through the door and tell me to go back to bed," Faith said about twenty minutes later as she dug a tortilla chip through salsa and contemplated it. Post sex, she'd been suddenly starving and had dragged Caleb down to the kitchen, where they now sat, wrapped in towels, hair still damp, eating whatever she'd been able to find in her pantry.

Caleb looked vaguely alarmed. "Is that likely?"

"No." She grinned at him. "She doesn't live here. Plus, Lou's no night owl. I'm sure she's been fast asleep for hours. She's the odd one out in the family. One of those annoying early birds."

"Well, I'm all in favor of going back to bed with you,"

he said. "But this salsa is amazing." He pulled the bowl a little closer to him, dunking his chip theatrically.

She made a mock insulted noise and grabbed the bowl back. "Throwing me over for snack foods already?"

"Think of it as necessary refueling."

"I have to sleep at some point." After all, she was working tomorrow—no, make that today. It was way past midnight already.

"At some point. Just not quite yet." He leaned over and ran his thumb over her lip and she suddenly didn't feel sleepy at all. But she was still hungry, so she nipped at his thumb and then reached for another chip as he pulled it back.

"Not until this is all gone," she agreed. "It is pretty damn good. Locally made. And no one knows what the secret ingredient is. Will said it drives his brother crazy because he can't figure it out."

"Will from the bar?" Caleb asked.

She nodded.

"You hang out with Will a lot?"

Was that a slightly jealous tone in his voice? "I eat there now and then. It's the closest place to this house where you can eat out. And I run into him around the island. Hard not too." She reached for another chip. "Don't worry, I'm not the Harper sister Will has eyes for."

"He and—Mina, isn't it—have a thing?"

"I suspect he'd like to," Faith said. "But Mina . . . well, her husband died a few years ago. She's kind of been keeping to herself." She nodded at a photo stuck to the fridge. "That's her."

The picture was of Faith and Mina hugging. Mina

taking advantage of the couple of inches she had on Faith to smile goofily at the camera over the top of Faith's head.

"She has the same eyes as you," Caleb said.

Faith nodded. "Yeah. All three of us got Dad's eyes."

"She also looks young," Caleb said, looking closer at the picture. "Too young to have been married let alone widowed."

"She's twenty-three. Childhood sweethearts. Announced she was getting married right after she finished high school and there was no stopping her."

"You Harper women like getting your own way."

"We do," she said. "We run to stubborn."

"I would never have guessed," Caleb said, tossing a chip at her.

She batted it away. Enough about Mina. Too serious a subject for this night and this man. Caleb was her escape. "I forgot to ask, did you have a good time today?"

Caleb nodded. "I did. Great music. I picked up Liam at the ferry at midday—"

"Liam's back?"

"Yes."

"Where does he think you are right now?" She was fairly certain Danny would be at whatever party was happening back at the festival site right now. He wouldn't be worrying about Caleb. But Liam was Caleb's friend.

"I told him not to wait up. I didn't give him any more details."

"Oh. Okay, good."

"All the bands we saw were amazing," Caleb said. "And the crowds were definitely into it all. Nice work if you can get it."

"Missing the roar of the crowd?" she asked, curious.

He shrugged but didn't answer.

Avoiding again. But this time she didn't want to let it go.

"You really don't know what you're going to do now that you've retired?" she asked.

"I'll figure it out. Maybe I can take up guitar. Never had time for music lessons as a kid. Too much tennis. Is thirty-four too old to become a rock god?"

"Not necessarily." She smiled at him. "Though between that and the mechanics course, you're going to be busy."

He looked blank for a moment, and then grinned. "Oh, right. Will's car. Well, even rock gods have to have hobbies."

She didn't want to tell him that rock gods tended more toward buying already fixed cars than fixing them up themselves. "Can you sing?"

"I can take lessons." He twisted, peering at the guitars hanging on the wall.

She doubted he'd know a Gibson from a Martin. Whatever he was going to do, it wouldn't be music.

He rolled back toward her. "What about you? Never had the urge to hit the road with a guitar strapped to your back?"

"Been there, done that," she said. Suddenly she wasn't hungry any more. At least not for chips and salsa. Nope, she wanted the distraction again.

"You have?" Caleb looked intrigued. "What happened?"

"Didn't work out," she said. If he didn't want to tell her everything, then she wasn't going to open old wounds either. "And that's too long a story for tonight." She wiped her hands on a napkin and then stood, letting the towel drop to the floor. Caleb's eyes were suddenly very blue as he watched her. She straightened her shoulders, liking that she could stop his train of thought just by taking off her clothes.

"I don't know about you, but I'm feeling kind of re-fueled now. Another set, Mr. White?"

"Game on," he said and let his towel drop too.

chapter fifteen

The next few days passed in a blur of music and Caleb, and when Faith woke on Sunday morning, she was, for a moment, not entirely sure what day it was. Or what had woken her.

A noise?

Yes. There it was again. An odd *thwock* followed by a softer jingling sound.

Puzzled, she went to the window. Her room was at the back of the house, looking out to the ocean. But it also looked over the tennis courts.

Where Caleb was currently standing, dressed in shorts and not much else, racket in hand.

The *thwock* noise came again and her sleepy brain finally identified it as their ancient ball machine. Grey had bought it when they'd had lessons as kids. But it still worked and it got pulled out every so often when Lou or someone staying with them wanted to practice. Maybe

Lou had been using the court recently. Faith hadn't had time to pay any attention.

Caleb hit the ball back with an easy swing of his racket that was such a graceful and perfect sweep of muscle, Faith could only stand and admire it.

Then she found out what the metallic noise was when Stewie bolted down the court after the ball, collar jangling. He found the ball and brought it back to Caleb's feet. Caleb grinned down at him and hit the next ball while Stewie bounced in excitement, tail wagging furiously.

The two of them made such a cute picture that Faith leaned on the windowsill to watch man and dog being silly together.

As Stewie started to bark when Caleb walked down the court to reload the ball machine, it finally sank into Faith's brain that if Stewie was here and running around loose in the garden, then Mina must be around somewhere. She occasionally brought Stewie over and left him downstairs in the kitchen if she was called out and couldn't take him, but she didn't let him just roam the main grounds by himself. Too many miles of beach for him to disappear down.

Gah. Mina.

With Caleb here.

In very plain sight.

Crap.

She turned from the window and found her robe, pulling it on as she hurried toward the door. She only just stopped herself breaking into a jog as she hit the stairs and the scent of coffee came wafting up to her. If there was a god, it would be Caleb who had made coffee.

But nope, no such luck. As she came into the kitchen, Mina was sitting at the table, the French doors open, giving her the perfect view of Caleb and her dog as she drank coffee, newspapers spread across the table in front of her.

"Hey, sis," Mina said as Faith froze in the doorway. "Sleep well?"

"Fine, thanks." Coffee. She needed coffee if she was going to have this conversation. She crossed to the counter, made herself a double shot espresso and downed it in a gulp.

"Don't mind me," Mina said with a smile that bordered on a smirk. "I'm just sitting here admiring the view."

Faith sighed and went over to the table. "Okay, you got me."

"And you have Caleb White apparently. Mom would lose her shit if she saw him playing tennis on her court."

"Mom" meant Lou. Mina called Emmy by her first name. "Ma" occasionally. It made sense. After all, Lou had raised Mina. Since Adam had died, Mina has started calling Lou by her first name most of the time like Faith and Zach did, but "Mom" was still Lou and Lou only to all of them. "You are not going to tell her about this."

"And why is that?"

"Because he's not going to be here for long. And she'd just get her hopes up." She frowned at her sister, hoping she was clear about that. "What are you doing here at this hour of the morning anyway?"

"Couldn't sleep," Mina said. "So I thought I'd come on over and tell you that I was going to come over to the festival tonight. See Danny do his thing. Stewie and

I were having a nice walk when he ran off. When I caught up, I found him with . . ." She jerked her head toward the door. "He was prancing around with one of the balls, looking far too proud of himself. Caleb said he didn't mind, so I left Stewie with him and came in to make some coffee and see if you were awake."

"It's six a.m. on Sunday."

"It's the last day of festival. You're usually at the site by seven on the last day."

"How do you know that?"

"Sis, I may not go to much of CloudFest, but I get the same security reports you do. I know what time you come and go. Just like you know what time I do."

Damn. She'd forgotten the stupid reports. Mina's lighthouse didn't come with a separate entrance onto the property so she had to use the main drive, just like Faith. Which meant she came and went via the main gates. Where the security system logged everyone who came in and out. Faith got e-mailed a copy of the report weekly. Daily at festival time, but she'd been too busy to read them. She'd forgotten that Mina received the reports too. She'd never mentioned them.

But if Mina had been reading the reports, then that meant she knew that Faith had had a guest the last three nights.

"So you read the reports and just randomly decided to walk my way at six a.m.?"

Mina blushed. Her sister's pale skin never really helped her hide her emotions. "I'll admit I was kind of curious to see what kind of guy was good enough to make you break your stupid island rule." She looked back toward the doors again. "I have to say, I admire your taste. He's a little big and brawny for me but he is definitely pretty. If you like older guys." She grinned at Faith over the rim of her coffee mug, expression innocent.

"Listen infant, he's only thirty-four. Not exactly ancient. Nor is he brawny." Caleb was strong yes, but it was lean strength. There was a certain breadth to his shoulders and yes, he was tall, but he was hardly built like The Rock.

"Don't bristle. I wasn't insulting him." She angled her head. "You're defending him a little vigorously if he's only temporary."

Faith blinked. "No, I'm not." She was, she realized. The thought was . . . confusing.

"Why is he only temporary?" Mina asked. "Because like I said, he's nice."

"How do you know he's nice?"

"Lou and I went to hear The Captains yesterday. We met Caleb backstage. He was fun. And lovely to Lou. Gave her the lowdown on Andy Murray. You know how much she loves Andy Murray."

Not as much as she loved Caleb White, apparently. "He failed to mention that he'd met you." Though they hadn't exactly had much time for long heart-to-hearts lately. By the time the festival wrapped up each night there was time for sex and sleep, and then the routine started all over again. "Mom didn't mention him either."

"Well she did say you hadn't returned her calls for the last day," Mina said.

Faith started guiltily. "Shit. I meant to call her back. Is it important?"

Mina shrugged. "To be honest, curiosity isn't the

only thing that got me out of bed so early." She reached for the purse on the chair beside her. Drew out a small black notebook. "Lou gave me this. Said the lawyers sent it."

Faith took the notebook, suddenly wide awake. "What is it?"

"One of Dad's. They found it in that Jersey storage locker. Open it."

The cover was soft under her hand. It wasn't as big as the notebooks Grey usually used. She opened it. The first page was blank, which was odd. Grey usually dated his books. She flipped through the pages curiously. The first few were blank, but then she turned another and Grey's familiar bold scrawl leapt out at her. She peered at the words. Lyrics. To what? She started to read.

"Do you know that song?" Mina asked.

Faith shook her head. The lines on the page spoke of a girl and loss. And regret. Familiar territory for Grey, but the words were unfamiliar. And Faith got the sense that they weren't written about a lover. The words were gentler. Full of . . . something like yearning? Who had he written this for? Her? Mina? "I've never seen this song before." She ran a finger down the page. Feeling for a trace of him on the paper. Stupid. The writing was unmistakably Grey's. But if he'd written a song for one—or both—of them, surely he would have at least sung it for them?

"Mom seemed pretty excited," Mina said.

Faith flipped through the rest of the book. The other pages were all blank. Apart from the last that said "see other book." What the hell? That was just like Grey.

"Why?" she asked absently, staring at the words. "It's

just one song." Then it clicked. "Tell me she doesn't think this is one of the songs from that damn lost album."

"She didn't say that in so many words . . ."

Faith sighed. "She needs to give that up."

"She loved him too," Mina said. "Maybe this is how she deals with that. Thinking that there's more of him out there somewhere." She sipped her coffee. "I don't mind the thought myself."

"It's a nice thought," Faith conceded. "But that doesn't make it real. I wish she'd just let it go. Maybe then she'd give Seth a chance."

Mina smiled. "Seth was with us last night for a while. I think she's thawing. She'll get there."

"She deserves to be happy."

That got her an eye roll.

"Hello. Pot. Kettle." Mina jerked her chin toward the tennis court. "I'm guessing you're not going to be asking that very pretty man out there to stay on after the festival."

"He doesn't live here," Faith said. "I do. That's why it's temporary."

"You don't have to live here. Ricky didn't live here."

"Ricky was Ricky. We both knew where we stood. He was temporary too. Caleb knows what the deal is."

"You never brought Ricky home though," Mina said. "In what . . . three years? You only ever saw him in L.A. And here's Caleb White, on the island less than a week and making free with your . . . tennis court already."

"He's only temporary," Faith repeated firmly.

"You know your stupid rule is ridiculous, right? Keeping them off the island isn't actually going to stop you from falling in love if you meet the right guy."

"I'm not going to fall in love," Faith said.

"That's dumb," Mina said.

"Why? What has falling in love ever got any of us?" Faith said before she could stop herself. "Grey broke hearts, Mom's included. Zach seems to be following in his footsteps. And you—" She stopped herself. She wasn't going to throw Adam's death in Mina's face.

"But there was happiness before any of that, " Mina said. "And no one can predict how anything will ever turn out. Doesn't mean you can't try for a little joy."

"I'm fine."

"You're not fine," Mina said. "You're stuck here. You came home for what was meant to be a few months while you and Zach figured out your next plan and then he took that gig with Fringe Dweller and Dad got sick and you just . . . stayed."

"Lansing is my home. I like it here."

"Me too," Mina said. "But I never wanted to leave. You and Zach did."

"People change," Faith said.

"So why can't you? Take a chance on Caleb? Stewie certainly seems to like him. Stewie's a good judge of character, you know." She wriggled her eyebrows at Faith.

"Your dog would love anyone who hit a tennis ball for him," Faith retorted. "And this conversation is dumb. I've known Caleb for a week. And as I said, he's leaving." The thought made her cranky and she tucked her feet up on the chair, resting her chin on her knees.

"Yadda yadda yadda," Mina said. "You're the one being dumb. You're not chained to this island. You have enough money to go anywhere and do anything you want, even without the estate being finalized. I'm guessing Caleb does too."

"I don't want to talk about this."

"So you say. But we've been sitting here for what, ten minutes, and you've been watching him more than you've been looking at me. I think you kind of like the man."

"Liking isn't love." She held up a hand, anticipating what Mina was going to say next. "Neither is sex. He's hot. And yes, he's a good guy. Maybe even a great one. But I'm happy with my life."

"So happy that you threw a fit when Zach pulled out and disappeared for most of the day?" Mina asked.

Faith blinked, sitting up straight. "How did you know that?"

"Leah told me," Mina said. "I do pay attention to what goes on around here. You are my sister. I assume you were with Caleb?"

"Maybe."

"So he was the one you ran to when you were feeling bad? After you'd known him a day or so?"

"I wanted something to distract me. Sex does that quite nicely, thank you."

Mina sighed. "Okay. You keep telling yourself that. But you gave up on music when Zach didn't come back for you. So don't make the same mistake twice and give up on something else that could be great too soon."

"I didn't give up. I didn't want it enough," Faith said. "Grey told me that. Told me that if I really wanted it, I would've gone after it again."

"Yeah, well, Dad could be a real son of a bitch sometimes," Mina scowled.

"He was right about that, though," Faith said. "I didn't want it. I liked the idea of it. But being out there, all the travel and the bullshit that goes with it. I didn't want the music enough for that. Or, at least, didn't need the same sort of validation from it that Grey did. That Zach does. They need to be the center of attention. I was kind of relieved to be out of it."

"Maybe so," Mina said. "But you did just kind of come back and take over when Dad got sick. You've never really stopped to work out if there was something else you'd rather be doing." She hesitated. "Or did you? You said you wanted to talk to Zach and me about something after CloudFest. And now he's not coming. But you can tell me, you know. If there's something else you want to do. If you don't want to do this any more." She waved a hand. "If you don't want to run Harper or CloudFest or whatever, then you don't have to. I don't care. And if Zach wants the recording studio to stay in business, then Sal and Leah have that under control. The same with Harper Inc. We could find a CEO. Hell, Theo could do it." She bit her lip. "You were there for me when I needed it. And I'll always be grateful for that. But I'm okay now. So if you need to get off Lansing or whatever, then go for it."

"I don't want to leave Lansing," Faith said.

"But there is something else you're thinking about, isn't there?" Mina said.

Dammit. Mina has always been far too perceptive.

"Yes," Faith said. "There is. But it doesn't mean leaving the island. In fact, the island is part of it. But it's something that would take too long to explain just now. We can talk about it after the festival is done and dusted.

If we have to we can Skype Zach in. Because I'd like to use some of Dad's money for it."

"You don't want to give me a hint?" Mina asked.

"It sounds a little odd."

"Odd is good." Mina shrugged. "I like odd."

"Well, I've been thinking a lot about me giving up music—I mean, it was the right thing for me in retrospect. But I just feel like for a lot of young musicians or singers, particularly women, that a setback early on can kill a career. Look at Sienna, she's out of action now for who knows how long with her wrist. If she'd just been starting out, on a tour, or trying to meet a recording deadline, her wrist could have stopped it all. She'll be okay because she's already successful, but it doesn't work out that way for everyone. This industry is just . . . so hard on people."

"So you want to . . . what exactly?"

"Start another foundation program. Sort of. Something that supports young female artists through the first few years. Gives them some backing and resources and support." Grey had set up a foundation that gave grants to a few of his pet causes way back when. It was still part of the Harper Inc. enterprises and Faith and Theo oversaw it in conjunction with the other board members. But this, this would be hers. As long as Mina and Zach agreed.

"Like . . . a record label?"

Faith shook her head. "No. I don't want to run a label. But I want something that provides some seed money, perhaps. And help hooking them up with mentors and advisors and the right kind of people who can help them get things started. Time at our studio. So that they can get some music out there and maybe do some tours and not have to sign some hideous 360 deal that means they have to be Taylor Swift–level successful to make any money."

Mina looked intrigued. "That sounds great. Just girls?"

"For now, yes. I feel like they have a harder time. I mean, look at me and Zach . . . a band came knocking on his door when he and I didn't hit straightaway, but no one came chasing me. And maybe that's because I didn't look right, or maybe I wasn't as good"—she held up a hand as Mina started to open her mouth to protest that statement—"but I don't know. I just want to see if I can help a few of the women who do really want it to get it."

"Well, I can't imagine that Zach would be against that."

"It's not quite so straightforward. For me to put time into this and for us to put money into it, there'd be stuff I couldn't keep doing."

"You already know what I feel about that. You need to do what you need to do to make you happy."

Faith pulled a face. "Maybe. But there's no time to start talking details now. So let's leave it at that."

"Sure," Mina said. "Sounds good to me. You have my vote, you know that." Stewie's bark drifted though the window, and she smiled. "And Stewie's. You deserve whatever you want. Or whoever." She stood then, before Faith could start arguing again. "And now, I'm going to go rescue your guest from my dog. Lou said keep the notebook."

"You don't want it?" Faith picked the notebook up again, running a finger along the spine gently.

Mina shook her head. "No. You keep it. I know where it is." She bent and kissed Faith's cheek. "I'll see you tonight. You and your mystery man."

An hour later, Faith had shooed Caleb away so that she could get ready. She'd showered and dressed and headed down to the kitchen to grab her purse. The sight of the little black notebook on the table stopped her in her tracks.

Grey.

She glanced at the time on her phone. She was late already. A few more minutes wouldn't matter. She scooped up the book and, moving on autopilot, walked over to the piano. Pulled out the stool and sat while she stared at the words on the page. Then swung herself around and lowered her hands to the keys. She hadn't played in months. But the lyrics Grey had written had been running through her head. How long since she'd sung one of his songs? She pressed a key, then another. Picking out a familiar melody, the notes and chords of Cloudlines—Blacklight's first hit—flowing out of her without any thought. She started singing softly before she realized what she was doing.

Her phone blasted into life beside her and she yanked her hands back, heart pounding. She looked down at the screen. Danny. Crap. Her heartbeat went into overdrive. She snatched up the phone. "Hey, Danny, everything okay? You all set for tonight?"

If it wasn't, if he was about to pull out too, then she

didn't know what she was going to do. God, let it be anything but that.

"It's almost set," Danny's voice said. "But I just need
one more thing to make it perfect."

She slumped in relief. "Anything," she said, fervently.
"What do you need?"

Danny's chuckle tickled her ear. "I'm happy to hear
you say that. Because, what I really need, kiddo, is you."

He knew this feeling, Caleb thought. This energy in the
air. Anticipation. The way it felt when you stood in
the tunnels leading down to center court before a final.
The crowd in front of the stage buzzed and hummed
and cheered, creating an entity and an energy that had
his gut tightening and his muscles twitching in response, his fingers instinctively tightening around the
racket that wasn't there even though he wasn't standing
down there with them.

He bounced on his toes, trying to ease the sensation
a little. He didn't know exactly why he was so keyed up.
After all, he knew exactly who the secret act was going
to be. And he was standing side stage, rather than surrounded by the people in the crowd going crazy.

"Pretty cool," Liam said in his ear, nudging his side.
He was grinning at Caleb, also moving restlessly as the
crowd started to clap and chant.

"Very," Caleb agreed, eyes still on the stage.

"I don't suppose your mystery girl has anything to do
with the fact that we're standing right here instead of just
in the VIP area?" Liam said.

"Dude, we're staying with the guy who's about to go
on and blow everyone's mind," Caleb pointed out.

"Yes, but you haven't been around much. And Danny Ryan doesn't owe you any favors."

"Maybe he just likes you," Caleb said. "You're the one he loaned his house to after all."

Liam shook his head at him. "Your poker face isn't as good as you think it is, buddy."

"You're telling me professional poker player shouldn't be on the list of second careers to consider?"

"Not if you don't want to lose all your hard-won millions."

"Thanks. I'll keep that in mind."

"You going to tell me what it is you are going to do one of these days?" Liam said.

Caleb gave him a look.

Liam held up his hands. "Just asking. You can't just sit around on your ass for the rest of your life. You'd go nuts." He paused, then smirked. "Unless you're making plans with mystery girl, of course."

"Shut up and listen to the music." Caleb turned back to watch the stage. Just in time to see Faith appear on the far side of it and stroll out to face the crowd. At the sight of her the noise went from a chanting buzz to a roar that he was surprised didn't knock the stage down.

Faith, looking like a total rock goddess, in a tight black mini, over-the-knee boots, and a top made of some sort of gold stuff that consisted of a complicated series of straps and panels that flaunted every one of her assets while really showing none of them, grinned at the crowd. She'd done something to her eyes, turning them smoky and golden at the same time, and her mouth was painted a deep shade of red. He couldn't take his eyes off her.

"Yeah, total poker face," Liam said.

Caleb gave him the finger but kept watching Faith as she grabbed the microphone and eased it out of the stand.

"Hello, CloudFest," Faith said. "Are you having a good time?"

The roar that answered her was even louder than before. A wall of noise that his brain couldn't quite process. Grand Slam tennis crowds had nothing on rock concerts.

"I'm glad," she said. "And are you ready to have an even better one?" She paused again as the wave of noise rose again, grinning at the response. Then made a little shushing movement with her hands, waiting there, looking perfectly comfortable with the spotlight, until the noise dissipated a little.

"For those of you who might not know, I'm Faith Harper." Another roar. "And my dad and his three best friends started CloudFest way back in 1990. Yes, before a lot of you were born." She laughed then. "This festival means a lot to my family because it meant a lot to my dad, Grey. And one of the things he loved to do was to sneak someone in to put on an extra little show before we say goodbye for another year." This time the scream that answered her words was almost solid in its intensity. It hit Caleb, and moved through him, like a jet engine, making his pulse pound wildly. But it couldn't shift his focus from Faith.

"So this year, we're going to do that again." She paused, that wicked red smile growing wider. "Do you wanna know who it's going to be?"

"Yes!" the crowd screamed.

Faith shook her head, put her hand to her ear. "Sorry, I can't hear you. Do you want to know who it is?"

"YES!" The sound was deafening. The energy pulsed from the crowd, the sense of anticipation palpable. The hairs on the back of Caleb's neck stood on end. His right hand curled at his side.

"That's better," Faith said. "All right. As much as it's fun to stand here and talk to you all, and to say a huge thank you for coming out to our little island to celebrate the music my dad loved so much, I'm going to leave you now. But first, I have one last thing to do. Ladies and gentleman, please welcome back to the CloudFest stage, a place that's missed him more than we can say for the last six years, Mr. Danny Ryan."

For a moment there was a silence so deep, Caleb wondered if the previous noise had actually deafened him.

But then the cheering started and the whistling and the screams, and he realized he could hear perfectly well. Whether or not he'd still be able to once this set was over was another question.

Danny walked out onto the stage, guitar in hand, as the rest of his band moved into place around and behind him. The bass drum started to pound as Danny reached center stage and the noise got louder still. Faith kissed Danny's cheek before she ran off into the wings, still on the opposite side to Caleb. Dammit. She caught him watching and grinned, then pointed to Danny.

Right. He was here to see this, not stare at Faith.

Danny lifted his guitar and took control of the crowd effortlessly.

Caleb had seen plenty of bands play in his day. Been

to concerts in front-row seats and private gigs at extravagant birthday parties and corporate events. But he'd never seen anyone own the stage quite like Danny Ryan owned CloudFest. And he hadn't even been Blacklight's lead singer.

Danny played some old songs—not Blacklight songs—and some of the songs he and Erroneous released over the last few years. And then, right at the end, he stood, a lone figure in a plain black tee and black jeans, holding his guitar, wiping sweat from his forehead with his arm. The crowd fell silent.

"I'm going to do one last song for you. And then I'll turn you over to the Merlins, because they're the headliners." This earned a protesting roar rather than a pleased one. Danny gestured for silence. "Now Faith told you that her dad, Grey, started this festival. And to be honest, when he first suggested it, the rest of us in Blacklight thought he was a little crazy. Well, we were wrong and he was right. Grey would tell you that was the case most of the time. I don't know about that." He smiled wryly. "But he was one hell of a friend and one hell of a musician and I'm going to do something I haven't done since he died and sing one of our songs without him. But I don't want to do it alone. So—and this took a lot of arm twisting so I hope you appreciate it—please join me in welcoming back to the stage, Miss Faith Harper."

Caleb's jaw dropped. Faith? What the hell? She hadn't mentioned any of this to him.

But apparently that didn't matter because sure enough, Faith was striding back onto the stage to take her place beside Danny, doing a little curtsy at the crowd as they screamed.

And then Danny started to play and she opened her mouth and sang the first line of "Cloudlines," the song that had made Blacklight famous. A song that was slow and sad and sweet. A song about hopeful hopeless love, broken hearts, and the sea. Her voice was low and strong and sure, maybe not as amazing as her father's, but pretty amazing all the same.

Incredible.

She looked like she belonged up there. Why the hell wasn't she a star like her father? Why the hell wasn't she in his arms right now because he wasn't sure he'd ever wanted anyone so much in his life as he wanted her right now.

The song went on—he knew the words but at that moment he couldn't have told anyone what they were—and he just watched her. And, at the last, when she turned and looked at him for a moment as she sang the last line—something about being lost and falling, Liam moved closer to him and yelled over the cheers and applause, "I hate to tell you this, but you, sir, are in trouble."

To which he had no reply. Because it was one hundred percent true.

He was in a world of trouble. Not the temporary kind. The real kind. The thunderbolt kind. Maybe he'd known it all along but hadn't wanted to say it. But he was in trouble. And trouble's name was Faith Harper.

chapter sixteen

She had forgotten what the adrenaline felt like. How it took you over, carried you up and out of your body. Forgotten the buzzing, shuddering rush of it through her veins. And she'd never sung in front of a crowd like this before. So big. So hungry for her.

It hit her like a shot of pure alcohol, making her giddy even as she sang the words that made her sad. But she stood and sang and let herself ride the wave of it for a while. Until, as the music headed into the last verse, she turned and saw Caleb standing at the side of the stage, eyes fixed on her, something like awe on his face. Awe and a look of total yearning want that made her almost lose her place in the song because the only other thing that had made her feel this good in years was him.

The look and the crowd made her dizzy and she could only stand for half a minute or so with Danny after they finished, acknowledging the applause and roars of approval before she turned and ran from the stage straight into Caleb's arms, throwing herself at him and kissing him.

It wasn't until the camera flashes started to explode around them, penetrated even her closed eyelids with flares of light, that she crashed back down to earth and realized exactly what she'd just done.

Kissed Caleb White. In front of Lou, who she knew was standing on the other side of the stage. In front of Mina. In front of Danny Ryan. In front of about thirty thousand screaming CloudFest attendees. And in front of a good proportion of the who's who of America's music press.

Apparently Faith and Caleb were no longer a secret.

Right at that moment though, she couldn't bring herself to care all that much.

She opened her eyes when a voice said, "Ms. Harper, we'll get you out of here." The flashes were still going off around them, blinding her. Through the spots of afterburn floating in front of her eyes, she just had time to register Caleb's face grinning down at her and several of the festival's security team behind him. She heard her name being called, pleas for her to look this way or that. But she didn't want to pose for photos. She just wanted . . . hell, she didn't really know. She ducked her head and, after making sure Caleb was following, let herself be hustled away to the relative safety of one of the portable site buildings they used for the admin teams.

Someone pushed her down into a chair and she sat obediently.

"Are you okay, now, Ms. Harper?" a man's voice asked. One of the security guards. She nodded, not sure she could speak yet, and shooed him away. She should know all their names. She did know all their names but right now she couldn't quite think over the pounding of her heart in her ears. It would be easier to be certain who was talking to her if she wasn't still half-blinded from the cameras.

"We're fine," Caleb said firmly. "You guys can go back to work."

She nodded again, agreeing to this plan. "What he said," she managed. "I'm fine."

"Fine" was a weird word. So small. So innocuous. Something she said every day. But right now she had no idea what she meant by it, much less what she wanted everyone else to think about it. Including the reporters and cameras that would no doubt be lying in wait for them when they reemerged.

The guards filed out of the tent, and Caleb closed the door behind them. "*Are* you okay?" he asked.

She blinked, waiting for her vision to clear. Caleb seemed to be unaffected. Maybe he was just used to it. He must get it all the time in press conferences. Or used to get it all the time at least. He said he'd wanted to fly under the radar as much as he could.

Well, she'd just blown that plan up fairly thoroughly.

Her hands flew up to her mouth. She hadn't even thought about what Caleb might want. Hadn't thought at all, if she was perfectly honest. Shit. What had she done?

"Faith?" Caleb's voice sounded concerned. He crossed the small room in about three steps and knelt down in front of her chair. "Talk to me."

"I'm sorry," she said, speaking in a rush. "I wasn't thinking. God. All those reporters."

"Faith," he said. "Look at me." He put a hand on her arm, thumb stroking her skin.

The spots dancing in front of her eyes had almost all gone. But now, all she could see was Caleb.

His face was serious. Blue eyes calm. "I don't give a fuck about the reporters. Unless you do?"

"But you wanted to stay out of the press."

He shrugged. "It was never going to work forever." His mouth quirked. "And hey, at least we've given them something to write about other than my retirement."

Her stomach twisted. God, they were going to be splashed all over the news sites. And the tabloids. She'd always hated reading about her dad's latest scandals. Now she was going to be one of those stories. "I'm sorry," she said.

"Honey, there'll be another story in a day or two. I'm retired and you're not famous in that 'we need all the pictures of her' way. I'm not sure we're big enough news for them to keep hassling us. There'll be a singer or a movie star who does something dumb soon enough." He leaned in and kissed her softly, then pulled back. "Though I have to say, I'm not entirely sure why you're not famous, with that voice. You were amazing. You should be topping the charts."

She shook her head. "Not my thing."

"Okay, but if that's not the thing you're good at, then I'm not sure I want to see the thing you *are* good at. Are you the da Vinci of spreadsheets or something?"

That made her smile. "No. Though I do know my way around a good formula."

"Whatever floats your boat. Seriously though, you and Danny rocked. Literally."

"That song's more a ballad really."

"Don't get all pedantic on me, Harper. No wonder that song made Blacklight famous."

"It's a good one," she agreed. Grey had written it about the girl he'd just broken up with when the band had first come to Lansing. Typical him. Turning his destruction of some poor girl's heart into a career.

"Do you want to talk about why it's not your thing?" Caleb asked.

"Not right now," she admitted. From outside the cabin, the sound of the Merlins storming through their first number was making it hard to think.

"Well, what do you want to do . . . right now?"

"I have to stay for the closing party," she said. "I can't bail on it. Particularly not after *that*." She put her head in her hands, realizing that she was going to spend the whole party fielding questions about her and Caleb. Either that or why the hell she hadn't ever gotten back on the road.

"Okay," Caleb said. "Parties are fun. Then what?"

She knew he wasn't asking just about tonight. There was definitely a "what" to be discussed. It was crazy. They'd known each other a week but there was definitely a "what." Which both delighted her and scared the crap out of her.

"Can you stay a little longer?" she asked, feeling her pulse start to pound again as the words left her mouth.

"Danny might want his house back," Caleb said.

"Plenty of room at my place," she said. "And I always take the week after CloudFest off work."

"In that case," Caleb said, leaning in again. "I can definitely stay."

He started to kiss her again but was interrupted by a knock on the door.

"Go away," Faith yelled.

"Faith, honey, it's me." Lou's voice sounded a little surprised. "I just wanted to make sure you're okay. Those reporters went a little nuts back there."

"I'm fine, Mom," Faith said. She looked at Caleb and mouthed "sorry," but he just smiled and shrugged as if to say "what can you do?" "I'll be out in a minute."

"Is Caleb okay, too?"

"Yes, Mom. Your favorite tennis player is one hundred percent unharmed." One hundred percent a load of trouble that she hadn't any idea how to deal with, but that wasn't the question Lou had asked.

"Judging by what I saw back there, he's your favorite tennis player too, dear," Lou said somewhat tartly. Caleb started laughing, clapping a hand over his mouth to stifle the noise. She scowled at him, which only made him laugh harder.

"Mom, you're just going to stand there until I come out, aren't you?"

Caleb's shoulders were still shaking, his eyes bright with amusement.

"Probably," Lou said. "After all, there's a party to go to. And I need to tell you face to face how great you were up there." She sounded proud. "And Mina and Leah and Ivy are here too," she added. "They all think you were great as well."

Faith heard Ivy start laughing at that. "Okay, Mom. You can all form my fan club later. We're coming out now. I need to go grab my party clothes from my car." Her miniskirt and boots were leather. It was definitely too hot to wear leather all night. She'd dragged them out of her wardrobe when Danny had talked her into performing with him. She still wasn't entirely sure how he'd managed that.

But she'd used to wear the boots when she was performing with Zach and she'd figured maybe donning some of her old clothes might make her remember what the hell to do on a stage. Armor of a sort. The skirt just happened to go with the boots, being black with many zippers and studs. A purchase she'd made under Ivy's influence on a girls' weekend to L.A. She'd never worn it.

She stood, stepping around Caleb. "You can stop laughing now."

"You have to admit, that was funny," he said.

She narrowed her eyes at him. "Just for that, I'm going to let Lou fangirl at you all night."

"I like your mom," he said. "She can talk to me all she wants. As long as I still get to go home with you, that is." He batted his eyes at her. He had ridiculously long lashes. They were lighter at their tips, so you didn't notice until you got up close. "Do I?"

"If you're very, very good."

"I am. Excellent, in fact. Top seed."

"Do you do your own PR?"

"Yep." He grinned. "And I know it's working. Because I have it on very good authority that I'm your favorite tennis player."

She rolled her eyes at him. "You're just lucky you're pretty."

"You're pretty too. Especially in that outfit. The boots are definitely a look that works for you. And as for this . . ." He surged to his feet easily. All of a sudden he was right behind her, one hand tracing a zigzag down her back, following the gaps in the fabric. Everywhere he touched, her skin flared and warmed. "I can see some of your tattoos."

"That's kind of the idea,' she said. His hand on her skin was starting to make her lose her train of thought. What was so important that she couldn't just drag him home and work off some of this buzz with him in her bed already? The party. Right. Whose bright idea was that?

Oh yeah. Hers.

Past Faith kind of sucked. She needed to give herself a talking to.

Which wasn't going to happen.

So she had to live with it. She wriggled out of Caleb's reach, so she could think again. "Okay, time for you to talk to my mother now. I need to change."

"I think you're perfect just the way you are," he said.

"And for that corny line, you get to talk to Mina, Leah, and Ivy too," she said and laughed when he finally looked a little daunted.

It turned out that nothing really daunted Caleb though. Over the next week, whenever she managed to drag him out of bed, he happily went with her to various town events, dinner at Lou's house, the post-festival celebrations Harper threw for the crew, and even a couple of nights at Salt Devil. It had been as close to a perfect week as she'd had in a long time. There had been plenty of stories about her kissing Caleb at CloudFest on the internet and in the press, but Caleb had been right, they'd only been of interest for a day or so until the next celebrity got the spotlight turned on them. And her days were too full for her to worry much about the news.

Full of Caleb.

Who always seemed to enjoy talking to everyone he met, fitting in with the residents of Lansing and the rhythm of island life as though he'd been born to it.

She'd even told him her idea for a foundation to help new female artists and he'd been as encouraging as Mina had been. Even given her a few ideas. Like he'd had her back.

Like he was going to be there.

On Saturday night, they found themselves back at Danny's for a beach BBQ or fish fry or whatever the heck Danny decided it would be. He was going back to L.A. the next day, to get back to preparations for his tour. He had, of course, managed to invite half the island to the party. Even Mina had turned up, which meant that Stewie and several other dogs were running up and down the beach spraying random people with sand or shaken-from-dog-fur seawater as they played.

Faith walked over to where Mina was sitting on a blanket, eating a burger the size of her head while she laughed at her dog.

"Hey, sis. Can I join you?"

"Dog watching? Sure." Mina patted the blanket beside her, shuffling over a little and tucking her legs up and out of the way. Her feet were bare and as sandy as her cut-offs and red-striped tee. She looked happy.

Faith plopped down beside her. She brought her own share of sand, having taken part in a wild bout of beach volleyball that had resulted in her landing on her butt quite a few times.

Caleb was still playing with a few of the other guys. He fitted in effortlessly. Everyone who'd met him this week seemed to love him. His side was winning, both sides exchanging amiable trash talk as points were traded back and forth. He'd taken off his tee, which meant the view as they played was not hard on the eyes at all.

"He plays well." Mina said, following the direction of Faith's gaze.

"He does." She smiled in Caleb's direction, watching all that lovely muscle flexing in the sun. Thinking about how she might make flex it in other ways later on.

"You know," Mina said, "this is going to sound weird, but he reminds me a little of Dad."

Well, that killed her mood. She squinted at Mina. "Really? I don't see it."

"It's not how he looks, it's more . . . I don't know. He's got that thing Dad had. Charm. Charisma. Whatever it is. People want to talk to him. And he makes them feel good when they do. Look at him out there—he's running the game and the guys all love it. Even the ones he's beating the pants off."

A little chill ran through her stomach as she followed Mina's gaze and looked. She was right. The guys were all circling 'round Caleb. Not obviously, but if you looked for it, it was there. They watched him play. Fist-bumped him. Cheered him on. She knew that dance, that subtle rearrangement of a group that puts one person in the center of it all. She'd seen it happen around Grey her entire life.

Grey had been charming. And very good at making you feel like you were the center of the world basking in sunlight while you had his attention. But then, when you lost it, then it was as though you'd been banished to somewhere dark and shadowy and cold. And Grey had never paid much attention to what lurked in the shadows.

But Caleb . . . he cared. She shook off the unease in her gut. Caleb wasn't Grey. "I think he just likes people. And I guess he's traveled so much with his career that he's gotten good at dealing with them."

"Dad liked people too," Mina pointed out. "Oh, don't get me wrong, I don't think Caleb is all about Caleb the way Dad was all about Grey. But you can't deny he's charming. He's certainly charmed you."

"You were the one telling me that was a good thing. Have you changed your mind?"

Mina shook her head. "No. I'm still in favor of you being charmed." She shrugged. "Sorry, it was dumb. Forget I said anything."

It wasn't that easy. Because Caleb had definitely charmed her. No denying it. But had she been denying that maybe he'd done it a little too easily?

She watched as he dived for a ball and missed, sprawling to his knees in the sand where he proceeded to fall backward, convulsed with laughter as the guys on the other team high-five and hooted good-natured insults in his direction. The knot in her stomach loosened. Grey hated losing. He wouldn't have been laughing. He certainly wouldn't have climbed back to his feet and picked up the ball, ready for the next round. Nope, Grey would've left the court, pretended to lose interest.

So. There. Mina was wrong. Caleb wasn't her father. He was just Caleb.

And, for now, he was hers.

The next morning, Faith found herself back at Danny's, to deliver one of Grey's guitars he wanted to borrow. Danny opened the door, smiling when he saw her. She and Caleb had left the party after midnight. She had no idea what time it had wrapped up, but Danny looked none the worse for wear.

He kissed her cheek in greeting, and then grinned as she held out the guitar case.

"Thanks, I'll take good care of her." He took the case from her carefully

"Of course," Faith shrugged. "Great instruments should be played. Dad would want you to use them. Zach has a couple of them he takes on the road. The travel case is in the truck. Caleb will bring it in, he's just on the phone."

"Who's calling at this hour on a Sunday morning?"

"Danny, it's ten a.m. That isn't early to most of the world."

"Still." Danny shook his head. "Sundays are for sleeping in."

"Says the man catching the eleven o'clock ferry."

"It was the only ticket I could get." He looked past Faith to where Caleb stood by the truck, one hand on its faded red hood, phone up to his ear.

"He looks like he might be a while. Business call?"

"His agent. Or manager. Something like that. I don't know exactly." Caleb had been ignoring calls most of the week. He'd taken a few of them—and had never looked happy while he did—but he hadn't told her much about what he was discussing.

"I guess retiring like that means he has all kinds of stuff to deal with," Danny said. "Sponsors and shit."

"I guess," Faith said. It couldn't be easy to unwind a career so abruptly. Caleb had to be more organized than Grey had been, but even if just the business side of things was anywhere as complicated as Grey's, it had to be a pain in the butt. She just wished he'd talk about it.

"Well, come in, might as well caffeinate while we wait for Wonder Boy."

Wonder Boy? Danny's tone was light but his words still made Faith's stomach tighten a little.

But she followed Danny to the kitchen and found mugs while he made coffee.

"Take anything in the fridge you want," Danny said. "Leon will deal with the rest."

"I'm good," Faith said. "Leave it for Leon." She didn't want to think about Danny leaving. It had been nice having him around again. She took the mug of coffee he offered and wrapped her hands around its warmth.

"Caleb say anything about what he's going to do with himself next?" Danny asked, voice casual. A little too casual.

Faith froze with the mug halfway to her mouth. "Why? Did he say something?" She'd found the two of them talking several different times over the last week. Conversations that had broken off when she'd appeared. Danny had lived through Blacklight coming to an abrupt halt. Maybe Caleb had been asking him for advice?

"No." Danny said.

"Oh." She relaxed.

Danny tipped milk into his mug. Stirred it thought-fully. "I have to say, he's not exactly the guy I thought you'd fall for."

"Who says I've fallen for him?"

"Everybody with eyes," Danny replied with a smirk. "Not like there's no evidence, Faithy. You two going around all googly-eyed. All that kissing. The fact he's now staying in your house and not mine. It all kind of adds up."

She gave him the finger, trying to calm the sudden thump in her pulse. She'd been trying not to think too hard about her feelings for Caleb. It was all too new. Too complicated. Better to just enjoy herself than overthink herself into a panic. Then she remembered what Danny had said. "Why isn't he the sort of guy you thought I'd fall for?"

Danny's mouth twisted briefly. "He's a front man."

Her stomach turned icy. She put the mug down care-fully, the coffee suddenly not appetizing at all. "What does that mean?"

"You know exactly what I mean. He's always at the center of things. Ambitious. Leader-of-the-pack type."

"You're a front man," Faith pointed out. "And you're not like that."

"I'm a front man now," Danny said. "But only because Grey isn't here to do it."

"Caleb's not like Grey."

"He's definitely a lot less wild than Grey," Danny agreed. "But he's still a front man."

"And that's a bad thing?"

Danny shrugged. "Not necessarily. Just not who I thought you'd want."

"Why not?"

"Front men go after what they want. They always have a thing they're chasing. A goal. Christ, the guy was number one in the world. You've got to be driven to get to that position."

"There's nothing wrong with being ambitious." She was twining her hair around her finger now. Wrapping it a little too tightly, so that the tip went white before she released it.

"No," Danny agreed. "But that's not the kind of guy who wants to spend the rest of his life on a tiny island."

"Grey lived here."

"Some of the time. The rest of the time he went out and raised enough hell that he needed to come back here to recuperate. Not sure Caleb's the hell-raising type. But he is the world-beating type. He's gonna want to channel that into something. And ever since you came home, I've kind of had the feeling that this is where you want to be."

Faith swallowed. "You're saying you don't think it will work?"

Danny grimaced. "Faithy, I'm not one to make predictions. And I've never been good at relationships. I just wanted to make sure you were seeing the man clearly. Good and bad. I'll admit, he seems like a good guy. But he is a front man. I know one when I see one. Zach's one too. You, well, you do a damned good job at whatever you turn your mind to, but you don't need the spotlight in that same way. Problem is that that might mean, with a guy who does, that you end up waiting in the wings. And I think Grey taught you a little bit about how that works out."

He looked sad a moment, bushy eyebrows drawing down. "Sorry, kiddo. I could be completely wrong. But Grey's not here to look after you and Lou, and well, Lou is too big a Caleb White fan to see him clearly." He shrugged. "But hell, maybe I'm talking out of my ass."

Faith shook her head, tried to smile. Trouble was, maybe he wasn't.

chapter seventeen

The drive back from Danny's was quiet. Caleb was driving, his fingers tapping out a rhythm on the steering wheel to the Springsteen he was playing through his phone. He looked happy. Content.

Maybe Danny was way off the mark.

But there was a coil of cold in her gut contradicting that thought.

As Caleb pulled the truck to a stop in front of the house, his phone rang again.

As he went to hit ignore for the hundredth time that week, Faith snapped, "Just answer the damn thing."

"Faith?" He sounded startled. But she wasn't in the mood to stay and talk, so she climbed out of the truck.

He caught up to her just before she reached the door. "What's going on?"

"Call them back," she said.

"Call who back?" he asked.

She pointed at the phone. "Whoever it is who's been

calling this week. It must be important or they wouldn't still be calling."

"It's nothing that can't wait."

"Really?" She stared at him. He was trying to charm her out of her bad mood. But he was also not telling her the truth. The cold spot grew bigger. She rubbed her arms, which were suddenly covered in goose bumps.

"Really," he said.

She turned on her heel. Headed for the house. As she walked through it, she could smell him. His cologne, and the rest of the things that made up Caleb, all in the air. He'd been here a week and he'd already become a part of the place.

She didn't want to give that up. She felt him come up behind her, and she twisted, throwing herself at him, kissing him wildly.

"Faith?" he said again.

"No talking," she said. "I want you. Now." She started tearing at his clothes, mouth moving back to his. He didn't take that much convincing. He lifted her and carried her up to her room—which had felt like *their* room for the last week—and then he laid her down on the bed and took her. Hard and fast and wild, the way she wanted. The way she needed. Driving away the cold with his body, reminding her what they had with every thrust and touch and every ounce of sensation he wrung out of her.

She came hot and hard, coiled around him, holding on as hard as she could, as he came with her.

For a long time, they lay there, just where they'd finished, breathing too hard, struggling to come back from the pleasure as their heart rates slowed. When she finally felt the fog of lust retreating, she was smiling.

This. This was what she wanted.

And then the damn phone rang.

Caleb looked around, expression somewhat guilty. His phone was presumably in the pocket of his shorts currently somewhere on the floor. She shoved him away, the mood lost again. The cold spot returning. Sex, it seemed, wasn't enough after all. "Answer the damn thing."

He shook his head, and she wanted to smack him. Instead she crawled off the bed, found the phone, and threw it onto the quilt next to him. He picked it up, his eyes narrowed, and he stalked out of the room, pausing only to grab some clothes.

And she suddenly knew what she had to do when he came back.

Which he did, after ten minutes that felt more like an hour while she'd sat on the bed, trying to remember how to breathe through the frozen ache that had suddenly taken up residence in her chest.

Caleb sat on the bed, expression wary. "Is there something we need to talk about here?"

She'd been steeling herself, but it was still hard to say the words. They stung like the ocean. "We need to talk about when you're leaving."

He went still. "Leaving?"

"You are going back, right?" There, she'd said it. She'd thought it would be a relief. But the knots in her stomach only felt worse. She rubbed her chest. Hell, everything felt worse. Even her skin felt suddenly wrong. "This was only ever meant to be a temporary thing."

His eyes were wary. He'd never looked at her like that

before. "I don't remember setting a date. I like it here. And I don't have anywhere pressing I need to be."

"That's not true. Your manager—or whoever it is— has been calling you for days now."

"So maybe I have to go back to L.A. or Malibu for a few days. That's not the end of the world."

She pulled the sheet she'd wrapped herself in a little closer. "You really think you can sort your whole life out in a few days?"

"I can start."

"Then what?"

"Then we figure things out." He stood then, took a few steps. Stopped. Came back and sat down.

But she could see he wanted to move. To leave maybe. His hands moved restlessly, the muscles in his shoulders tensed. His body knew the truth, even if he didn't.

And seeing that made her want to run. But she had nowhere to go. She had to stay. This was her home. Her island. Her life. She'd chosen it. He wouldn't. "Or maybe we should just keep this simple."

"Define 'simple'?"

"Admit that this was a fling. A mutual distraction."

"A fling?" His voice was low, puzzled. Almost cracking. He sounded like he'd never heard the word before.

She tried to sound casual. She at least managed to keep her voice steady. "You can't tell me this is the first time you've had a fling. You must have had girls throwing themselves at you in every country you've ever been to."

"It's not the first time, no. But that has nothing to do with this. We're not like that."

"Why? After all, we've known each other less than two weeks. Maybe that's all it's meant to be."

He shook his head. "Maybe I want it to be more."

God. Why couldn't he make this easy? She hugged her knees to her chest. "Why?"

His mouth twisted. "Because I like you, Faith. I like you a lot. I like talking to you, I like the way you hum when you're washing dishes. I like those tattoos that run down your spine and the way your eyes change every second. I like the way you taste on my mouth. I like that voice of yours that can make me shiver. I like the way you think and the way you make me laugh. Because every night this week, I've fallen asleep wishing the day was just a little longer so I could have some more time with you. Because I want to be with you. . . . Don't you want to be with me?"

He was killing her. She was going to crack in two. But she needed to be strong. "That's not the point."

"I think it is. It's all that matters. Isn't this what most people want? What most people are always trying to find? Someone they like? Someone they can't get enough of? That they can have the kind of sex we just had with?" He shook his head at her. "You can't tell me this was just about sex for you."

She was so damned cold. Dammit. Why was he making this complicated? "I can't make that decision after two weeks."

"Why not?"

She shook her head and climbed out of the bed. So cold. She needed to get warm.

"Where are you going?"

"To take a shower. Because I think you and I want

different things here. If you're looking for love, I'm not your girl."

Caleb scowled. "What the hell does that mean?"

"Why are you getting upset? Aren't you the one who was all 'everything has a time then you move on' at Salt Devil the night we met? I thought we were on the same page here." That part was a lie. Because she'd been letting herself believe there was more.

"I don't give a damn what page you're on. I want to know why you're so freaked out."

She found her robe, slipped it on. Then faced Caleb again. He was sitting on the edge of the bed, dressed in just shorts, looking golden and rumpled and gorgeous. Too bright. He'd burn her up. "Look at you, you're Mr. All-American Boy. And I'm . . . I'm not the kind of girl All-American Boys take home to their mothers. I told you that too."

"My mother isn't the kind of mom who sits around waiting for their sons to start having grandkids and trying to control who the mother of those kids is," he said. "But even if she was, she wouldn't get a say in who I choose to be with. I don't understand. This last week, it's been so good. It's been fucking great, in fact. Don't you want to see if there's anything in that?"

She shook her head at him. "It's not that simple."

"Explain it to me then."

"Harpers aren't good bets," she said and then headed to the bathroom, locking the door firmly behind her.

Caleb stared at the bathroom door wondering exactly what had just happened. Other than him apparently totally misjudging the whole situation. He'd had some

awkward post-sex conversations in his time but this . . .
this was a new low. He had no idea why Faith, who'd
just spent the whole week with him acting like she was
happy—delighted even—to be with him, like she felt
the same way as he did, was suddenly telling him she
had thought all along that the whole thing was temporary. Shutting him out. Pushing him away. He thought
they'd gotten past that. From the moment she'd kissed
him after she sung at CloudFest. That was when it had
moved from fling to . . .

To what exactly?

From beyond the door, he heard the shower turn on
and his fingers dug into the fabric of the quilt as he resisted the urge to go over there and try to get her to let
him in.

If he was in there with her, maybe he could make up
for the blunder. He wasn't sure exactly what he'd done,
but whatever it was, surely he could sweet-talk her into
forgetting he'd been an idiot. But the locked door meant
she wanted to be alone.

So he had to wait.

And while he waited, there wasn't a lot to do except
think about what had just happened.

She was right, of course. He did need to go back to
Malibu. And spend some time in L.A., mopping up
some of the mess his retirement had created. Settle ruf-
fled feathers with sponsors. See what deals he might
keep.

Look after his team. He wasn't a one-man band, after
all. He'd never been one for having an entourage trail-
ing after him at all times—he preferred to find local
physical therapists or masseuses when he traveled—but

he had a coach and an agent and an assistant. All of whom were currently waiting for him to make his move so that they could figure out what to do in the wake of the bomb he'd set off by retiring.

He'd discussed the possibility of returning with Eddy, his coach, before, of course. They'd looked at the possibility after his surgery. But ultimately, he'd made the decision alone. He'd certainly announced it without telling anyone else, which in retrospect was kind of a dick move, but he'd sat down at the post-game press conference, with cameras flashing at him and people shouting, and the words had just kind of fallen out of his mouth.

Much like they had just now with Faith.

Maybe he should look into a muzzle.

Might make things easier.

Though, in Faith's case, her reaction baffled him. He was no expert on women, but most of them, in his experience, were hoping for something more than a "thanks, that was nice" thrown over a guy's shoulder as he headed for the door in the morning.

But if he'd learned anything in the last two weeks, it was that Faith Harper didn't fall into the category of "most women."

Question was whether or not he was going to get the chance to figure her out.

The door to the bathroom remained shut. The water in the shower was still running. Two options. Either sit here and wait for her or do something else.

Liam was about the only one he might talk about Faith with, but Liam had his own shit going on, judging by the radio silence since he'd left Lansing.

Of course, he had friends in other time zones but all of them would want to talk about his retirement. He'd been avoiding talking to anybody for two weeks now.

So, no using the phone as a distraction. He definitely wasn't going to check his e-mails or social media. He'd been avoiding those even harder than the phone. He'd had to take the phone calls. Or some of them, but he'd ignored the rest of it. He could only imagine the e-mails waiting for him.

He'd been imagining—or trying not to imagine maybe—them since he'd left the press conference, not quite believing what he'd just done.

The sensation had been a strange mix of relief and horror. He'd floated in the middle of it, feeling not quite connected to the world. There'd been a bubble around him that had made the roaring of the reporters and the camera flashes and Eddy's steady stream of "what the hell" type comments in his ear sound like they were coming through several feet of water.

That bubble had carried him into the car waiting to take him back to his hotel, where he'd left Eddy standing in the corridor, still wanting to know what the hell was going on. It had gotten him through the flight home. Numbness, it turned out, was useful.

But his bubble had vanished when he'd woken up in his own bed less than twenty-four hours after making his announcement. Then he'd been left facing the fact that he'd just walked away from his whole life and had no idea about what came next.

That had kicked off a hunt for a bottle of whiskey. But drinking only helped for a day. Then he'd decided the hangover was worse than facing reality. He'd started each morning determined to start to deal with things. Only to find himself frozen . . . inextricably drawn to the couch and mindless movies and takeout to avoid going anywhere—particularly not with the scrum of photographers camped out on his doorstep. Eddy had turned up a couple of days after Caleb had arrived home, but Caleb had sent him away. His agent, Ivan, got pretty much the same treatment. Eventually Caleb had just pulled his landline out of the wall and let his cell go to voicemail. It had sat on his kitchen counter buzzing accusingly every so often, but he'd ignored it.

It was only chance that he'd seen Liam's name flash up on the screen when he'd been scraping leftover Thai noodles into a dish to nuke for dinner.

Liam had no skin in the Caleb White Tennis Star game. Liam was a friend. One who didn't need anything. Caleb hadn't heard from him in a while and he'd been getting sick to death of his own company, so he'd picked up. Which had led, in one way or another, to him sitting on this bed, contemplating the sound of the shower and what to say to the woman who was seemingly determined to maybe let herself dissolve away entirely under the water rather than come back out and talk to him. Maybe she hoped that if she stayed in there long enough, he'd leave. But, nope. That wasn't going to happen.

He didn't know exactly what he was going to do, but not that.

The shower suddenly shut off, the lack of sound somehow frighteningly loud.

He climbed out of the bed, unable to just sit there and wait for her to emerge. He found his T-shirt, pulled it

on. Much as he might have liked to drag her straight
back to bed and convince her she was being dumb that
way, he didn't think that was likely to fly with Faith.

So, clothes.

He couldn't do much else. He smelled like sweat and
sex. The room smelled like sweat and sex and Faith's
perfume despite the open windows. The breeze only
added the sharp tang of salt to the mix. Which was a
goddamn heady combination. He liked the smell of her
around him. On his body.

The bathroom door was still shut, the stark-white
painted wood mocking him.

He glared back, then realized that he probably looked
like a crazy person, standing just a few feet away from
the door, scowling. That wasn't going to improve Faith's
opinion any. He retreated back to the bed, sat down
again. Tried not to scowl.

Eventually—after what felt like another century or
so—the door opened and Faith walked out, wrapped in
a massive gray towel. Her hair was wet, slicked back
from her face.

She looked about eighteen. Like she had in the Blacklight videos.

It was a weird kind of mental whiplash. A spike of
the same rush of "that is one gorgeous human" he'd
had when he'd first seen her all those years ago mixed
with the fact that the real live person was standing here
with him.

And that for all her Faith swagger, and that face and
the confidence with which she generally attacked the
world, for all the fact that she was the daughter of a rock
star who should really have no cares in the world, she

was just a woman standing there. Looking stupidly beautiful and kind of lost.

The kind of lost he knew about.

When she saw him, she stopped as though she hadn't expected for him to still be there.

"Hey," he said.

"Hey," she said, tugging the towel tighter. She looked around the room. For her clothes? He didn't know where hers were. He hadn't been paying attention at the time.

"I should get dressed."

Crap. "Don't," he said. "Talk to me. Please."

Her brows drew together. "I'm not sure there's much to talk about."

"Don't I at least get a right of reply?"

"This isn't a debate. I get to choose who I let into my bed. And how long they get to stay." She moved then, to the far side of the bed. Bent to pick up her dress, looked at it critically, and then shook it with a snap of her wrists that was almost savage. It still looked pretty wrinkled when she'd finished, but she put it on anyway.

"Of course you do. But don't I at least get to know why?"

Her eyes came back to him. They were gray like ice. No hint of the sea. No hint of life. "Because you're in no place to know what you want."

"What does that mean?"

"You just blew up your life. You've been focused on tennis for what, twenty years? And now that's gone. And I know what happens to guys like you when they have something they love that much in their life. Something they're driven to do. Particularly when they can't get their fix."

"Oh? What happens?"

"Well, if you're my dad, you fuck up three marriages and three kids and take drugs and alcohol. If you're my brother, you throw your sister away to chase the first thing that let you keep chasing the dream. In your case, well, let's just say, I don't know. But I don't want to find out either. Been there done that."

"So because I quit tennis I can't be in love with you?"

Was it possible for someone to actually slap you with words? Because she definitely felt his words hit her.

"You're not. You just need a distraction. A temporary high while you find your new thing."

"Why can't you be my new thing?"

"Because guys like you can't sit around making somebody else the center of your universe. You need more."

Her words were like a slap. And something in him snapped. He wasn't going to let her do this. Let her decide he wasn't good enough for her. That she couldn't trust him or whatever the hell story it was that her brain had cooked up. "You know what, Faith. I am not your fucking father. Or your brother. You never did tell me exactly what happened with you and Zach, but I assume he's part of the reason you stopped doing what you did with Danny up on that stage at CloudFest. But I'm not him. I'm not going to ask you to give anything up."

"You will. You'll want to start a business empire or something. You won't be happy here." Her hands clenched at her sides.

"You run quite the business empire from Lansing, in case you haven't noticed."

"I was born here. I belong here."

"You feel safe here," he said, voice rough now. He was holding onto his temper with a death grip. "That's not the same thing."

"I could be anywhere I want. I want to be here. You have no idea what you want. You can't possibly. Not this soon. You've just grabbed onto me because I was the first thing you stumbled across that caught your interest again. Gave you a taste of that high. But I can't be your methadone, Caleb. I won't be. You need to work your life out. Figure out what you really want to do. Otherwise, one day you'll wake up and realize I'm not what you need. Then you'll be gone. And it'll only hurt more then than it does now."

"Faith." His voice cracked. "Don't do this. Didn't you hear me? I told you I loved you."

She shook her head. The crack in his voice matched the one in her heart. But she couldn't show him that. She had to be the strong one. For both their sakes. "You just think you do. But once you get off this island, you'll realize just how wrong you are."

chapter eighteen

It would be two weeks tomorrow, Faith thought as she trudged through the sand. Two weeks since Caleb had left. Two weeks since she'd told him to go. It had been the right thing to do. So why did she feel so broken?

Two long crappy weeks. And every morning of those two long and crappy weeks, either Mina or Lou had turned up to make her leave the house and go for a walk along the beach. Neither of them had pressed her to talk. But they'd been there.

Today it was Lou's turn. She walked in the soft sand, beside Faith, wearing bright red shorts and a white linen shirt, bending occasionally to examine a shell or a piece of seaweed.

Faith hadn't been much interested in her surroundings on these walks. She just kept moving. Until today. When suddenly, she had to stop. Couldn't do it any more. She sank to her knees in the sand, like someone had cut the last few threads of willpower that had been holding her upright.

Lou studied her a moment, then knelt too, moving in close. "You want to talk about it now?"

Did she? No. But if she didn't, then she was going to go crazy. "Not sure talking will help." Her voice shook a little and she pressed her lips together as the knowledge of it hit her in the gut again.

"You've been saying that since you were a teenager. And have I ever let you get away with it?" Lou settled back on the sand.

"No," Faith muttered.

"So talk. About Caleb. I still don't understand why he left," Lou said.

Faith hugged her knees, staring out to the sea. It was a little wild today, whitecaps dancing as the waves rolled endlessly in. Usually she found the rhythm of the water relaxing. Today it was depressing. "I told him to go."

Lou's mouth dropped open. "Oh, honey. Why?"

"Because he has a life to figure out."

"He can't do that here?"

She shook her head, blinking behind her sunglasses. She wasn't going to cry all over her mom. She was done crying. "It just . . . wasn't going to work."

"But you two adore each other. That's obvious to anyone who sees the two of you together."

"That doesn't mean it's going to work. And it's ridiculous, we've only known each other two weeks."

"Sometimes it doesn't take very long," Lou said. "I met Grey and I knew in hours. Sometimes love just happens. And you have to go with it."

Faith flinched. "Not if it's just all going to end in tears. Caleb's used to being in the spotlight. Like Dad. He hasn't been away from that long enough to know who he is without that. Or if he can handle it. I don't want to be the thing he uses to hide from that. Because one day he'll wake up and realize he can do without me when he figures it all out. I'm not going to be left behind again."

"So you're just going to be alone forever?"

"That's not the only choice, is it?"

Lou shook her head. "It is if you won't take a chance. That's how love works. You have to take the risk. The sadness is part of the price of the happiness."

"That sadness almost broke Mina," Faith said. Her throat ached and she swallowed. "It's taken her three years and she's only just breathing again. I have friends. I can have lovers. I'm happy enough."

"Oh, Faith."

She lifted her head. "Don't 'oh, Faith' me. If you believed what you were saying, you'd be married again. But you've been alone since Grey left you."

Lou shook her head. "That's not entirely true. I made a choice when Emmy left Mina with me. To give you kids some stability. I didn't want the three of you to go through any more change. And then life kind of happened. It takes a lot of time to raise three kids and work." She paused. "It doesn't mean I haven't had sex from time to time."

"Mom!" Faith blurted despite herself. Then she clamped her mouth shut.

Lou's smile was smug, though Faith couldn't see her

eyes behind the sunglasses she wore. "Did you think I was a nun?"

"I didn't think about it!"

Lou laughed. "Well, I'm not. You're not the only one who goes off-island you know. I even had a Ricky for awhile."

"How do you know about Ricky?"

"I asked Leah once what friends with benefits was and she let it slip."

Faith groaned and dropped her head back down on her knees. She didn't really want to think about her mom making booty calls. She was happy that Lou had had someone to make them to, but she didn't want to think about it any further than that. "Sex is different though. You haven't let yourself fall in love." She sighed. "Sometimes I feel like there's a price we're paying."

Lou lifted her glasses, shoved them onto the top of her head, expression quizzical. "For what?"

"For Dad's success. I mean he did some damage in his lifetime and he paid a price, but maybe it wasn't enough. Sometimes it feels like the rest of us have to make up for it. Mina lost Adam, and Zach gave us up for music. And you and me. Well, we're alone."

"Faith Elizabeth Harper. That might be the most ridiculous thing you've ever said." Lou said, looking incredulous. "This isn't ancient Greece. No one's cursed or being manipulated by gods. Yes, your father could be a bastard at times. And yes, he wasn't the dad you deserved all of the time. But that doesn't mean you have to let that define you. You don't have to be alone. You can be better than him. You don't have to make his mistakes. You can be happy and it will last. You just have to make the leap. "

"You haven't," Faith objected. It was all very well for Lou to make that speech, but it didn't mean anything if she didn't really believe it. "Seth Rigger is standing there ready to catch you, Mom. You know that. And you won't make the leap. But you expect me to? Where do you think I learned to be so careful?"

Lou flinched, suddenly looking old. "Well, then I'm sorry for that. That's not what I wanted you to learn from me."

Crap. Now she was making Lou feel bad. Really, she was terrible at this. "I'm not blaming you. I'm just saying that Caleb and I . . . well, it's crazy."

Lou's hand came down on her back, rubbing gently. "Like I said. Sometimes love is crazy. Sometimes it just is. And I had Grey for five years. They weren't five years of unending bliss, but I was really happy for most of them. He loved me in his way. And Mina had Adam for three. Longer if you count all the time they dated. Do you think she'd choose to give that time up? If she could go back, would she give him up rather than lose him in the end?"

Faith thought about Mina. About the look in her eyes whenever she'd looked at Adam. "Probably not."

"Then maybe you should take your sister as your role model, not me. Do the crazy thing. You can't go back and get married at eighteen but you can have Caleb. If you decide you really want him."

She made it sound so easy. And Faith wanted to believe. She just didn't know if she could. She breathed in, tasting the salt in her mouth. You couldn't get away from it on the beach. The cost of enjoying the water was the sting of the ocean on your tongue. Grey had told her that once. And now she suddenly realized he hadn't just been talking about the beach.

"What about Seth?" she asked. "Are you going to do the crazy thing?"

Lou smiled. "I'm thinking about it."

"You are? You've acted like you didn't know he liked you for the last few years. What changed your mind?"

Lou pushed up from the sand, started brushing it from her shorts. "Well, honey, that's easy. I decided that it was time to see myself looking as happy as you did whenever you saw Caleb again."

The ferry ride to the mainland had never seemed quite so slow. In fact, she wasn't entirely sure they weren't going backward at times, the Pacific Ocean apparently feeling cranky today and sending up enough chop to make the ferry fight for its path through the waves.

But Faith had always been good on boats and didn't abandon her post on one of the front seats on the outer deck, even though she was getting thoroughly drenched with spray in the process.

Well, she'd dry soon enough.

She was ready to dive off the bow and swim the last few feet by the time the ferry finally docked. Of course, that would mean abandoning her car, which would probably stop everyone else from getting their cars off because she'd sweet-talked Bill at the ferry company into giving her prime position so she could be the first car off.

So she didn't abandon ship, instead bolting back

down to her car so she'd be ready to roll as soon as they let her. Her palms were sweaty where she gripped the steering wheel, as she wondered—for the thousandth time since she'd talked to Lou on the beach yesterday—if she was crazy to do this.

She had Caleb's address in Malibu, thanks to some more sweet-talking she'd done with Liam. Who had been reluctant to give it to her until she'd practically begged. She had a feeling she wasn't Liam's favorite person just now. She couldn't blame him for that. She didn't feel that kindly toward Ivy or Leah's exes either.

Malibu was a long drive, so she decided to stop and get coffee and something to eat before she set off. She pulled off the ferry and drove around the terminal building to the small group of cafés that serviced the ferry traffic and parked in front of the last of the stores, a bakery. When she climbed out of the car, sniffing the air to try to figure out what smelled so good, she thought she heard someone call her name.

Then she almost had a heart attack when she turned to see Caleb standing just a few feet away. He wore a baseball cap pulled low and sunglasses, and his chin was stubbled. He looked so much like he had the very first day she'd seen him driving off the ferry at Cloud Bay that for a moment she thought she must be imagining him. Some sort of weird stress hallucination.

"Faith," he said, sounding unsure. Hallucinations didn't sound uncertain, surely?

She waved with one hand then wondered what the hell she was doing. She must look demented. She shoved her hands into the pockets of her jeans. "Um, hello."

Caleb came closer. Stopped about two feet away from her.

She wanted to touch him so badly she had to clench her hands in her pockets to keep them there.

"What are you doing here?" They spoke in unison.

A nervous giggle welled up in her throat.

"Ladies, first," Caleb said. He took his sunglasses off, tucked them into the neck of his blue T-shirt. The color suited him. Made his eyes bright. But it also highlighted the shadows under the eyes. He looked tired. Unhappy.

She'd done that. She bit her lip and curled her fingers tighter, fighting the urge to reach out and try to smooth those marks away. Which wasn't even possible. Wondering what he'd do if he saw the matching smudges of purple under her own eyes.

Maybe he'd think she deserved them. But if he did, well, she'd just have to live with that. She owed him honesty, at least. If they were going to start again. "I was coming to see you," she said finally.

His brows lifted. "You were? But I was coming to see you."

"I must have missed that memo," she said drily. "Wait, you didn't leave me a message or something, did you? I swear I didn't get one." Her inbox and voicemail had remained stubbornly Caleb-free for two long weeks. She was sure of it. She'd only checked them about a thousand times a day.

"No. I thought maybe it would be better to use the element of surprise. In case you'd decided to get me banned from Lansing or something."

"Angie Ritter seemed to like you, she'd probably overrule anything I tried to do in that department."

That earned her a half smile. God, she'd missed that smile. But she didn't want to get her hopes up.

"I'll keep that in mind."

There was a pause. Was he waiting for her to say something else? The silence stretched out. Yep. Apparently the ball was in her court. "How have you been?"

He shrugged. "Not the greatest two weeks of my life. But I've been busy, at least."

"Doing what?"

"Somebody told me I needed to sort my shit out. So I've been doing that."

"You have?" God. Did she sound pathetic?

Caleb nodded. "I've made a start. That somebody gave me some ideas actually.

"They did?" She couldn't remember giving him anything resembling advice. Just marching orders.

"Yeah. I've been looking into a foundation as a start. Thought maybe starting a tennis camp for kids might be a good thing. Kids who can't afford to go to the kinds of schools that have good sports programs. That kind of thing. Somewhere they can come and just . . . have fun for a week or so. Fresh air. Lots of room. That kind of place. Know anywhere like that?"

Her heart was starting to pound. "I could maybe come up with some suggestions."

"Good. So, Malibu. Seems like a long way to go to see a guy you told to get the hell off your island."

"I didn't say that," she protested.

"That was kind of the gist of it. Maybe you were more polite. Didn't feel so polite though." There was a flash of sudden fierce pain in his eyes that made her wince and look away.

"I'm sorry," she said. "I screwed up, I think. That's what I was coming to tell you."

"You think? Or you know?"

"That kind of depends on what *you* think."

"I think I'm not your father. Or your brother. I think that I'd like to be allowed to show you that. To show you that I'm never going to willingly hurt you."

A smile was tugging on the corners of her mouth. She resisted it. She had no idea if she should be smiling yet.

"But I also think that you need to be the one who knows I'm not them."

"I do," she said. "I was scared."

"Of what?"

"Of how much the thought of losing you was starting to scare me."

"So you decided that making sure you lost me was the way to go?"

She lifted her chin. "I come from a long line of people who do dumb shit when they're scared. That's something you need to understand about me."

"What kind of things?"

"In my father's case, lots of whiskey. The occasional hit of cocaine. That kind of thing."

"What about you?"

"Not whiskey. Definitely not drugs. I do better at walling myself off than wiping myself out."

Another half smile. "You gonna work on that?"

"Do I have a reason to?"

He nodded. "I think so. Because you know, you were kind of right. Maybe I was looking for the next thing to make me feel as good as tennis did. But you were kind of wrong too."

"About what?" She managed to squeak the words against the happiness that was starting to bubble up in her throat.

"You're not a distraction. You're the good stuff. The real thing. The addiction I'm pretty sure I'm not going to ever kick. Which is a kind of screwed-up way of saying what I told you once before. That I've fallen for you, Faith Harper. I don't know how to quit you. And everything else is just details that we can figure out."

She was grinning now. Grinning and pretty sure she was going to explode if she didn't touch him soon. She needed a fix of Caleb White.

"Me either," she said. "I don't know how to quit you either. I'm sorry I screwed up. Can you forgive me?"

He grinned at her. "I think that can be arranged."

"Will you come back to Cloud Bay with me?"

"Will you come to L.A. or wherever when I need to go? Because I don't like being without you. It sucks."

"I think that can be arranged," she said. Then she reached out and pulled him close. "In fact, I think you're going to have trouble getting rid of me."

"Sounds good to me," Caleb muttered. Then he leaned down and kissed her.

THE END